FOAL

the trouble
with
shooting stars

meg cannistra

Simon & Schuster Books for Young Readers
NEW YORK · LONDON · TORONTO · SYDNEY · NEW DELHI

SIMON & SCHUSTER BOOKS FOR YOUNG READERS
An imprint of Simon & Schuster Children's Publishing Division
1230 Avenue of the Americas, New York, New York 10020

SIMON & SCHUSTER BOOKS FOR YOUNG READERS
is a trademark of Simon & Schuster, Inc.
For information about special discounts for bulk purchases, please contact
Simon & Schuster Special Sales at 1-866-506-1949 or business@simonandschuster.com.
The Simon & Schuster Speakers Bureau can bring authors to your live event.
For more information or to book an event, contact the Simon & Schuster Speakers Bureau at
1-866-248-3049 or visit our website at www.simonspeakers.com.
Jacket design by Lucy Ruth Cummins
Interior design by Hilary Zarycky
The text for this book was set in Bembo.
Manufactured in the United States of America
0719 FFG
First Edition
2 4 6 8 10 9 7 5 3 1

Library of Congress Cataloging-in-Publication Data
Names: Cannistra, Meg, author.
Title: The trouble with shooting stars / Meg Cannistra.
Description: First edition. | New York : Simon & Schuster Books for Young Readers, [2019] |
Summary: Twelve-year-old Luna, who is recovering from a disfiguring car accident, is inspired to heal by two magical neighbors who take her up to the heavens to sweep the moon and stars.
Identifiers: LCCN 2018049035 |
ISBN 9781534428966 (hardback) | ISBN 9781534428980 (eBook)
Subjects: | CYAC: Stars—Fiction. | Magic—Fiction. | Disfigured persons—Fiction. | Self-esteem—Fiction. | Family problems—Fiction. | BISAC: JUVENILE FICTION / Social Issues / Self-Esteem & Self-Reliance. | JUVENILE FICTION / Family / General (see also headings under Social Issues). | JUVENILE FICTION / Fairy Tales & Folklore / Country & Ethnic.
Classification: LCC PZ7.1.C368 Tro 2019 | DDC [Fic]—dc23
LC record available at https://lccn.loc.gov/2018049035

To my dad, John Cannistra, for always supporting my writing and for never telling me to become a lawyer like my sister.

And for the rest of my family, which is too big to name individually (though I'm sure I won't hear the end of it for not doing so).

You—you alone will have the stars as no one else has them. . . . In one of the stars I shall be living. In one of them I shall be laughing. And so it will be as if all the stars were laughing, when you look at the sky at night. . . . You—only you—will have stars that can laugh.

—*The Little Prince*

Chapter 1

It's easier being yourself at night. When the only eyes on you belong to the stars and the sky wraps you up in its darkness like a big, soft blanket. The nighttime is special because the world opens wide and not even the moon cares what you look like or who you are.

I used to like the sun, but not anymore.

I wiggle my fingers under my mask, scratching my cheek. My skin is sweaty and soft underneath the plastic, like the jiggly clams Uncle Mike makes every Christmas Eve. It's not a pretty, lacy mask. It's a hard white shell that covers the right half of my face, and Mom says I can't take it off, even if the tight Velcro straps give me headaches.

When I was seven Mom, Dad, and I took the Staten Island Ferry into the city to see *The Phantom of the Opera*. He had to wear a mask like mine. An ugly, uncomfortable mask that covered half his face. But maybe it's better we have to wear these masks. Maybe people would be scared of me, too, if they saw what I looked like without it. People usually dislike anything that's not normal. But most people never see me way up here in my tree. They're so busy looking ahead, they forget to look up.

I adjust the sketch pad splayed out in front of me and take up my pencil. Mom and Dad used to be fine with me sitting on the little wooden platform Papa Ranieri built into the tree outside my window. It's the best place for drawing because it's one of the tallest points in the neighborhood. The perfect spot to see all the interesting things happening on my street. But ever since the accident, they've said I can't be out here. It's too dangerous in my current condition. But I don't think it's any scarier than when I'd sit up here before.

Mom and Dad didn't always treat me like a porcelain doll. Bianchinis are rough-and-tumble—made from tough stuff. Before the car crash, falling off my bike or a twisted ankle from soccer were nothing. They became stories of heroism told at Sunday dinners. The old Luna didn't have time to cry over minor injuries. She was too busy having fun.

But sitting in my tree is worth whatever danger my parents now think exists. From one side of the platform, the entire cul-de-sac is on full display. On the other side, I can peer into the recently sold house next door. It's quiet and calm. A place where I investigate the neighbors without them knowing I'm snooping.

The streetlamps glow softly, like little planets all lined up in their own solar system. If you squint hard enough, you can see the top of One World Trade Center over the trees and houses, even though I live all the way on the north shore of Staten Island, a great big rock at the bottom of Manhattan. Kind of like how Sicily sits all the way at the bottom of Italy, always being kicked by the giant boot.

A gust of cold wind whistles through the trees and whips up the pages in my sketch pad. I wrap myself tighter in my rainbow comforter and take a sip from my mug of chamomile tea.

Chamomile was my aunt Marie's favorite. Before she passed away, she'd invite Mom and me over for tea Fridays after school. She'd drink Earl Grey on Friday afternoons, but chamomile at night when she couldn't sleep because she said it calmed her stomach. I started drinking it when sleeping became hard after the accident. So far it hasn't done much of anything except make me think of Aunt Marie.

I push aside my pencils and sketch pad and look through the binoculars Dad got me for sleepaway camp in the Catskills last year. Light fills up the third window on the third floor of the tall house across the street.

I count out loud: "One, two, three . . ."

Mr. Anderson shimmies into view, dancing in his undies. I laugh so hard tears form in the corners of my eyes and my sides begin to ache. I bury my face into my comforter to muffle it. Mr. Anderson's dance is the one thing that makes me laugh nowadays.

I inhale the lavender scent of my freshly washed comforter, then sit up straight and bring the binoculars back to my eyes. It wasn't until after Dad and I got into the car accident, when I didn't want to sleep, that I noticed how different the world is at night. Even boring old Tompkinsville.

It's as if parents make their kids go to bed early so we don't realize all the awesome things that happen once the moon rises. It's like a secret you learn when you become an adult. A mysterious other world that's one giant riddle filled with the shadows of passing cars and a chorus of crickets and the hush of whispered conversations. It's bigger too—more room to stretch out, to explore, to draw. Once you learn all this, going to bed at nine p.m. is impossible. Not happening.

I don't spend every night in my tree sketching the world. Drawing used to come easy, but now I can't hold on to a pencil or a piece of charcoal for too long without feeling jolts of pain in my left hand. When drawing isn't an option, I toss and turn in bed. Or I sneak downstairs to watch horror movies, eating toast dripping with butter and brown sugar. Still other nights I actually get more than a few hours of restless sleep. But those are rare. It's not like back before the accident, when Mom would have to shake me awake from the middle of a good dream.

A bang echoes down the street, and a dog barks. Maybe it's a bunch of raccoons making a new home inside the Perigos' garage. Or maybe it's a burglar trying to get into the Kim family's house while they're out of town. I scan the empty driveways until the Jamesons' security light catches my eye.

I drop my binoculars, and they thump against my chest.

Cecilia Jameson knocks over the trash can as she sneaks out of her house. Her room's over the garage, and it's a careful slide down the sloped roof and a short jump from there into the shrubs.

A red car idles out front, and Cecilia scurries across her now well-lit driveway and into the passenger seat. The car peels down the street and takes a sharp left out of the neighborhood. It's not fair that she gets to leave. She could be going somewhere incredible, like a late-night diner that serves disco fries or a secret slumber party at the Metropolitan Museum of Art. Jealousy lodges in my throat, and I slurp down some more of my tea.

The security light goes out again. I lean through my

window to check the time on my alarm clock. Only ten thirty. I stifle a yawn and pull my comforter around me. The neon-bright diamonds of color almost glow under the moonlight. Red, orange, yellow, green, blue, indigo, violet. Granny Ranieri bought it for me. She thought it would look nice with my blue walls and dark canopy bed. She said it'd be like sleeping under a rainbow. That it would help me heal. I trace the diamonds with my fingers. Feathers poke out in some places, pricking my skin.

Ten thirty. *Only* ten thirty.

I stretch my legs out across the platform and wriggle my sock-covered toes. Usually the nights go fast when I stay up drawing. There's so much to get down in my sketch pad that light will be rising over the tops of houses before I even finish my tea. But tonight I'm restless. My mask feels like a face-prison, and sketching is making my hand cramp up.

I stare into my mug. The bloated bag of tea leaves pokes out of the milky brown slurry like an iceberg. I press down on it with my pinkie, and more tea spurts out. My stomach turns. There's nothing worse than cold tea. All the sugar sits at the bottom like sand and crunches between your teeth.

Another gust of wind bursts through the leaves, too strong for my comforter. With a sigh I start moving my stuff back into my bedroom. It's always around November that the nights get too cold and the wind forces me inside, ruining all my sketching plans. At least sneaking down-stairs to watch horror movies is a good plan B.

A loud beeping cuts through the neighborhood.

I freeze.

A large white truck backs into the driveway next door. Weird since the other family living there moved out only last week. Someone's moving in. In the middle of the night.

I press my trusty binoculars to my face. In large black lettering on the side of the truck reads:

LE SPAZZATRICI, SAPIENTI-FAMILY-OWNED BUSINESS, ESTABLISHED AT THE BEGINNING OF TIME, STELLE, ITALY.

"Spazzatrici?" The word feels strange on my tongue, but not entirely unfamiliar. Like a story your mom would read every night before bed, or a song your choir teacher taught you for Christmas Mass. I pick up one of my pen-cils and write the word onto the left corner of one of my blank pages in large, looping cursive.

I don't know much Italian. They teach Spanish, Latin, and French at Saint Mary's Catholic School, and I chose French because I want to live in Paris and work at the Louvre when I'm older. Mom and Dad know a little more Italian than me, but aren't at all fluent. Mostly words they say I'm not allowed to repeat. Nonna Bianchini tried to teach me, but I've already forgotten a lot of it. I reach inside my bedroom window for the laptop I left on the bench, so I can look up the word, but it's not in there.

I lean over the tree platform to get a better look at the van. Painted underneath the large black lettering is a swooping, dizzying constellation of fireflies glittering in a purple-blue night's sky. They glow just like stars.

I blink twice, then readjust the binoculars. The fireflies move across the side of the van. Twinkling and zipping between the black letters.

The hairs on my neck prickle.

It must be a trompe l'oeil. I've seen those before in the city. The ones painted on walls to look 3-D and go on forever. Definitely an optical illusion of some kind. A very cool one.

A short man with a thick mess of black hair, olive skin, and a round face jumps down from the truck and surveys his parking job, hands on hips. The passenger door slams shut, and an equally petite woman appears at his side. Bringing up the rear are a young boy about the same height as his mother and a little girl with a long black braid trailing her back like a cat's tail.

The man wraps his arm around his wife and kisses the side of her head before moving to the rear of the truck and unlatching the door.

"We're so early," the boy says when his dad is out of earshot. I readjust so I'm lying on my belly and lean even farther out over the tree to spy on the new neighbors.

"Why couldn't we have stayed at home longer?"

I raise my eyebrows.

"Oh, hush." His mom opens the driver's door. "There's much to prepare before winter, Alessandro," she says, rustling about in the back seat of the truck before retrieving a hot-pink backpack. "Go help your papa unpack the equipment." She pats him on the head and sends him on his way. The woman turns to the little girl and hands her the backpack. "Just like I taught you. Do you need my help this time?" She smiles. Her Italian accent is heavy, like my Nonna Bianchini's.

The little girl shakes her head and unzips the backpack, retrieving what looks like a dollhouse-size wooden china cabinet, which she clutches to her heart. She runs through the front door, and the empty house blinks with light. The girl hurries down a hallway and reappears in the dining room's lit windows toward the back.

She stands in the middle of the big room before heading to a wall and disappearing from view. My binoculars remain trained on the spot where she vanishes. The freezing air blows under my mask and chills the sweat on my cheek.

What is she doing? I crane my neck to try to find her.

She pops back into view. The girl grins, rubs her hands together, and closes her eyes. Tossing her shoulders back, she snaps her fingers and the dollhouse china cabinet falls apart into several different pieces. I hold my breath, the pressure growing in my chest. Cabinets don't break apart on their own.

She moves her hands through the air, wiggling her fingers as if conducting an orchestra. Her head bobs up and down to a melody I can't hear. The girl breathes deeply and stomps her left foot on the ground and, in the blink of an eye, the cabinet's two left feet grow. She stomps her right foot and the cabinet's two right feet grow. The binoculars are pressed so hard against my skin that they're digging into my cheek.

The cold breeze turns warm, and the air feels different. Lighter. The sound of cars fades to a hush. The streetlamps flicker until they go completely dark. It's as if the entire night has shifted to make room for the girl's performance. She flicks her wrists and stretches out her arms. The cabinet's platform expands and positions itself atop the feet. She moves her arms again, and soon the cabinet's sides grow seven feet tall and pop onto the platform.

The girl pushes her hands together, and the tiny drawers spring to regular size and begin to assemble themselves as if being put together by ghosts. Finally, the drawers slide into the cabinet and the doors screw themselves onto golden hinges and carefully close themselves.

My stomach drops like it does when you jump off a swing. I lean farther over the wooden platform, and it groans as I move. I take a deep breath and grip on to its edge for support. I *have* to get a closer look.

What was once a china cabinet fit for a dollhouse now towers over the little girl. Her eyes snap open, and she claps her hands together. She runs back through the house and out the front door. "I did it, Mama! Alessandro, Papa, I did it!"

"Oh, Chiara. What a good job," her mom says. The boy, Alessandro, and her papa pause their work to congratulate the girl.

My heart beats wildly in my ears. I quickly grab my sketchbook and scribble down "Stelle, Italy," and the kids' names—Alessandro and Chiara—underneath "spazzatrici," and put my binoculars back up to my eyes.

Chiara runs back inside, pink backpack in hand. She opens it and retrieves a small table. She places it in the center of the dining room. Again she takes a step back and squares her shoulders. This time she keeps her eyes open while snapping her fingers. The table falls apart, and she begins her performance once more. The pieces grow large. The table starts rebuilding itself on its own. The once tiny piece of furniture that fit comfortably inside her little hands is now a regular-size table, standing tall in the room.

Three sharp knocks echo from the other side of my bedroom door.

Panic rushes up to my chest.

I scurry through my window on hands and knees, losing my balance on the window bench and falling to the floor with a *thud*. Tea splatters everywhere.

"Great," I mutter, sopping up the tea with a dirty T-shirt.

"Luna?" my mom says as she opens my bedroom door. Her thick blond hair is tied up in a messy bun; her dark-brown roots are nearly an inch long. Mom hasn't gone to see Janet, her hairdresser and Tailee's mom, in a couple of months. She looks down at me, eyebrows raised. "What are you doing on the floor?" she asks, moving farther into my room. "And why is the window halfway open? Were you outside again—and on that platform after we told you not to? You catching a cold would not be good for your recovery."

"I fell off my window bench." I stagger up to my feet, pulling the comforter around my shoulders.

"You shouldn't be awake to begin with." She presses her forefinger and thumb into her eyelids and shakes her head. "You need to rest. Sleep will help you heal."

Everyone says Mom and I look alike—all the Ranieri side of the family. We both have curly hair, big brown eyes, and freckled tawny skin. The only part of me that looks Bianchini is my big nose. But that was before the accident. I don't look like much of anyone now. Not even myself.

"I couldn't sleep." I pick up the mug and scramble to my feet. "Mom, there are some seriously weird people moving into the house next door. In the middle of the night."

"You're spying on the neighbors? Again, Luna? You know that's an invasion of people's privacy."

"I wasn't spying." I shake my head. "I was *investigating*. And anyway, this is different. They're like wizards or something." I bounce onto the window bench and pull the curtains back farther. "Come on. Come look." I hold the binoculars out to her. Mom hesitates in the doorway. "Seriously. The girl did this magical spell to make tiny furniture grow to full size. I swear on my grave."

"Luna Andrea Marie Bianchini, don't you go swearing on your grave. You know how that makes me feel."

"Sorry." I tap at the window with my fingernail. "But you've got to come look. Please? After you look I'll get into bed. Promise."

Mom rolls her eyes, but she steps out from the doorway. "Let's see." She grabs the binoculars and peers down at the house.

My heart pounds against my chest as I watch her expectantly.

"I see a white truck in the driveway." She lowers the binoculars and gives me that look only moms are capable of. "No wizards. No magic growing furniture.

They probably moved in this afternoon and are finishing unpacking now."

"What?" I snatch the binoculars from her hands and stare out the window. A few lights shine in the windows, but the house looks quiet. The truck parked outside doesn't say anything about spazzatrici on it. There are no fireflies dancing on its side. There's nothing on it at all. "No, that's not right." I shake my head, curls bouncing back and forth across my face. "I saw them. I saw the little girl make the cabinet grow. The truck had all this writing and a really real trompe l'oeil on the side." The words fly out of my mouth in a jumble, each one stumbling over the last. "I know what I saw, Mom."

"You probably fell asleep, sweetheart," Mom says. "You must have dreamed it."

"No, I know I didn't dream this."

Mom reaches beyond me and shuts the window, locking the gold clasp at the top. She closes the curtains. "Luna, it was just a dream."

"I'd know if it was a dream." Mom ushers me off the window bench and toward my bed.

She rubs my shoulders. "Seeing things that aren't there wouldn't be good, Luna. Maybe you're just overtired. Or the medication is causing you to have lucid dreams. I'll call Dr. Tucker tomorrow."

"I know what I saw," I whisper.

"Please," Mom says, her shoulders slumping forward. Little horseshoe-shaped shadows are bruised into the skin under her eyes. "No more sitting outside in your tree tonight. Or on the window bench. Just get into bed and try to get some sleep. We all need some rest." She smiles that tired half smile she gives when her mind is elsewhere. "I know it's hard, Luna, but please."

"Okay." I look over at the window once more, before climbing into bed and letting Mom tuck the rainbow comforter around my body. "I'll try. For you."

"That's all I ask."

"Hey, Mom?"

"Hm?" She brushes the curls from my forehead and kisses me.

"Do you know what the word 'spazzatrici' means?"

"It's pronounced *spa-tsa-tree-chee*," she says, sounding out the syllables. "It means 'sweepers.' Try saying it slower."

"Spaz-za-tree-chee," I say again.

"Close."

"The word was on the truck next door."

"Okay, Luna," Mom says with that tone in her voice that means she doesn't believe me. "Don't forget to say your prayers."

I haven't done much praying lately. Ever since the car crash, talking to God feels uncomfortable. I used to say my prayers every single night and go to Mass at school once a week. But even with all that praying, God still didn't stop my dad and me from getting into a car wreck.

Mom walks to the door and shuts off the light. "And don't forget Jean."

I turn Jean Valjean, my sleep turtle, on, and the stars carved into his shell illuminate across my bedroom ceiling in soft whites, greens, blues, and purples. My cousin Rocco says I'm too old to have a night-light, much less one that's also a stuffed animal. But I can't give Jean up. He's been with me since I was little, and he's stuck with me through everything. Having him around is extra comfort and makes the tossing and turning a little less difficult.

"I love you, Luna," Mom says from the doorway.

"I love you too."

She closes the door.

"Spazzatrici," I mumble. "Sweepers. What in the world could they be sweeping?"

My toes touch the floor just as she turns off the light in the hallway. I scurry across the room and push back my curtains. The lights are still out in the house next door.

Maybe it *was* a hallucination. It *has* been weeks since I slept through the night.

I grab my sketch pad and pencils and head back toward my bed when a small flicker of light catches my eye. I pull the curtains back an inch and peer out from behind them.

All alone in the vast and quiet darkness is a single firefly floating near the window across from mine.

My breath catches in my throat, and I leap onto my bed, turning Jean Valjean off and my bedside lamp on. "Sorry, Jean. I know I promised Mom I'd sleep. But it'll have to wait just a little longer."

I hurry back to my window bench and pick up a pencil. Underneath "spazzatrici," I begin to draw a big house filled with little furniture and a small girl at the center of it all.

Chapter 2

Bursts of red and orange leaves shoot across the drizzly late-autumn sky like flare guns. They rise up off their branches before tumbling from the trees and collecting in wet piles on the yellowing grass in our backyard. I stifle a yawn, my eyes fixed on the small corner of the next-door neighbor's house that is visible from the kitchen window. No one has come or gone since they moved in last night. At least I don't *think* anything happened. I did fall asleep on my window bench sometime around two thirty and woke up as the sun started peeking over the rooftops.

Since last night, I've done thirteen drawings of the Sapienti house. Each one time-stamped like the photographic records private investigators keep on TV. I would've done more, but Mom made me come down to eat breakfast and do some homework. She's got me on a strict schedule. Homework between breakfast and lunch on days I don't have morning doctors' appointments and between lunch and dinner on days I do.

"What're you looking at, Luns?" Uncle Mike asks, pronouncing my nickname like *loons*. He comes by every day. Most days after closing at Bianchini's Deli to talk business with Dad because Dad misses being in charge at the deli. But today he snuck away at lunchtime to have one of Mom's famous chicken parms.

We all sit at the kitchen table, devouring our sandwiches. They're my favorite, the breading crispy and flecked with cayenne to give the chicken a bit of a kick. Even better than Nonna Bianchini's. Mom's is light, and she toasts the hoagie roll with butter, chopped garlic, melty mozzarella, and grated parmesan to make it a garlic-bread sandwich. Then she tops it with homemade gravy. Nonna's is too greasy and sits in my stomach like a horseshoe. But I'd never tell her this. It's an unspoken family rule: Never, *ever* tell Nonna Bianchini her food tastes anything less than delicious.

"It must be something special that's piqued your interest," Uncle Mike adds. "Can't even get any attention from my favorite niece and goddaughter."

"It's nothing." The word "magic" scratches at the back of my throat, wanting to be said aloud, but I swallow it down with the chicken parm.

I pause from monitoring and take a big bite of my sandwich. I shouldn't tell anyone about what I saw just yet. Especially after Mom's reaction. This can be my secret for at least a little while. Inspiration for my latest collection of drawings. I'll find out more about them and fill my sketch pad with their strange magic.

"Delicious sandwiches, as always." Uncle Mike wipes bread crumbs from his beard and grins at my mom. Uncle Mike looks just like my dad even though he's younger— same black hair, same bushy eyebrows, and same big sloping nose with a hook at the end. The Bianchini beak. Mine used to look like that.

"Thank you, Mike. You and your brother are always such good eaters," Mom says.

"We got it from our pa, who got it from his." Dad moves his hand from his wheelchair's armrest to jostle his brother's shoulder. "A Bianchini knows good food and knows never to turn it down." He grins, always smiling when Uncle Mike is over for a visit.

I pop the last bit of sandwich into my mouth, savoring the oozing mozzarella, spicy chicken, and sweet tomato sauce. I need to go outside and get a closer look at that house. Their arrival next door is stuck in my brain like a piece of pepper between my teeth.

"Slow down, Luna."

Eating became difficult after the accident because my jaw gets sore from all the chewing. Sometimes it makes me not want to eat much at all. But my stomach is always roaring and Mom's chicken parm sandwiches are too good to pass up. Like my dad said, we never say no to good food.

Mom smiles at my empty plate. "A gold star," she says, picking up everyone's plates and putting them in the kitchen sink to wash later.

"I haven't gotten a gold star for eating everything since I was little," I say.

"Maybe we should bring them back," Dad says. "Get you to eat more."

I shrug. "Or maybe Mom can make chicken parm for every meal."

"You'd get sick of it after a while." She wipes her hands on her jeans and sits back down at the kitchen table. "And then what would I bribe you with?"

"New art supplies? A huge easel made of nice wood. Not the cheap kind from those craft stores."

Dad laughs, a deep bellowing sound that emerges right from his diaphragm. He should have been an opera singer with such a rich, musical laugh. "My little da Vinci. I didn't know you were interested in painting."

"Painting?" Uncle Mike says, a glimmer in his dark eyes. "I knew you'd be an artist like me. Ever since you picked up your first crayon."

I smile at him. "I'd like to try it. Watercolors aren't my thing. I like the thick oil paints. We got to use them once in art class."

"You could paint something like that." Uncle Mike gestures to one of my last drawings from art class. Mom hung it on the wall. Gloria, one of my cousins, is dancing at her ballet studio. Her tulle skirt twirls around her legs as she spins on one slipper. It's one of my best drawings. Even my art teacher, Ms. DeSario, thought so. She said I was great at getting out into the world and capturing life on the page. I don't go to Gloria's dance classes anymore to sketch the ballerinas. I don't sketch much of anything beyond what I can see from my tree.

For a moment this all feels normal: eating chicken parm, talking about art, having lunch together. When Dad could still work and didn't have to be in a wheelchair. When Uncle Mike wasn't coming over every single day to keep Dad in the loop about the deli. When I was in school on Tuesdays and eating tacos in the big, busy cafeteria with Tailee and the others instead of at home with my family.

Maybe a chicken parm sandwich can heal me after all.

The phone rings, and Mom jumps from her seat to check the caller ID. "Luna," she calls from the kitchen. "It's Tailee."

My stomach rolls over. Tailee and I first met in kindergarten, when I accidentally sat in wet paint. Her mom had packed her a spare dress since she was prone to spilling milk all over herself. Tailee let me borrow it. Ever since, we've shared a love of neon colors, scary movies, and spicy foods.

The rings grow louder.

Tailee must be sneaking in a phone call from the girls' bathroom during lunch. She knows not to try texting or calling my cell phone anymore. I haven't charged it in a few weeks. There's no point in having a cell phone when you don't really go anywhere.

"Do you want to talk to her today?" Mom asks, her voice light.

Right after Dad and I got out of the hospital things still seemed hopeful. The doctors said my face would heal, the burns would fade, and the mask would be needed for only a month at most. In that month, Tailee called me every day and came over nearly every other day. We'd talk like things were fine. Or at least close to fine. I felt okay, even though I'd wear my hair in a way that covered most of my mask whenever she stopped by. But then the doctors said my mask needed to stay on another month. Then the word "surgery" sprouted up in doctors' appointments like a prickly weed. It was harder to believe I'd ever get better.

After that first month, Tailee would still try to fill the silence with jokes and stories from school. But my voice was trapped in my chest. Buried under the debris from the car wreck. Talking became more difficult the longer the mask stayed on. Strained and awkward. So I stopped. Now I hide whenever she brings my homework or asks to hang out on the weekend. I don't want to wonder about what she thinks of me now. The word "ugly" wriggles up in my head, but I beat it down. Tailee wouldn't think I'm ugly. But maybe.

Now it's been two and a half months since the accident and nearly a month since I've seen Tailee. The longest we've gone without seeing each other.

When you've been changed so completely, it's nearly impossible to be the same person for your friends. Pretending to be yourself is hard when you don't even look like yourself anymore.

I stare down at the table and shake my head.

Mom clicks her tongue, but she says nothing. The answering machine picks it up. My stomach flips again. Tailee hangs up without leaving a message.

Half of me is relieved she didn't; the other half wishes she did. Maybe so I could hear her voice or know for sure whether she's mad at me for avoiding her.

"I'm dropping you off at the deli around two, right?" Mom says to Dad, then looks at the clock. "I still don't know if it's a good idea for you to be going to the deli today."

"Why?" Dad asks, anger immediately rising in his voice.

And just like that the bubble pops.

"It's hard for you to get in and out of there. You don't want to overexert yourself. Dr. Madan says—"

"He doesn't know everything." Dad dismisses the idea. "I used to be there every day at four a.m., handling shipments and making sure the lights stay on. I can handle a few hours of doing paperwork in the back."

Mom squints at him. She knows it'd be more than him sitting in the back office looking over the books and reviewing schedules.

After Dad's parents got married, they opened a small store and lived above it. Bianchini's Deli. Old black-and-white pictures of the storefront dot Bianchini's walls like a timeline of sorts, spanning its forty-four years in business. Dad and Uncle Mike started working there with my nonno when they were kids. As Nonno got older, Dad took over, bought the old tailor's shop next door, and made it even bigger. Everyone in Staten Island knows Bianchini's. The newspapers call it the best Italian deli in the whole borough.

When I was little, Mom and I would go in every Saturday and Sunday morning. I was just tall enough to peek over the counters and see my nonno and Dad busy managing deliveries, slicing meat, and laughing with customers. Their work was so precise, so artistic—even when they were just wrapping deli meat in butcher paper. Nonno says art is in everything. From the way you slice the prosciutto to the way you treat your employees and deliverymen. The art you put into your work is what makes it special.

Mom pinches the bridge of her nose. "Fine, but we need to get you cleaned up a bit first."

He glares down at his hands, at the wheelchair he's had to use since the accident. "I'm fine the way I am."

"You got gravy on your shirt," Mom says. "It'll take ten minutes."

"C'mon, Frank." Uncle Mike pats him on the shoulder. "Don't be a grump."

"I'm not a grump," Dad snaps.

Mom stares at him, her eyes narrowed. The clock ticks out the long, uneasy silence. It finds its way under my skin and into my body, squeezing around my heart until it aches. I can't stand it, so I jump up from the table and walk over to the map of Italy hanging on our wall. I run my finger over the glass, catching a thin layer of dust, and distract myself as the silence between my mom and dad deepens. Their tense quiet is like the seconds between thunder and lightning, with the rest of us getting all soaked from the storm.

I look for Stelle, Italy, the town from the side of the Sapientis' truck. I trace the map with my finger, lingering on the places I know best. Nonno and Nonna Bianchini were both born on the boot, in Tuscany. Granny Ranieri was born all the way down in Messina, Sicily, and Papa Ranieri is from Naples.

My eyes travel from Naples down the coast and

toward Sicily. A little black dot, all the way in the boot's heel, leaps out at me. I almost press my face to the glass. My heart jumps into my throat. Scrawled over the little dot is the word "Stelle." I've never noticed it before. Though I guess I never had reason to notice it until now.

There it is.

The city that disappeared from the white truck in their driveway.

The city I scrawled in my sketch pad next to the word "spazzatrici." *Sweepers*.

"C'mon, Frank," Uncle Mike says.

Dad sighs and tosses his hands in the air. "Fine. Do what you must, Sofia."

I look over my shoulder. Mom plasters a smile on her face and wheels Dad from the kitchen. Uncle Mike drums his fingers on the table but doesn't say anything.

I let out a deep breath once they leave the room.

"Tough, huh, kid?" Uncle Mike says.

His words don't register with me.

"Stelle." I tap the dot repeatedly, as if doing so will make it spill all its secrets. It is real.

"Stelle's a beautiful place."

I whip around. "You know about Stelle?"

Uncle Mike scratches at the scruffy beard on his pale face. "I went once. To their Cielo Stellato celebration way back before my first year of art school. Talk about inspiration!" He stares at the map, a dreamy look in his eyes. "It's such a teensy little speck of a town with all these incredible stone towers that cut right into the skies."

"Really?" I move closer. "What's Cielo Stellato?" My tongue stumbles over the words, too big and awkward to handle the musical syllables.

He smiles. "It means 'starry sky.' Stelle has the best view of the stars in all of Italy. Maybe all the world. My pa would say they were blessed by the goddess of the moon, whom you're named for."

"Nonno told you that?"

He nods. "Yeah. He'd tell us all these Italian folklore stories when we were kids. Luna loved Stelle and the towers they built to reach her and the stars. So she shines brightest on them. Every summer they pay thanks with a huge celebration. There's tons of dancing and food. It goes all night long, and then everyone sleeps the next day.

"It was amazing, Luns. The food, the wine, the music." He laughs again and runs a hand through his long, curly black hair. "The people of Stelle know how to live. The sky was filled with fireflies—thousands of them."

Fireflies. Like the gold, glittering ones on the Sapientis' truck. A tingle zips through me.

Uncle Mike stretches his hands out above his head. "The night stretched on forever. As if it were twice as long. Like the whole town convinced the goddess Luna herself to extend the night for the celebration.

"And Luna smiled down on the whole thing, bigger and brighter than I've ever seen her. Her face beaming as she watched the entire city honor her." He closes his eyes and leans back in his chair. The most relaxed I've seen him since he's taken over the deli. "I ended up lying down on a hill and tried my best to fit the billions of stars in a drawing, but I couldn't."

"I want to go," I say, bouncing up and down. "We went so long ago that I don't remember Italy at all."

"You don't remember going to Italy?"

"I was only six." I furrow my brow. "I do remember the sunflowers in Tuscany."

"Well, maybe one day we can go again." Uncle Mike opens his eyes, the smile on his face wavering. "But it'll have to be after your dad is back in charge of running the deli. I barely have time for anything else now."

I sit back down in my chair. "You haven't gotten to work on your art for a while."

A shadow of Uncle Mike's grin returns. "You need to see what I did with the deli."

"What did you do?"

"Your dad isn't a big fan, but I spruced up the seating area. It's a place people want to sit and enjoy their pastries and coffee now. Think murals and softer lighting. Not that old-school deli your nonno was running. It's good for business."

"It looks like an art museum," Dad says. Mom's wheeling him back into the kitchen. He frowns. "Not a deli. People will get confused."

Uncle Mike rolls his eyes. "You just hate change."

"What I hate is that you're not taking this seriously."

"Ease up. Both of you," Mom says, her eyes darting from Dad and Uncle Mike over to me. "Luna, go grab your coat."

"I don't feel like going," I say. My eyes drift to the window and a glimpse of the house next door. There's no way I'd be able to properly investigate the new neighbors if Mom and Dad are at home watching my every move. "I want to stay home and read."

"Are you sure you don't want to go to the deli?" Dad asks. "I thought you loved coming with us."

Salty slices of prosciutto, sweet ricotta-filled *sfogliatella*, and fresh-out-of-the-oven biscotti pop into my brain. My thoughts travel to fixing a plate of my favorites and spending the afternoon at the deli poring over my sketch pad. There's nothing better than being at Bianchini's. But my eyes drift back to the window, the corner of the Sapientis' house just visible. I can't get distracted from my investigation. Especially not when I know Stelle is a real place. There's just too much to uncover.

My fingers graze the hard plastic of my mask. "I want to stay home."

Mom frowns. "You should get out. Get some fresh air. You could run errands with me. We wouldn't be gone long."

"I'm fine staying home alone." I shake my head. "I'm old enough."

"Are you sure?" She loosely wraps a scarf around her neck. "You know I don't like leaving you here by yourself."

"You used to be fine with it before the accident."

The word "accident" sets off a firecracker in the room. Everyone flinches.

"I'll be fine. I know where my medicine is, and I can call if there's a problem. Promise."

Mom furrows her brow but says nothing. She grabs her keys off the kitchen counter. "Just be careful. You need to finish up your science homework while we're gone. Chapters five through seven," she says. "And call your dad or me if something happens. Right away. Don't wait."

"She knows the drill, Sofia. She's twelve." Dad's head is already at Bianchini's. Too far gone to contribute much else to this conversation. Already dreaming of the cream puffs and arancini he'll need to make to fill upcoming holiday orders.

"Okay, fine. We love you, Luna," Mom says, kissing

my cheek. Uncle Mike pushes Dad outside, followed by Mom closing and locking the door behind them.

The house is quiet. I run to the front door and peek out the window just in time to see Mom's and Uncle Mike's cars pull out of the driveway.

Finally! I grab my binoculars off my closed science textbook, snatch my coat from the rack, and tuck my sketch pad under my arm. The cold wind smacks me in the face as I launch myself out the back door and jump from the patio steps onto the crunchy grass.

I trail the fence separating us from the Sapientis, peering through into the backyard. Maybe I can look through the back windows and see what's in their house now.

There's a loose slat in the fence dividing our backyards. My cousin Rocco and I found it last summer when we were looking for secret passageways we could use to sneak between our neighbors' backyards and over to each other's houses. He and Gloria live five houses down. I used the loose slat only one time. Rocco had a bad cold and couldn't attend a family barbecue. I snuck him a piece of lemon cake and no one knew I'd even left.

I kick the loose slat with my boot, ready to squeeze through into their yard, when a muffled squeaking sound pierces the quiet afternoon. I stare between the posts. The screen door to the Sapientis' house slams shut. Chiara rushes from the house with a large wicker laundry basket in her arms. She hops down the porch stairs and runs through her backyard, her black braid trailing behind her on the wind. She darts full speed into the woods like a comet. A bright November sun hangs high in a cloudless sky, but its rays seem smothered by the woods.

The woods don't look the same. They're thicker, darker—like a forest has sprung up overnight. We never had this many trees in my backyard. They're twisted and gnarled, tree limbs crisscrossing and tangling together in a mess of red and orange leaves. Their trunks are solid and dark. Almost impossible to see beyond. I gaze behind me at my favorite tree and my secret platform. Even it looks a little different.

I linger at the gate in the fence that leads to the woods. My brows knit together, and I pull up my binoculars to get a better look. Flickers of gold sparkle in the darkness, ducking between tree branches like little stars trapped in the trees. I think of Uncle Mike's stories of Cielo Stellato and the words on the Sapientis' truck.

Spazzatrici. Sweepers. I need to know what that could mean.

The wind picks up, rustling the leaves hanging from the branches. It's like they're whispering to one another, sharing secrets about what's hidden behind their backs.

I take a deep breath.

If I want to know, I'll have to follow Chiara into the dark.

Chapter 3

The gloomy trees close behind me, their limbs tangled together in an impossible knot. It's darker than it was on the other side of the gate. Even the little bursts of light seem to have disappeared. The once well-worn path is now overgrown with branches grabbing and scratching at my jacket. The air feels warmer in here than it is in my backyard.

I stumble forward, trying to avoid fallen trees. A cold sweat beads on my forehead and collects beneath my mask. My breath comes out in ragged puffs. I squeeze my hands into fists.

I stand still for a long moment, thinking about turning around. I may actually be afraid of the dark now—the eerie darkness that persists in the daytime where no sunlight can reach, like the woods or basements—and may be too much of a weenie to do whatever it takes for this investigation. After the accident, my whole family told me how brave I was to survive such a bad car crash. That I bounced back like all Bianchinis. But there wasn't anything brave about what I did. I was scared when the car hit ours, terrified when I woke up in the hospital. I almost leapt out of my own skin when I looked at myself in the mirror for the first time. I panicked so bad that Mom took down all the mirrors in the house so I wouldn't have to look at myself. And there's *definitely* nothing brave about being too scared to sleep because you're afraid of the nightmares.

A loud screech echoes through the woods. A large raven swoops down so close I can see the sheen in his black beady eyes. I stumble backward over a tree root and bang into the side of a tree. I barely hold on to my sketch pad.

My shoulder throbs with a hot, prickling pain, and the voice in my head screams: *This is a bad idea—ABORT!*

I stare down at my mud-caked boots. Ugh!

"Maybe Operation Sapienti is over for today," I whisper to myself, but when I look up, a small golden firefly drifts between the trees above me.

I squint at the little bug and watch as it blinks on and off.

It's the middle of November—too cold for fireflies—but another joins it. Then another. Soon there are seven fireflies glittering in the dark like a car's headlights on a lonely road. Safe. Calming. A warm breeze circles around me. They fly just a bit closer, weaving between tree limbs and braiding back together, drawing me deeper into the woods.

I follow them. They hover around me when I lag and speed up once I reach them, swirling and spinning between the leaves.

I hear a girl's giggle up ahead. Then a strange squeal.

I stop.

Maybe it's a baby pig. People sometimes keep little pigs as pets even if they don't live on a farm.

I hold my breath and listen for it again. Another squeal. I tiptoe forward, getting closer to the sound.

The noise repeats just beyond a cluster of dense trees, followed by a shushing sound. The fireflies disappear beyond the underbrush. I creep up and carefully push back the leaves.

I gasp. In a clearing just beyond the trees is a large stone castle that looks like it has been standing in these woods for thousands of years. Its exterior is covered in a thick layer of ivy, but the roof is gone and the stones are crumbling away.

I know these woods. Or at least I thought I did. They'd never been this big and there was never an old castle sitting in the middle of them.

My hands shake, and I grip the tree trunk to steady myself.

Fireflies drift on the edges of the clearing and light up the castle like candles at Midnight Mass. Another squeal erupts from a weathered spire to the right. I look at its base and there's the girl, her hands stretched out to the sky.

"You're being too loud, Chiara," her brother yells down from the castle's spire. "People will hear you!"

"No one will hear us all the way out here, Alessandro." Chiara tosses big, fluffy pillows in a wide circle. "You're always too worried about everything."

"Are you ready for the first one?" Alessandro asks.

Chiara positions herself in the circle's center and lifts a large wicker laundry basket stuffed with even more pillows and blankets. She's grinning, and adjusts her stance so her feet are planted firmly on the ground.

I pull up my binoculars and follow her gaze up the side of the castle. *What are they doing?* I think.

Alessandro stands on the edge of the spire, his legs shoulder-width apart to keep from falling. An old-looking wooden ladder rests against the thick ivy. A wicker basket sits next to his feet—practically teetering on the edge—stuffed with pillows and blankets like Chiara's. But the blankets inside his keep wiggling.

"Be careful. They're still just babies," she says.

My heart leaps into my throat. I stand on my tiptoes to

get a better look at what's inside the basket. More pigs? Puppies? Kittens? Are they throwing baby animals off the castle?

Alessandro unwraps the blankets. I shriek, then quickly cover my mouth and hold my breath.

"What's that noise?" Alessandro pauses and leans forward to look beyond the ring of fireflies.

I duck farther behind the trees. My heart beats so hard against my ribs that it's bound to burst through my chest. It booms in my ears like a drum. Can they hear it?

"What noise?" Chiara asks. "I didn't hear anything."

"I heard something."

"It's probably an animal. Stop worrying. We need to get going."

I should run. My feet get all tingly, my nerves telling my brain it's time to go. But I press my binoculars tighter against my face. I can't stop watching.

They're not puppies or kittens. It's like nothing I've ever seen before.

Inside the basket sit six tiny balls of light. Each one glows a soft white-gold, but they look a bit jagged to be perfect spheres. Little points run alongside their bodies, wiggling like tiny fingers and toes.

They're not just balls of light, though. Are they fairies, their magic so bright their small bodies can't contain it? Or are they something else entirely? My head swims with the possibilities. Trying to fit whatever they are into the world I've known for the past twelve years is impossible. They can't be from this earth. A dull pain clusters between my eyebrows, as if my brain is expanding to make room for these tiny, ethereal creatures.

"They're stars," Alessandro says. "They'll be fine."

"*Babies,*" Chiara repeats. "They're still little. They don't know how to fly yet."

Stars.

Stars?

My brain pushes even harder against my skull.

The stars bounce up and down, that squeaking noise even louder now. I lean out past the trunk to get a better look. Each star has a face. Little pebble eyes, like mice, and small, thin mouths. Their faces animated, each with a different expression, as if they have emotions.

My stomach churns, the chicken parm sandwich threatening to spill out. *This is impossible.*

I readjust my binoculars, clean off the lenses, and try to blink the stars away like a daydream, but there they are: The stars sit in their cozy wicker basket on top of the spire, bouncing and squealing like little baby animals.

Alessandro picks one up from the litter and cradles it in his arms. The star glows a bit brighter as it wriggles around. "Stay still. You're going to fall," he says. The star settles a bit as the boy tickles its tummy. He smiles. "There you go. Are you ready?"

"Remember, be careful!" Chiara yells from the ground.

"One." Alessandro raises the star up into the air. "Two." He swings the star back. "Three." He lets go of the star. It wiggles and flutters its arms, trailing bits of shimmery, silvery grit like clumps of sand—*stardust*—in its wake.

The star bounces through the air before floating slowly down toward the girl. She runs about with the pillow-filled laundry basket while trying to gauge where the star will land. "Keep going," she yells. "Don't fall yet. You can do it!"

The star chirps and dives. It does its best to stay afloat, face strained, eyes shut tight and mouth turned down in a frown. The star squeals again and lands face-first on a pillow with a small *tuft*, sending plumes of feathers into the air.

Chiara rushes to its side and cuddles the star to her chest. "Shhh, it's okay, little one." She bounces it in her arms. She grabs a bottle from her basket and presses it to the star's mouth. Whatever's in the bottle doesn't look much like a liquid. Instead it looks like a stormy, silver-white swirl of energy. The star's eyes open wide, and it takes hold of the bottle in its tiny arms.

"Don't baby it," he calls.

"But it *is* a baby, Alessandro." She pats the star on its pointed head before placing it gingerly in the basket. "You need to be nice to them. They're new to this, and it's our job to teach them."

He rolls his eyes at his sister and rocks the next star in his arms. "Okay, little buddy," Alessandro says. "You can do this. It's your turn. I know you can." He tosses the next star into the air, and even though it whirls and flutters a bit higher and for a little longer than the other star, it still makes a hard landing onto one of the pillows near Chiara.

"They're not gonna be able to stay afloat up there on their own for a while." Chiara picks the star up in her arms and snuggles it against her cheek. "These poor little stars."

I watch mesmerized as one by one Alessandro tosses stars into the air. After the last floats down from the castle, he quickly scrambles down the ladder with his basket to bring them up to the spire again for more training.

The forest grows even darker. The fireflies glow brighter, but it's still hard to see. I step a little closer. I need to soak up every detail. I need to be able to draw this, get this scene just right.

I move out from behind the tree to peek through the bushes in front of it, palms sweaty, hands shaking, sketch pad tight under my arm. I duck and push aside the branches of a bush. My hand slips and the bush shakes loudly. The leaves smack back together hard.

The noise echoes through the clearing.

Everything stops.

Chiara lowers her arms and stares in my direction.

Alessandro quickly tucks the star he was holding back in the basket. The baby stars stop their cooing.

"I told you I heard something a couple hours ago!" Alessandro yells. "That's too loud to be an animal."

"Who's there?" Chiara calls.

My breath catches in my throat. Chiara's eyes meet mine. Her mouth opens in surprise. But before either of them can say anything, I run.

Chapter 4

I scramble back through the woods. A tree branch scratches my hands and its roots catch my shoes. I wince and swallow a yelp while pushing through the darkness. My chest aches, throat sore from the cold.

My yard comes into view as the sun begins dipping behind the houses. The pinks and oranges of its last rays pool over the dusky sky like spilled watercolors. I swing open the gate and dart toward my house. It must have been a long time since I started watching Chiara and Alessandro. Mom will know I've been gone if she's back.

I give one last glance behind me before opening the back door and locking it quickly. I lean against the wall, clutch my sketch pad to my chest, and try to catch my breath. The room spins around me. I close my eyes. All I see are baby stars dancing in a dizzying display.

I have a conversation with myself:

"Did that happen?"

"Yes, Luna, you saw baby stars."

"But baby stars aren't real, are they? They definitely don't have faces!"

"Luna?!" Mom calls from the kitchen.

I scramble out of the mud room and through the kitchen door.

"Where on earth have you been? I got home twenty minutes ago and you were nowhere to be found," Mom says. "I've looked everywhere for you. And don't say you were out in the backyard or in your tree because I looked there, too."

"I walked down to Aunt Therese's," I say. "Wanted to see if she had any . . ." I close my eyes tight, trying to think of something—*anything.* "Sugar? Sugar for my tea."

"Sugar? We've got plenty in the pantry." Mom crosses her arms over her chest. She taps my science textbook with her finger. "It looks like this was barely touched while we were gone. Did you do any reading at all?"

She's like a human lie detector machine. If I try to cover it up, she'll just punish me. And that'll take way longer than telling the truth. My eyes drift to the stairs at the end of the hall. All I want to do is race up them and sprawl out with my sketch pad and pencils.

"No. I was out in the woods."

Mom's eyebrows jump up. "You were *where?*"

"But it's because I saw the neighbor kids run back there and I wanted to see what they were doing." I gesture toward the window. "Except the woods aren't really woods anymore. Have you seen them? It's a forest full of spooky trees now. Thousands of them. Like really big ones with tons of leaves."

"You shouldn't be out in the woods, Luna."

"But look, Mom!" I grab her by the arm and pull her toward the window. "Look how many . . ." I pause, squinting out into our dusky backyard at the shabby number of trees. No longer a forest. Just the same old neatly planted trees my cousins and I used to play tag in. You can see straight through them like a row of toothpicks. "No." I shake my head. "No, no, no. There were way more. I swear. And a huge castle in the middle."

"A castle? On Staten Island?" Mom frowns, the lines around her lips deepening. "Were you really out there today?"

"I *was*, and the forest was humongous." I pull up my binoculars. Maybe looking at the woods through the binoculars will make them go back to the way they were this afternoon. But no. If anything, there are even fewer trees.

"I don't know what's gotten into that head of yours lately."

"Mom, I was there. I *know* what I saw." My voice turns whiny like when I was little and used to throw tantrums.

The kitchen gets heavy with silence. The grandfather clock in the foyer chimes five. "I'm making that appointment for you to see Dr. Miles. That therapist Dr. Tucker recommended," she says.

"What?" I blink at her several times. "Why?"

"You need to talk to someone even if it isn't me." Mom turns away from me and busies herself with chopping onions. "We're having tacos for dinner."

"I'm not hungry." I grab my sketch pad off the dining room table and run up the stairs to my room, shutting the door behind me.

My whole body buzzes. I sit on the window bench and open my sketch pad, pencil poised over an empty page.

Everything pours out onto the page: the stars, the castle, the fireflies, the dark, scary woods. And the Sapientis.

My hand aches, but I keep drawing until the page is full and my mind is empty. Maybe Mom would believe if she saw my drawings. Maybe with this proof she'd realize I'm not imagining things. I peer at the Sapientis' house, trying to see through their dark curtains and into their fantastical world.

Or maybe she'd worry about me even more.

We all see things so differently.

But that's how it is with a lot of things.

I touch the edge of my mask; its hard plastic is cold after being exposed to the chilly air for so long. I stare down at the mess of magic in my sketch pad, the hasty draw-ing of everything in my head. If Mom can't see it, what would Dad or Uncle Mike or even someone else see if they looked at this drawing? Would they understand it the way I do? Or would they be too busy to pay close attention?

I tear a clean page out of my sketch pad, quickly writing my name and address and a rambling paragraph that reads:

Hi there,

You've been selected at random to participate in my project. My name is Luna. I'm twelve years old, and I live on Staten Island. I love art and draw every day. I'm interested in what you see when you look at my drawing. Will you please take a look at it and write me back? Tell me what exactly it is that you see.

And.

Be.

Honest.

I've included a stamped envelope with my address, so don't worry about postage costs. Remember: Be honest.

—Luna

I fold the paper in half and rummage through my desk for the envelopes from the stationery kit my Granny Ranieri bought me for my birthday last year. Carefully, I place the note in an envelope, along with my drawing of Chiara using magic to grow furniture in their house.

There have to be more people out there who see what I see.

I put the envelope on my desk, placing my bright red pen right on top so I don't forget about it, and sit back down on the window bench.

With the stack of envelopes sitting across from me, I turn to a new page in my sketch pad and keep drawing.

Chapter 5

I don't need help." Dad grabs the wheels on his wheel-chair and tries to pull himself away from Mom.

"Your hands are all calloused," she says. "It's going to hurt in this cold."

"Why do we have to do this?" I ask. "It doesn't make me feel any better."

We stand on our driveway, the Wednesday morning sun hidden behind gray clouds fat with rain. I watch the Sapientis' house. Still and quiet. Almost as if it's empty. No one's been around all morning. I haven't even seen their parents since the night they moved in.

"Dr. Madan says Dad needs fresh air." Mom's walks have been an ongoing routine for the past month. Every morning at ten. And if Dad or I have a doctor's appoint-ment in the morning, she makes us go in the afternoon.

A light breeze stirs up the chilly air and sends dead

leaves skittering across the street. I readjust the envelopes nestled between the pages of my sketch pad. Sometimes Mom and Dad like to sit in the small park at the end of our street and I have time to draw the birds and squirrels. But I wish I was still at home spying on the neighbors and drawing pictures of bouncing baby stars instead. Mom would never let me miss one of our family walks.

I finger one of the envelopes. Drawings for my new project. Last night after I drew the stars, I kept going— drawing other fantastical things, like the full moon against a starless sky and unicorns guarding castles hidden deep in the woods. When I couldn't think of any more magic, I drew ordinary things that are sometimes overlooked.

No two people see something the same way. Or correctly. I learned that on one of the crime shows Mom and Dad used to watch together. On every episode, the cops talked to several witnesses and each one had a different idea or opinion of what happened at the crime scene. No story was 100 percent right.

That's where my experiment comes into play. I asked Mom this morning and she said I could leave the folded drawings in our neighbors' mailboxes with our address and ask for their interpretations. As long as I didn't pester them for responses. I'm curious if people can see the magic too, or point out any extra magic that I missed. I want to know what other people notice.

I wrap my thick wool scarf around my face and pull my hood over my head. If it weren't for my experiment, I wouldn't be too excited to be out here. I don't want anyone to see me. Or my mask.

Dad looks about as miserable as I do. He doesn't want anyone to see *him* either. His pale skin echoes the gray sky. His big brown eyes are sunken and sad. Even his large, hooked nose looks droopy. And it's hard for him to shower now, so his thick black hair doesn't have the spring it used to.

Mom tugs my scarf down a few inches, so it's not in my eyes, and smiles. "These walks will do us all some good," she says. "We need to get out more."

"I hate them," I say, walking past my parents. "I don't like people looking at me."

"Look right back at them, Luna. Be brave. There's nothing wrong with you," Dad calls after me a bit too forcefully.

I cringe. It's like he thinks he can shout the courage right into me. Into us.

"Frank," Mom whispers, thinking I'm too far ahead to hear the edge in her voice. "That's not what she needs right now."

"What? She needs to be tough." Dad's voice is firm. It presses down on the crisp autumn morning like an iron. "It's already unfair for a kid her age to deal with all these doctor visits. She doesn't need to deal with people staring at her all day too."

Face flushed, I quicken my pace, running out onto the street so I'm farther away from them.

Tompkinsville has a lot of different kinds of streets, but mine is my favorite. Our street, Marigold Court, is the very first one in the neighborhood. It ends on a cul-de-sac and looks a little bit like a big key amid all the other, labyrinthine streets. All the houses are old and look unique, not like the gated communities where every house comes out looking the same. Here some are short and squat brick homes; others are tall and spindly with big turrets and wood siding. Ours sits smack-dab at the end of the cul-de-sac with the woods at its back. Those strange woods that transform into a twisted, secretive forest. How could an ancient crumbling castle I've never seen before sprout up like it has always been there—and then disappear? Fantasies like that don't just happen on Staten Island.

"What do you think of the new neighbors?" I call over my shoulder. Mom and Dad go silent, their eyes moving over the Sapientis' house.

"New neighbors?" Dad says.

"They just moved in the other day," Mom replies. "They're from Italy, I think." She tilts her head to the side.

They both shrug.

"The dad was in the garage the other day. We saw him

on our way back from Dr. Madan's office." Mom pulls her blond hair into a ponytail as she stares at the house.

"Did you see inside?" I turn to face them. "What was in there?"

"I don't remember," Mom says. "I wasn't snooping."

Dad rolls his wheelchair after me, just a yard behind. "They seem quiet."

"And their windows are dark," Mom adds.

"I want to know what they're up to."

"Don't be so nosy, Luna. It's not polite."

"You don't need to tell her what to do all the time." Dad's voice carries on the wind and stings my cheeks.

I tuck deeper into my coat.

Adults always say it's not the kid's fault when parents fight, but when your name comes up more than anyone else's, it's kind of hard not to feel like you're the problem.

It might have been nice having a brother or a sister. I have my cousins, but now it would be good to have someone when you can't talk to your parents. Like Chiara has Alessandro.

I walk farther ahead of my parents, pull out my sketch pad, and press my palm against the drawing of the baby stars. My parents' voices fade on the breeze. The drawing feels warm against my cold hands, as if it carries its own magic.

I turn the pages to one of the time-stamped drawings

from last night. It's hard to imagine such a quiet Italian family existing. The only time my family is ever quiet is when we're all asleep. Even then my aunt Therese's snoring could wake a grizzly bear out of hibernation.

But the Sapienti family is different, I guess. No activity last night. None since I saw the baby stars bouncing around in the forest yesterday afternoon.

The breeze wraps itself around me, and I close my eyes. I can still see those glimmering stars twirling. When I finally fell asleep sometime after two a.m., my dreams weren't nightmares about the car crash. They were filled with dancing baby stars flying out of the forest and high up into the heavens. No twisted metal or screeching car tires. Just happy dreams of Alessandro tickling the stars' bellies before tossing them from the roof. And of Chiara laughing as the stars floated down onto the feathery pillows strewn about the forest. If I could, I'd live in those dreams forever.

"Just let me push you," Mom says. "It'll be better."

"I'm a man. I can do it myself," Dad snaps. "You just don't get it. You don't see this situation like I do."

I wince and move in front of the Kims' house, a cozy two-story that looks a lot like a gingerbread cottage tucked among many Christmas trees. The Kims are visiting their grandchildren in Florida. Mom's getting their mail and watching their cat. She said they wouldn't be home for two weeks, making them bad candidates for my experiment.

Mom takes hold of Dad's wheelchair and pushes him forward. He crosses his arms over his chest, lips pulled tight in a straight line. The same face he always makes when he's unhappy. For someone as loud and funny as Dad, it's hard to get him to the point where he's too upset to speak. But lately that's become his usual expression.

"What if I went to work on a more regular schedule, you know, to get out of the house?" Dad says. "Instead of these 'walks.'"

"You know you can't yet. Yesterday was an exception. It's so hard to maneuver behind those counters and with all those people." Mom pinches the bridge of her nose. "Mike told me Eddie crashed into you when he was carrying a cold-cut platter. You're lucky he wasn't carrying a pot of meatballs and gravy or something."

Dad waves the incident off with his hand. "Please. It wasn't that big of a deal."

"There was capicola and salami all over the floor. Besides, Dr. Madan says you need more rest."

"He doesn't know anything."

"He's one of the best doctors in the area." Mom sighs. "The deli is too stressful. It's clearly not very wheelchair-friendly. It's okay for once in a while, but not full-time yet."

"Mike's working on getting a ramp put in. It'll be ready in a month."

"Well, then we can discuss this again in a month."

"You're impossible."

"I'm practical."

Dad shakes his head, but he doesn't say anything more.

"Walks are good for you. It's important for you and Luna to get out of the house."

"You should just go back to work," he says. "We'd be fine at home."

"Frank," Mom begins. "You know I can't go back right now. Someone needs to be here to take care of you. Luna can't do it."

"We'd be fine during the day. And you wouldn't be bothering us."

"Bothering you?" Mom frowns, too tired to argue. She's a speech pathologist and works in the school district, but she had to take the first half of the school year off so she could be with Dad and me. I can tell she misses it. Every day she'd come home, excited to tell us about how the kids she's working with were progressing. But now nothing new happens. She's stuck at home and at doctors' offices all day. It doesn't help that Dad and I aren't as easy to be around as the kids she works with in the schools.

I walk faster, trying to lose them again.

ed in my throat, tossing my hair back over my shoul-
"I just don't want to be the town monster."

Come here, Luna," Mom says.

walk over, and Mom crouches in front of me and
hold of my arms. She squints, tugging the scarf
a bit, and then looks at me some more. "I don't see
er," she says. "I see my daughter, Luna. A brave girl
ckled cheeks, bright brown eyes, and a mass of
dark hair." She looks at Dad and smiles. "What do
Frank?"

ans forward in his wheelchair and looks at me
e puzzled way Mom did. "I don't see a mon-
he says. "And if anyone thinks otherwise, they
their eyes checked."

a baby anymore." I ball my hands into fists
p away from them. "I know what I look like.
ok down all the mirrors because I got upset.
"

om begins.

hands in the air. "No. Don't say my name
now everyone says my name like I'm some
the pound." *Ugly, ugly, ugly.* I stare past
if I look at my parents I'll start crying.
I can see my reflection in windows
ying to hide the truth from me doesn't
ing exactly what others see." My voice

If Dad didn't have to take me

day, he and Mom would still be a

in school.

I'd still look normal.

I close my eyes tight, tuck

back corners of my brain.

Two older ladies in tr

opposite side of the street

my parents and me. I pull

One of the women tilts

bly enough to melt m

eyes and she whispers

another appraisal. Th

craning to get a bett

they're thinking: *u*

and look down, p

back home. Sadr

to boil over. I f

cheeks.

"I want

"Luna,

says. She

"That's

"I'

push r

brave

lo

ders.

I

takes

down

a mons

with fre

springy

you see,

He le

in the sam

ster either,

need to get

"I'm no

and take a st

I know you t

I'm not stupi

"Luna," M

I throw my

like that. I hate

sad, ugly dog at

them, afraid that

"Don't you kno

and spoons? You t

stop me from know

catches in my throat. I glare at them. "But I'll be fine, okay? I always am. I just like being by myself."

Mom and Dad exchange a glance, worry etched on both their faces.

I touch the envelopes in my sketch pad and straighten my back. "If you want me to stay out, then I will. I've got stuff to do. Alone."

Dad sighs. He looks at Mom, who nods. "Okay, we'll head home," he says. "But we expect you back in fifteen minutes."

Mom narrows her eyes. "You understand? No detours into the woods."

"I guess."

"Don't give me that, Luna Andrea Marie Bianchini! Keep up the sass and you won't be allowed to do your experiment."

"Fine. I won't go in the woods." I press my lips into a firm line. Better to keep it at that instead of say anything more.

Mom gives me one last look before turning Dad's wheelchair around and heading back home.

I stomp over to the Anderson family's mailbox, a simple white metal one with a red plastic flag. Two pieces of mail and a catalog already sit inside. Good. That means they haven't brought their mail in yet.

I pull out an envelope and take out the drawing. It's the

one I drew early this morning with the charcoals Nonna Bianchini gave me. It's a picture of a boy in Grand Central Station. Commuters rush past him, hurrying to their trains, while he stands at the center of it all in a bright blue coat. Cradled in the boy's arms is a bright star. None of the commuters see him or the star; they're alone in the middle of a sea of people. I want to know if the Andersons see him. If they see any other magic that I might not.

I fold the drawing back up, put it back in its envelope, and place it in the mailbox.

I hurry on to the next house and place a different drawing inside. A breeze carries the scent of burning fireplaces with it. Fall and winter are my favorite seasons. They're crisp, like they've got bite to them. Spring and summer are nice too, but nothing beats eating fresh apple-cider doughnuts and drinking a mug of hot chocolate while curled up on the couch. Or going upstate to pick apples and finding the tallest hills for sledding. But the best part is the trees and the way they transform. They change the entire landscape. It's those great pops of reds and oranges amid the gray skies that are my absolute favorite part of it all. When they become skeletons in the winter, all spindly limbs, the landscape changes again. Mom and I go to the park in the fall to collect the prettiest leaves and press them between wax paper in books so they dry evenly.

It's already transforming into winter. The trees are

starting to look bare. We haven't gone to the park yet and it's already getting too late. A knot forms in my stomach. What if all the best leaves are gone by now?

I place another drawing in a green scaly mailbox shaped like a trout. If I get even one interpretation back, this walk will be worth it.

I pause outside the Sapientis' house. Their house is bright white and sectioned off by intricate dark wood-work. Its roof is high, like a mountain. The big truck is still in their driveway, its side still a blank white instead of emblazoned with the name and fireflies I saw two nights ago. Could they have been the same as those fireflies in the woods yesterday?

Everything looks different, and it's strange what a little sunlight can do to make it all seem so normal. As if I didn't see that little girl make the furniture grow ten times its size. Or watch her and her brother throw stars into the air and catch them in laundry baskets.

My eyes fall on their mailbox and my hand instinctively touches the last envelope.

I sigh and shake my head, shoving the drawing deeper into my sketch pad. The envelopes have my name and address on them. They'll know who I am. My heart leaps into my throat and I continue walking home.

Electricity tingles in my stomach and shoots down through my legs, compelling me to turn around. I run to the Sapientis' mailbox. The envelope is like a brick in my hand. I take a deep breath and open their mailbox. It's the best drawing I've done in a long time and the one that gave me the idea for my project. It's of them in the forest with the stars.

I shove it in between the catalogs and letters, then race back to my house.

My parents left the garage door open for me. I pause at the door and hear muffled voices reverberating through it. Dad's is low and forceful. Mom's is higher but just as aggressive. My hands shake as I press the button for the garage door, and the motor creaks as it lowers to the ground with a gentle thud.

"Mom? Dad?" I shout while walking through the laundry room and into the kitchen. "Can we go to the park—"

Their eyes shoot toward me, as if they had forgotten I was only a few minutes behind them. They quickly look away. Dad stares down at his lap, Mom up at the ceiling. Their silence is so thick it fills the room like smoke, blackening our lungs and choking the words from our throats. Anger swells up inside me, traveling from my chest, up my neck, and onto my face.

I frown, heat flushing my cheeks. Neither of them can look at me.

"I'm going up to my room." I'm gone before they can say anything.

Luna Bianchini
236 Marigold Court
Staten Island, NY 10301

I Know What I Saw

You didn't see anything.

—A. S.

Chapter 6

"Will you please fill those pie crusts with the apple and cherry fillings?" Mom gestures to the bowls of pie filling we prepared last night. She opens the oven and squirts another basterful of drippings over the turkey. "I'll make a plate of pigs in a blanket and prosciutto for you and Dad in a second."

"Do I have to?" I say.

She flashes me a look, and I get up from the kitchen table, shoving Alessandro's note back into my sketch pad. Dad and I didn't want to have Thanksgiving this year. Especially Dad.

Mom rushes around the kitchen, trailed by the smells of fresh rosemary and melted butter. It's Mom's first time hosting a family dinner in a long time. Her chance to trick everyone into believing things are normal around here.

It's been a while since I've seen the entire family.

I steal a glance at my sketch pad, longing to analyze Alessandro's note some more. His letters were sloppy, like he wrote it in a hurry. But his handwriting could just always be that bad. The *A* he used to sign the note is sharp and pointed.

I spoon the goopy cherry and apple fillings into their individual pie crusts and top them with the layers of crust Mom pre-rolled for me.

Maybe he was angry when he wrote it.

Or maybe he's scared I know too much.

The phone rings.

"Will you get that?" Mom asks, hands greasy from prosciutto.

RUIZ blinks on the caller ID. My stomach flips. It's Tailee. The phone rings again.

"Who is it?"

"I don't know."

My ears burn, the ringing like an alarm sounding out through our kitchen. Finally, the answering machine picks it up.

"Luna? I know you're there. Please pick up." Tailee's voice is tinny coming through the speaker, but she sounds annoyed. I wince. It reminds me of that time Damian pushed me down on the playground in the second grade and she called him a jerk before helping me up. But that time her annoyance wasn't directed at me.

66

Mom looks at me, eyes narrowed.

"Look, I just wanted to talk to you and wish you a happy Thanksgiving. You never want to talk to me anymore," Tailee continues. "You're never there when I drop off your homework." She sighs. "I miss you."

Tailee hangs up and the answering machine beeps. One missed call flashes in red. The knot in my stomach tightens.

"You need to see your friend, Luna," Mom says. "All this time alone. It's not good."

"Where should I put these?" I pick up the pies.

"Your therapy appointment is tomorrow."

"Umm-hmm," I mumble.

"Did you hear me?"

"Yes," I reply, putting the pies in the fridge and slamming the door shut.

"Take these into the living room." Mom presses two plates with prosciutto and mozzarella pinwheels, pigs in a blanket, and crusty slices of bread into my hands. "Give one to your father, please."

I nod.

"Tonight will be good for you." She kisses me on the forehead. "For all of us. Baby steps, right?" Mom turns her attention to peeling a fifteen-pound bag of potatoes.

"We never eat that many potatoes," I say. "We always have leftovers."

"There are more mouths to feed. Cousin Tina's bringing her boyfriend this year, and your aunt Giovanna is pregnant," she says. "Not to mention all the usual cousins who'll be here too." Mom attacks the potatoes with a frenzy. Potato skins get everywhere and stick to the tile floor like discarded Band-Aids. Gross.

The grandparents and uncles and aunts should be easier to deal with than my cousins. My grandparents generally ruffle my hair, shake their heads sadly, or look at me like they're about to cry. But they don't say much else. I know my younger cousins will be curious. Staring too long, asking questions no one really knows how to answer, or maybe even grabbing at my mask with their tiny hands. A shudder crawls down my spine. I swallow the fears and walk the plates of food out to Dad before I completely lose my appetite.

He sits in his favorite recliner, the same spot he spends most days now. He's watching the football game. He used to watch football standing, pacing in front of the TV and swearing under his breath whenever his team messed up. Now, unable to, most of his anxiety over the game is directed at the recliner's armrests—much to Mom's annoyance.

"Mom put these together for us." I place one of the plates on the end table next to him.

"Thank you, baby." Dad picks at one of the pinwheels,

pulling the prosciutto off and eating the mozzarella.

I sit on the couch and start leafing through my latest drawings of the Sapientis' house. No activity. Again. At 4:37 this morning, I thought I saw another firefly glowing in the window across from mine. But when I went to grab my sketch pad off my desk, the light was gone.

Just what are the Sapientis up to on Thanksgiving? Do they even celebrate it?

Maybe Mom wouldn't notice if I snuck off with one of the pies and brought it over to them. That way I'd be invited in and I could get a better look around.

"Aw, fumble!" Dad yells, leaning forward in his recliner.

I look up at the TV. "What does a linebacker do exactly?"

I put my sketch pad aside and dunk one of the pigs in a blanket into ketchup.

"They're defensive players," Dad explains. "They try to tackle whoever has the ball."

The doorbell rings, and I jump.

Dad raises his eyebrows. "The circus is here."

Everyone in the family has already seen me. But most, like Rocco and Gloria, haven't seen me since the hospital. When I was hooked up to machines and my face was freshly scarred, pink and red, the skin shiny like an icy pond. I've got the mask covering up most of my skin now. I can't look worse than I did then. Though I wouldn't *really* know with all the mirrors gone. It's hard getting a good look at yourself in the back of a spoon.

The doorbell rings again. I take a deep breath and place my food on the coffee table. Now is a good time to start practicing being brave.

"I'll get it," I holler into the kitchen.

I open the door and am greeted by both sets of grandparents. Nonna Bianchini reaches me first. She wraps me in her doughy arms and presses her bright red lips against my left cheek while squeezing me tight. She's a short, round woman with pinkish-white skin, like Dad's, and curly dark-brown hair. But despite being so small, she could knock the wind out of a hippo with her hugs.

"My angel," she says, her accent slightly heavier than my other grandparents'. She was born in Tuscany and moved here with her parents when she was around my age—old enough so some of that Italian lilt still hugs her English. "It's been ages since I last saw you."

"I saw you two weeks ago." My voice comes out in a gasp against her chest. "It really hasn't been that long."

"Too long when you live right down the street." She lets go a little, holding me at arm's length. Her brown eyes search my face and rest a moment too long on my mask. She clucks her tongue and cups my chin in her hand. "This is no good. I hate that this contraption hides your beautiful face."

"You know it's to help with the healing." Granny Ranieri pushes through the door. She's taller than Nonna Bianchini and stands as straight as a needle. Her gray hair is cut short; curls frame her angular face. Being from Sicily, her skin is darker, like Mom and me. She adjusts the gold-rimmed glasses that sit precariously on her sloped nose. "You're looking better, Luna." Granny Ranieri nudges between Nonna Bianchini and me and kisses me on the cheek.

"Thank you." I adjust my mask carefully, making sure none of the burns or scars are showing.

Nonno Bianchini and Papa Ranieri push past their wives, each greeting me with a kiss on the forehead, and then off to the living room to sit on the couch until dinnertime. They care, but unlike my grandmothers, they don't like to hover.

"You need to eat, you know," Nonna Bianchini says. "To build up your strength. Has your mother been feeding you?"

She pinches the skin under my arm, and I squeak. "Yes, obviously."

Nonna Bianchini shakes her head. "Not enough."

We move from the entryway into the kitchen, where both grandmothers greet Mom with big hugs and kisses.

"You poor, poor woman." Nonna Bianchini walks over to the oven and pokes around at the turkey. "So put

71

out with my Frankie and Luna that you've barely had time to properly dress the turkey."

Mom puts down the potato peeler and wipes the sweat from her brow with the back of her arm. "I've had plenty of time, Ma, but I could use both of your help."

Granny Ranieri rubs Mom's shoulder. "You're doing a fine job. You've got a lot on your plate."

"The turkey's going to be great," I say, looking between both of my grandmothers. I smile at Mom. Sometimes they don't know how to talk to her. Or to anybody. "I'll even have seconds."

"Thank you, Luna."

The doorbell rings again. But before anyone can answer it, the door swings open, and the sounds of Uncle Mike and the rest of the family trying to talk over one another flood into the hallway. Cousin Tina and her boyfriend; Aunts Victoria, Therese, Pearl, and Giovanna with her swollen belly; cousins Rocco, Joey, Gloria, Paulie, Rita, and Angelo; and Uncles Paul, Billy, Lou, Joe, and John all barge in and begin taking off their coats and shoes.

My heart flutters in my chest like a butterfly caught in a cage, banging against the wires trying to find a way out. The kitchen suddenly feels small. And warm, too. The skin under my mask itches. I look around, trying to find a way out and up the stairs to my bedroom, but my cousins are sitting on the stairs to take off their shoes.

"What's the matter, Luna?" Granny Ranieri asks. "You look whiter than a *fantasma.*"

I shake my head. "I'm fine."

"Bring the desserts and sides in here," Nonna Bianchini shouts. "We need some help."

Mom looks at me and gestures toward the entryway. "Go play with your cousins."

I open my mouth to protest, but close it again. I swallow hard and look at my purple-and-blue socks. The only two my age are Rocco and Gloria. The last time they came over with my aunt, I hid in my bedroom and pretended like I was asleep. It's one thing for them to see me in the hospital. That's when the doctors were more optimistic about my progress. Like when Tailee came over that first month and things seemed okay. Now the mask has stayed on so long that everything is different and I can't be the same cousin I used to be. That funny, chatty Luna is hidden somewhere inside, but she's having a hard time coming out.

My lungs are heavy, filled with too much air. Sweat pours down my neck. It all feels too overwhelming. I close my eyes tight and wish myself away to anywhere but here.

"Luna? Are you okay? Do you need to rest?" Mom looks at me like she's trying to stare into my brain. Sometimes it feels like she really can. I hate when she does this.

I shake my head and take a deep breath before walking into the entryway to greet them.

"Luna!" Rocco yells. He kicks off his sneakers and tosses his jacket on the floor. Even though he's only six months older than me, Rocco stands nearly a foot taller. If he keeps up at this pace, he'll be the tallest person in our entire family. He wraps me in a hug, nearly picking me up off my feet before putting me back down a little too gently. "I've missed you at school," he says, taking a step back. "Everyone has." Rocco directs his eyes over my shoulder, at the ceiling or the glittery cat on my sweatshirt—anywhere but my face.

"I missed you too, Luna." Gloria kisses me on the unmasked cheek. She casts a worried glance at my face before running into the living room to greet our Papa Ranieri. Gloria is also already taller than me by a few inches. But everyone's always said how much we look alike. Twins. Sisters. But now, not anymore. My face feels hot.

The others stare at me momentarily, eyes locked on my mask. Some look nervous, others sad.

"Oh, sweetheart," Aunt Giovanna says. She wraps me in a big hug and kisses my cheek. "I'm so, so sorry."

Cousin Tina is next, her long brown hair combed and styled into one of the same poufy updos she used to do for me when she'd babysit. A sad smile, eyes filled with concern. She introduces her boyfriend, who looks at his shoes the entire time. She hugs me and rubs my back before following after Gloria into the living room. The rest of the family follows suit, either kissing my forehead or smiling politely before making their way into the living room or kitchen.

My stomach flips. The entire procession makes me feel like a circus attraction. I don't want to make anyone sad. I don't want anyone feeling bad for me. I wonder if the Phantom of the Opera felt this way too.

"How are you feeling, Luns?" Uncle Mike asks, squeezing my shoulder. He towers over me—Bianchini tall at five eleven.

I shrug. "Fine, I guess."

Uncle Mike looks at me, *really* looks at me, his black bushy eyebrows knitting together. "Tonight will be okay. Pinkie promise." He wraps his pinkie finger around mine. "I'll even keep that ma of mine in line. I know how she can get."

"Thanks." I shake out my hair so it covers my burning cheeks. "I'm sorry."

"Sorry?" he says. "Why are you sorry?"

"I don't want everyone to feel bad."

"Oh, honey. It's not your fault." He frowns. "I got to help prep dinner, but just come get me if you need me." Before I can say anything else, Uncle Mike disappears into the sea of cousins crowding into the kitchen.

Rocco clears his throat. "Did it hurt?"

"The accident?" I ask.

He nods. His dark eyes are focused on the grandfather clock.

"Yeah." I adjust my mask again. "It burned," I say, unable to look at him. The scars on the right side of my face prickle at the healthy skin underneath. It's a dull, constant pain that's hardly noticeable until someone brings it up. My voice breaks, sounding not quite like my own—as if I'm outside my body and listening to some other Luna tell this story from far away. "It felt like suffocating. Like being torn apart, but then everything went black and I woke up in the hospital. I don't remember much else."

Rocco's shoulders slump. He opens his mouth like he has something to say, but quickly closes it. I don't know what's worse: all the worried glances, prayers, and "I'm sorrys" or not being seen or spoken to at all.

"Luna," Mom yells from the kitchen. "Can you please help me?"

I turn from Rocco and do my best to keep my tears in check. "Coming."

Before heading back into the kitchen, I rush into the guest bathroom and lock the door behind me. The tears fall, my shoulders shaking with the weight of them.

I undo the Velcro straps and remove my mask. My entire mind spreads and grows bigger after being trapped in the tight, constricting plastic. Like when Mom takes

76

out all the vacuum-sealed sweaters she put away during spring and they expand to their original shapes and sizes. This stupid mask. The only good thing it does is hide my scars. But everything feels more relaxed without it. There's room to think without getting a headache. I'd never take it off in front of people if I can help it, though.

I splash some cold water onto my face and wipe it off with Mom's decorative Thanksgiving-themed hand towel. The burns sting, but not as bad as they were when I was talking to Rocco. "You can do this," I say, staring at the empty wall where the bathroom mirror used to be.

Tears threaten to well up again. I'm not good at giving myself pep talks. My breathing comes in short, shaky rasps. I hold my breath and count to three, releasing it slowly once more.

"Get it together," I whisper.

I grab a tissue and blow my nose before putting my mask back on and leaving the bathroom.

Chapter 7

The kitchen is busy with all sorts of activity. It smells like flaky crescent rolls, buttery mashed potatoes, and juicy turkey. My stomach rumbles, and I remember the plate of pigs in a blanket and pinwheels I left in the living room.

I weave around cousins, my grandmothers, and Uncle Mike, all moving through the kitchen as if performing an intricate dance I never learned. Cooking with my family is fun, but it's always so hectic. I prefer when it's just my mom or Uncle Mike. It's easier to follow along.

Mom takes hold of my arm and presses a warm crescent roll into my hand. She brushes the hair from my face and looks at me. "You've been crying," she says.

I shake my head.

"This is too much for you." Her shoulders slump. Guilt shows on her face. "I shouldn't have volunteered."

"No. I'll be fine."

Nonna Bianchini stares at me. She drops the wooden spoon she was holding and it clatters on the floor. Flecks of brown gravy spatter across the kitchen cabinets.

"Fine?" Her eyes are watery.

"Is something wrong, Ma?" Mom asks, helping Nonna Bianchini sit down at the table.

"Her cheek. Her nose!" Nonna shakes her head. "If it weren't for that mask, everyone would see. My sweet little girl," she cries. "She's not the same."

"You haven't seen her face since the hospital," Uncle Mike says.

"Because I can't bear to." Tears wet her eyes. "I can't bear to see my little Luna hurt in such a way."

"Ma, calm down." Uncle Mike's eyes dart between me and his mother.

"Calm down?" Nonna's voice rises. "This is all *your* fault." She points a shaky finger at my mom. "You know Frankie shouldn't be driving when his mind is elsewhere."

Before I can try to understand why the accident would be Mom's fault when she wasn't even in the car, a wail escapes Nonna's lips. Her shoulders heave up and down. "What about Christmas pictures? What about when we go to Midnight Mass? She's never going to be normal with everyone staring and whispering." She cries freely, cheeks blotchy and red.

My face is hot. My pulse booms in my ears. The cousins and aunts in the kitchen stare at me from the corners of their eyes. The others trickle in from the living room and watch from the doorway. I'm stuck in the middle of it all, too tense to move from my spot. Trapped in the eye of Hurricane Nonna.

Mom's eyes widen. She takes a step closer to Nonna, her shoulders squared.

"Ma—" Uncle Mike begins.

"*My* fault?" Mom's voice crashes against the walls of the kitchen like a wrecking ball. "Where do you come off saying these things in my home? It was your son driving. And you've got no right speaking this way about my child."

"You're the better driver. You know how Frankie is. Always speeding and stressed out." She tries to catch her breath between sobs. Aunt Therese fills a glass with water and places it in front of her. "You know! It's your responsibility to take care of *your* daughter."

"She's his daughter too! And who cares about Midnight Mass and what other people think?"

It feels like the world is closing in on me. I try to take a deep breath, but it is trapped under the weight pressing down on my chest.

"The world is too cruel," Nonna says. "And you can't yell at me like this!" Her words are thick with tears, making it even more difficult to understand what she's saying. "Where's the respect?"

"That's it." Dad's voice rises above Nonna's crying. He wheels himself into the kitchen, his face red. "Great job, Ma. Thanksgiving's ruined before we've even eaten." He tosses his hands in the air. "If you're going to talk about my family like this, then you're not welcome here. No more Sunday dinners. No more hosting holidays after this."

The kitchen falls silent. Even Nonna Bianchini's sobbing has stopped. Everything starts to spin, and the few pigs in a blanket I ate are about to end up on the floor. Heat rises in my chest and travels up my neck to my face. Everyone is looking at me. My mask feels too tight. My eyes sting, and my breathing hitches. Crying or puking in front of my family isn't an option.

I dart from the kitchen, grabbing my sketch pad on my way up the stairs and locking my bedroom door behind me. I rip the mask off my face and fling it on the floor before throwing myself across my bed. I'd toss it out the window if I didn't know Mom would yell at me.

"Luna?" Mom's voice is soft on the other side of my door. "Luna, will you please unlock your door?"

"No." I shove my pillow against my face and scream. Hot tears slick my cheeks and soak the pillow through. I hurl it at the door. It hits the wall and slides down to the ground with a dull thud. "I'm never leaving my room again."

I pull Dad's cornicello out from underneath my shirt and squeeze it in my fist. Dad gave me his tiny gold horn amulet after the accident, just before my first surgery. He said it would protect me.

If only he gave it to me before the accident.

Then maybe I wouldn't be this big disappointment for my family.

"Please, Luna?" Mom says.

No amount of bargaining is going to make me go back downstairs and face my family. This isn't like one of her morning walks or weekly trips to see Dr. Tucker. I tug my rainbow comforter over my head and curl my knees up against my chest. Chatter begins to pick up again downstairs, but my family doesn't sound like they usually do. Not excited or happy. There's a tension. A strain to their voices. They're afraid Nonna's outburst is a fracture that'll lead to an even bigger break. I curl deeper into myself and shut my eyes. What my family doesn't seem to realize is that it's too late. Everything's already broken.

A muffled shout wakes me up. I open one eye, then the other. My room is dark. It's late. Everyone must have left. Mom's and Dad's voices rise and fall on the other side of my door. I roll over on my side. The red numbers on my alarm clock beam 10:27.

Eyes bleary, I pull my hair into a bun and crawl out of bed. I grab my mask off the floor and put it back on. My face won't heal properly if I'm not wearing it all the time.

Dad shouts and I flinch. Mom responds, but I can't hear what she says. I don't want to hear it.

It's too cold to sit out in my tree tonight, which makes their fighting all the more real.

I stare out at its gnarled, dark branches. It's the only place that feels safe and normal.

I sit on the window bench, sketch pad on my lap, and take up my binoculars. As usual, there's nothing going on at the Sapientis'. Mr. Anderson dances in front of his window, but tonight even his shimmying can't make me smile. Cecilia stares out her window, her phone up to her ear.

So much for the night sky wrapping me up like a big, warm blanket. I feel frozen. Mr. Anderson dances off to bed and Cecilia closes her blinds, the light winking out in their rooms. One by one the other houses follow suit, each window going dark as people wind down for the night.

Mom's and Dad's muffled shouts come in bursts through the vents. It's like counting the seconds between thunder and lightning. There's a science to it.

Outside, the night calm settles over the neighborhood

and I breathe slowly, wanting that calmness to push into my house too. Nonna Bianchini's tearful sobbing repeats over and over in my head. "She's never going to be *normal!*"

I press my head against the cold window glass. Maybe she's right. Maybe my face is broken for good and all the doctors in Staten Island won't be able to put me back together again. A wave of tears pushes against my eyelashes. I squeeze my eyes shut, not allowing them to fall. I take another shaky breath and reopen them.

A small flicker of light catches my eye.

It's not big, hardly significant, a tiny white dot in an ocean of blackness coming from the Sapientis' house next door.

I hide behind the curtain and watch the little lone firefly dance on the wind.

Alessandro emerges from the shadows. He pushes the second-floor window open farther and tosses a wooden toy connected to a silver string out onto the breeze. It falls a foot or so before catching on the wind and floating into the woods behind our houses.

I inch out from behind the curtains and press my hand against the glass. He lets some more of the silver string go, giving the toy enough slack to float farther away.

The glass vibrates. A buzzing grows in the palm of my hand and shoots up my arm. It travels all the way under my mask and pulses against my skin.

I snatch my hand off the window and open it up a

crack, bracing myself for the chilly end-of-November wind, but the air is warm. Almost hot.

I lean an inch out the window. The vibrating starts up again, coursing through my body. My hair floats just above my shoulders, bouncing around my head like when you press your hands against the electric static ball at the science museum. My eyes widen, and I'm afraid that if I blink I'll miss something. Excitement stirs in my chest, buzzing in time with the electricity surging in the air.

Alessandro's mom comes up behind him and puts an arm on his shoulder. "You need to be more careful." Mrs. Sapienti's voice carries on the breeze between our houses. "Da Vinci constructed it himself."

"It's made it this long," Alessandro says, smiling. "A little turbulence won't hurt it."

She plants her hands on her hips. "I don't know what I'm going to do with you."

"Chiara," Alessandro calls. "It's time."

The little girl appears in the window carrying a lantern. Chiara stands with her hands on the window-sill while her mother braids her thick dark hair into two plaits. "Don't let the stars nibble on your hair this time." Mrs. Sapienti finishes both braids with two dark-blue ribbons. She helps Chiara into a big down coat.

"I won't," Chiara says. "Promise."

Then about two dozen fireflies float from the forest,

85

joining their lone brother to illuminate the space between our houses.

Where did the rest of these fireflies come from?

I duck farther behind the curtains, my heart in my throat.

The fireflies form a circle like they did in the forest, bobbing up and down like fishing lures.

Alessandro tugs on the silver string. Emerging from the forest like an ancient warship is a large zeppelin.

A squeak escapes from my lips. I clasp my hands against my mouth to stifle the next one. This is bigger than the baby stars. Much bigger. The zeppelin looks nothing like the Hindenburg or the blimps that sometimes circle Manhattan. It looks centuries old. Like a flying Viking boat or pirate ship that belongs in some alternate history where ships ride upon soft, voluminous clouds instead of giant waves.

The fireflies open up their circle, and the ship floats into the middle. Their glow bounces off the side of the ship's dark wooden carriage. It's shiny with deep red accents. Narrow, too. Above it is a large black balloon the shape of a bullet. But unlike the zeppelins we learned about in history class, the balloon on this one is decorated with long gold ribbons.

At its bow is a wooden figurehead of a woman with silvery-blue skin. I grab my binoculars to get a better look at her. Her hair and eyes glitter as if she's been coated in stardust, and she wears a delicate-looking gown. Perched on her finger is a tiny, sparkling star.

I close my eyes tightly. When I open them again, the zeppelin is still there, floating just above the Sapientis' house, as normal a fixture as a satellite dish or a weather vane.

I pinch the skin under my right arm and yelp.

"I'm not asleep," I say. "This is real."

"I packed cookies, apples, and two sandwiches each." Mrs. Sapienti presses two lunch boxes into Chiara's hands, who passes them to her brother. She hands her daughter two brooms, two mops, and two buckets filled with what appears to be washcloths and cleaning supplies. "Remember to take stock tonight of all the supplies we have on board. It's been a while."

"Yes, Mama," the pair says in unison.

"And remember to be safe," Mrs. Sapienti says. "It's not an easy job."

"We always are." Alessandro rolls his eyes and grabs the mops and a bucket. "We'll be fine."

The ship lowers and fits snugly between our homes, docking close enough to the window. Mrs. Sapienti blows her children kisses before disappearing back into the room. The children climb onto the ship.

I hold on to the wall to steady myself.

"Hey!" Chiara's voice booms between our houses. She stares directly at me, pointing. "You! From the woods."

My pulse hammers against my head.

I shut my curtains tight and catapult back into bed, diving headfirst beneath my comforter. She couldn't have seen me. It's too dark to see into my room. Chiara saw a shadow. That was it.

I peek my head out from underneath the comforter. From the sliver between my curtains, I can see the hulking ship hasn't left. It looms over my bedroom. There's a soft tapping at my window, and I duck further under my comforter, like a groundhog.

The window. In my rush to hide I forgot to shut it. The bench creaks, and a soft *thud* hits the bedroom floor. I pull my knees up under my chin. I clutch my dad's cornicello, holding it tight in my fist.

I should have locked the stupid window.

"Hello?" Chiara says to the darkness. "I know you're in here."

Chapter 8

Chiara's footsteps echo throughout the quiet room. I hold my breath, praying she doesn't see the obvious girl-shaped lump in the bed. Hiding has never been a talent of mine. When my cousins and I used to play hide-and-seek, I was always found first.

I push off the covers and sit up. "Hi." Nervousness cracks in my voice.

Chiara turns, directing a little lantern in my direction. The candlelight cuts through the dark and lands square on my face. "Why are you in bed?"

"I was hiding."

"Oh." She walks over to the bed and flops down on the end of it like she's been in my room thousands times and has known me her entire life. "Why would y hide?"

It's only the little neighbor girl, but who knows

other kind of magic they're capable of. After all, they're probably not too happy that I know their secret.

"Because I'm scared."

Chiara laughs. "That's silly. Why would you be scared?"

I pluck at the feathers popping out of my rainbow comforter. "I know that you and your family are different. I saw the zeppelin and the stars."

"Silly! We already knew that from the drawing you sent us."

Of course they would have known from my drawing. My cheeks heat up.

"Besides, I *knew* I saw someone in the woods the other day. You're very nosy."

"I'm not nosy. I'm observant."

She shrugs. "Same thing."

"You're not mad that I know?" I ask. "You're not going to turn me into a frog and keep me in a cage, or make me into a statue to put in your backyard because I know your secrets?"

She puts a finger to her lips as if in deep contemplation. Finally, she shakes her head. "Nah. That's not how it works exactly. Also, Mama wouldn't let us keep a pet frog."

"Then what's going to happen?"

"Nothing, I guess."

"Nothing?"

"Well, it's really only a problem if everyone in all of New York knew. Most people don't even notice us. They're too busy to look up."

"I won't tell everyone in New York." I shake my head.

"Good." She smiles. "That would've been bad."

"So," I ask. "What do you do with it? That big ship?"

"We are spazzatrici." Chiara grins. "We tend to the stars and moon."

"You fly?" I point to my ceiling. "Up there?"

"Yes, all the way into the heavens." She laughs and mimics my pointing. "Beyond the roofs and up into the sky."

"That sounds dangerous." My heartbeat quickens. So many things could go wrong flying up that high. Especially in an old wooden zeppelin and not something more stable like a rocket ship. I swallow hard, my hands tingling. It also sounds wonderful.

Chiara looks at me, her big brown eyes pale in the candlelight. She stares so long, her gaze burning holes into my mask. *Ugly, ugly, ugly*, bounces around in my brain. That awful word I can't shake. I want to sneak back under the covers and hide once more.

But her smile only brightens. No sadness. No pity.

"Why are you staring at me?" she asks. "Do I have food on my face? We ate dinner in a rush tonight, and Alessandro always says I'm a messy eater."

"No. You're fine," I say. "Why are you staring at me?"

She shrugs. "We've got the same exact eye color. It's neat."

With that, Chiara hops from the bed and walks back over to the window. "You could come with us tonight, if you wanted. Your drawing was nice," she says. "Alessandro can be annoying, so don't listen to him. You could draw all the pretty things you see in space with us. It's *bellisima* up there. Do you want to come?" She tilts her head to the side, her dark braids floating around her.

I jump off the bed, the comforter falling to the floor. "Come with you? Up into the stars?"

Chiara nods. "Yeah. Where else would I mean?"

I look at Jean Valjean sitting on my bedside table, his starry turtle shell not at all like the real night sky. The zeppelin's shadow floats on the wall, rising and falling like the tide.

Mom's voice filters underneath the door. It's angry but hushed. Dad's chases after, his shouting louder than hers. Their voices are a muffled mess, tangled together in a wrestling match, trying to pin the other down.

I thought they went to sleep.

Chiara looks at the floor, pretending like she didn't hear my parents' yelling. "You should come with us," she says.

I take one last look at the bedroom door before pulling an old, too-big hoodie over my pajamas. I follow Chiara through the window and into the cold November night, my parents' arguing drowned out by the wind.

Chapter 9

"You know how dangerous it is bringing a non-spazzatrici into the heavens, Chiara," Alessandro says from behind the ship's wheel. "Do you realize how much trouble you'd be in if Papa found out?"

"As much trouble as you'd be in if Papa knew you forgot me on the moon two weeks ago." Chiara stares at her older brother, her gaze unblinking.

I stand behind her and awkwardly toy with the hair floating around my shoulders. Alessandro has a point. Bringing me along doesn't seem that safe, but I don't want to be at home.

"Fine. She can come along." Alessandro sighs. "But I'm not happy about it. She'll have to help out." He looks me up and down as if I were a soldier before nodding his head. "At least you're taller than Chiara. You won't need help reaching ropes or equipment. Name's Luna, right? Like the goddess."

I nod.

The ship is massive. Much bigger than it looks from the outside. It's impossible to take it in all at once. My eyes dart around, trying to collect each piece of the ship. To memorize every angle, every curve, every single bit of it.

I look back at my window, the zeppelin already at least four feet above it. It doesn't feel like we're moving.

My heart leaps into my throat. I'm *really* going up to the stars. I'm going to see the moon up close.

"How fast does the ship fly? And how does the whole atmospheric pressure thing work?" My fingers itch for my pencil and sketch pad, but I forgot them in my excitement to board the ship. I'll need to remember all of this. "How can any of this work? This isn't a dream, right?"

Alessandro rolls his eyes. "Are you going to ask a million questions all night?"

"Leave her alone and steer the boat, will you?" Chiara yells. "Papa said you passed out you were so excited on your first trip."

"Did not!" Alessandro shouts back.

"Just ignore him," Chiara says. "That's what I do." She tugs at my hand. "I'll give you a tour." Chiara walks me around the middle portion of the deck. Past groups of old-looking barrels and long, twisting pieces of rope, neatly coiled like snakes.

"What's your ship's name? And who is she?" I point at the lady at the front of the ship. She's beautiful.

Chiara places her hands on the smooth railing and looks down, the wind lifting the braids slightly off her shoulders. "She's named *Stella Cadente*—Shooting Star. And the lady at the front is the goddess Luna. I like her, too."

The trees tickle the bottom of the ship, trying to grasp at us with the tips of their branches, as we move past the Sapientis' attic.

"The zeppelin's balloon can expand and retract depending on the size of the space we're in," she says. "That's what it's doing now. It's like a set of lungs. Breathing in and out."

"And what happens when we get up into outer space?" I ask. "How do you even travel to the moon in one night?" My eyes widen. "And how do our heads not explode from all the pressure? Do we change into spacesuits and helmets? Do you have one for me to borrow?"

Chiara laughs. "You do have a lot of questions."

"I'm sorry," I say. "It's just that this is the most exciting thing that's ever happened to me. Ever."

"It's okay," she says. "It must be very weird."

"Just a little."

"We don't have space suits. Or helmets. But our heads have never exploded." She pushes off from the railing and dances back into the middle of the deck. Both sides of the ship have clean, polished wooden staircases that lead to the stern and bow. Alessandro stands at the wheel, his back to us as he directs the zeppelin out from the wedge between our two houses.

"Then how does it all work?" I spread my arms wide. "You don't run out of oxygen?"

She shakes her head. "Papa says it's magic."

"Of course it's magic," Alessandro yells over his shoulder. "You saw the stars in the forest. What else would it be?"

"It's just that we learn all this stuff in science class and then that's not how any of it works?"

"Atmospheric pressure is real. Science is real," Alessandro says. "But so is magic." He shrugs. "These things aren't mutually exclusive. Magic and science can coexist. Sometimes they're the same thing."

Chiara points overhead. "This is my job. I've got to turn them all on and off." Ten brass lanterns hang along the deck, illuminating the darkness with their bright flames.

Between the staircases leading to the bow is a silvery-blue door with a large brass knob. A sliver of a moon is etched into its front. "What's in there?" I ask.

"That's where we keep our equipment." Chiara smiles. "And it's the ship's nursery. We keep the baby stars in there—the ones you saw in the forest."

Chiara skips toward the door and waves for me to follow. "I need to check on them. Depending on how good they do getting used to the atmosphere, we're going to release them tonight. Wanna see them?"

"Yes!" I almost shout.

The zeppelin's balloon pushes out from between the roofs. It squeezes to fit into the small space before blooming to its full capacity as if it were taking a deep breath. Just as Chiara said. Like a healthy set of lungs.

I follow after Chiara. She opens the door about half a foot and pushes in through the small gap. "Stars run hot. We have to keep the warm air inside until they're used to the cold."

I shove my way into the room and close the door quickly behind me. A glaring white light hits me in the face. It forces its way beyond my eyes and into the darkest parts of my skull. I close my eyes and try to shield myself from its reach, but it burns through my eyelids.

"Oh, I forgot," Chiara says. She hands me a pair of round dark-lensed gold and leather Amelia Earhart goggles. "Sorry. Put those on quick."

At first it's difficult to fit them over my mask, but Chiara helps me yank them down. When I reopen my eyes, the light is no more powerful than a small flickering candle in a dark room. "Why was it so bright?" It felt like a high-powered X-ray machine—much more powerful than the one at Dr. Tucker's office.

"The little stars. They get brighter the closer we get to space. Aren't they adorable? Poor babies!" she says. "They've haven't been feeling well."

It takes a moment for me to spy them in their little bassinets. I gasp and step back until my heels collide with a bucket, sending a mop and broom clattering to the floor.

"Sshhh," Chiara scolds, her big brown eyes framed by matching goggles. "You're going to make them even more nervous."

Inside the room are five dark-blue bassinets.

And in each bassinet is a star.

"What are they?"

"Stars, obviously," Chiara says.

"But they're . . . babies?"

"Aside from shooting stars, all stars come from the souls of humans who pass on. It takes a long time for a star to be born though. These baby stars are the souls of people who died nearly thirty years ago."

Chiara must see the confusion on my face, because she starts to giggle.

"Humans—everything inside us, even our souls—are made from stardust," she explains. "When we die, we're reborn and spend the rest of our days as stars. Watching our families on earth, bouncing around, shining bright."

Catholic school teaches us that if we do good deeds

on earth, our souls will be rewarded and sent up to heaven. I imagined heaven to look like a big, fluffy cloud kingdom with a huge golden gate. Something about that idea always felt a little stuffy. Like an exclusive country club that makes you pay to get in. After all, why does heaven need a gate?

Chiara's explanation is a much better afterlife than standing around in white robes with golden halos. Being a star and floating around in the heavens with other stars. That sounds like a much less stressful way to spend eternity.

The stars blink like lightbulbs that could go out at any second. They don't seem as cheery as they did the other day in the forest. Their tiny faces twist and contort. Tinny wails echo from their mouths.

Chiara grabs a hot water bottle and thermometer off a table in the back and proceeds to fuss over the stars. She places the hot water bottle on one star's belly while checking the temperature of the one right next to him.

"What's wrong?" I ask. "Why are they sick?"

"Oh, it's just a mess." She frowns at the thermometer's reading and scribbles down some notes at a nearby table. "They're not like animals or human babies with mommies or daddies to teach them how to be stars. Spazzatrici have to take them to earth for training. There was a huge rainstorm when we were bringing them down, and they all caught colds. They're actually hotter than they should be right now."

"All that heat is coming from them?" Sweat collects on my forehead and under my arms. I wipe it off with the back of my hand.

"Usually it's hot, but not this bad."

One star cries out the farther away Chiara moves, its little howls helpless and sad. My heart twists at the sound and I move forward, wanting to do something, anything to make it feel better. But what could I do for a star? I don't even know how to take care of a human baby.

"The colds are just regular colds, but since they're babies—baby *stars*—it's harder for them to shake."

"So it's like they don't have strong enough immune systems to bounce back?"

She nods. "Poor dears. They do like singing, if you want to help," she adds as if reading my mind.

"I'm not the best singer. My dad says I sound like a cat howling at the moon."

Chiara laughs while preparing a small syringe of a purple liquid from a medicine bottle. She feeds it to the star on her right and dabs its face with a washcloth. "Cat howling makes up a lot of a star's lullabies," she says. "Just try it. But they only understand Italian."

"My granny used to sing one to me they might like," I say. "It's the only Italian I really know."

"Try," Chiara says.

The other stars around the one crying begin to yowl

too, their little voices feeding off one another. The noise rattles around in my head.

I close my eyes and begin Granny Ranieri's favorite lullaby. *"Stella, stellina, la notte si avvicina. La fiamma traballa. La mucca nella stalla."*

The stars' cries soften, their loud wails now gentle little coos.

I open one eye and look at Chiara. "My Italian isn't great."

"That was good!" She claps her hands together. "Look how peaceful they are now," she says. "My mama used to sing that one to Alessandro and me. I can sing the rest with you, if you want." Chiara starts the lullaby where I left off: *"La mucca e il vitello, la pecora e l'agnello."* She smiles. "Do you remember the rest?"

"A little."

Chiara sings again, and I join in with her, our voices warbling and only slightly in harmony. *"La chioccia con il pulcino, ognuno ha il suo bambino, ognuno ha la sua mamma, e tutti fanno la nanna."*

The little stars wiggle in their bassinets. Eyes heavy with sleep.

"Worked like a charm." She looks at the chart on the table. "Hopefully the rest will help them start feeling better, but we might not be able to release them tonight." Chiara moves toward the door. "We need to let them sleep."

We exit onto the deck and close the door, and then Chiara takes our goggles and hangs them on a nearby hook. She blows into her hands, snuggling deeper into her plush down coat.

I curl my hands into my hoodie's sleeves and stuff them into my pajama pockets. The wind is blowing faster now. It stings at my burned, unhealed skin. My breath comes out in plumes of white smoke. I wish I had my coat from the downstairs closet.

"How're the little stars?" Alessandro asks from his station behind the wheel.

"They're not doing too well," Chiara says, frowning. "Still have temperatures. Acting fussy."

Alessandro tosses his hands into the air. "We need to release them sometime, Chiara. They aren't your pets."

"I know they're not." She crosses her arms over her chest and wrinkles her tiny nose. "But it's still not safe."

We travel even higher. Nausea hits me in waves, and I take deep breaths to settle my stomach. I don't even risk looking over the railing. Even from the middle of the deck I can see the New York City lights far, far beneath us.

The ship zips through the sky, surrounded by darkness and the twinkling, curious eyes of millions and millions of stars. It all moves so fast, like shooting through the subway tunnels at lightning speed.

I gulp down my seasickness—cloud sickness?—and follow Chiara up to the stern.

Alessandro pulls out a strange-looking device, like a compass but much larger and with more doodads affixed to its sides. It's gold, old-looking, and several little metal spirals and knobs poke out of it.

"What's that?" I ask. A tingle of excitement rushes through me, and I wish again that I had my sketch pad. There are so many things I want to remember about this strange trip.

He grins and buffs some dirt off the gadget's side with his sleeve. "This is my family's pride and joy," he says. "It's the moon tracker our nonno built. Now all the spazzatrici use it. The best, most accurate moon tracker available."

I lean forward, getting a view of the gadget's face. It looks a little bit like a clock face, but instead of numbers, a moon, constellations, other planets, and what looks like earth circle the perimeter. In the middle are three arrows, like a clock's hands. One sits steady on earth while the other two rotate in opposite directions. On the very outside of the gadget, surrounding the moon and other images, are five shooting stars, moving in slow progression around the edge.

"What do the knobs sticking out of the sides do?" I ask.

"One flips the device's face to show more locations.

This spiral one twists and helps us navigate to the part of the earth that's closest to the moon."

"Doesn't that take a long time?"

He shakes his head. "The zeppelin's fast. Much faster than any airplane or rocket."

"That's incredible," I say, tugging at the sleeves of my hoodie.

"*Spazzatrici* are incredible." Alessandro straightens a bit, pride shining in his eyes.

The idea of magic still feels strange to me, almost impossible—like trying to hold on to a dream right as you're waking. I point to the twinkling rubies on the edge of the gadget. "What do these mean?"

He smiles. "Shooting stars. You do know what those are, right?"

"Of course I know what shooting stars are," I say with a huff. "You make wishes on them and they're supposed to come true." The Fourth of July before Dad and I got into the accident, my cousins and I spent the night lying on a blanket at the beach. A shooting star flew by and we all made wishes. I wished for the next year of school to be the best one yet. Dad and I got into the accident the Wednesday before Labor Day weekend—right before the first day of school. My stomach drops. "It's never worked for me."

"They do come true!" Chiara says. "But not in the way you might think."

"What do you mean?"

Alessandro looks at his sister, and Chiara shrugs. "It's rare for them to answer wishes asked from people on earth. Too many wishes at once."

"If you're up here and you see one flying by, you can catch one with a net and it'll grant your wish," Chiara adds.

"Sometimes. They don't grant *every* wish." He frowns. "It needs to be a good one."

The cogs in my brain click together as realization sets in. A wish for my family to be normal again. My dad and me fully healed. There is hope. "Have you ever caught one?"

"Once, but they're difficult."

"And usually kind of mean," Chiara explains.

"But it's possible." I bounce on my tiptoes. "Did your wishes come true?"

He shakes his head. "I didn't wish for anything. That would be unprofessional."

Chiara snorts. "He couldn't convince the star that his wish for an endless supply of chocolate was a worthy wish."

"But maybe *I* could convince a shooting star." My thoughts flood with what I'd say to the shooting star if I caught one. It would have to grant my wish. It's important. It's not about chocolate or fame or fortune or anything like that. I just want my face fixed. It's a simple wish.

"Well, if we see one maybe you can try?" Chiara says.

"And *you'd* have to catch it. That's tough." Alessandro looks down at his moon tracker. "We'll be to the moon in about five minutes. Start preparing the cleaning supplies, Chiara."

"I'm going. I'm going." Chiara tosses her hands in the air as she rushes down the staircase and begins gathering all their equipment.

"And you." Alessandro fixes his dark eyes on me. "Even though I'm not too happy having you on my ship, it'll be good having someone other than Chiara to help get things ready."

"What do you need me to do?"

He pulls his coat's furry hood tighter around his face. "First, grab a spare coat from the closet. It's going to get colder the higher we go, and a sweatshirt won't keep you warm. Then help Chiara." Alessandro pulls the wheel to the left, and the moon's huge glowing face peeks out from behind the zeppelin's big balloon.

The moon's light is soft, humming with energy the same way a lightbulb does, warm and inviting. I want to live in the moonlight forever. I take a step back; my eyes widen to take it all in. It's so bright.

Alessandro smiles. "I looked the same way the first time I saw her up close. Incredible, isn't she?"

"Amazing," I say, the only word I can grab from the millions of other thoughts swirling in my head. "It's ... I ..."

"We'll be there soon, so get ready."

I take the stairs two at a time and first head for the supply closet to grab a coat. All of them are a little too big, but I find what looks like an old pilot's coat from the 1940s: a soft brown leather, lined and trimmed with wool.

I zip it up over my hoodie and snuggle deep into its warmth. It smells like chocolate and basil and feels like home, like my family's deli.

Chiara runs past, juggling mops and two large pails. "Have you seen the polish?" she asks without stopping.

"Polish?" She turns, both of her furry eyebrows rising high on her forehead. "You know, the moon polish. It's due for another shining. It gets one every twenty-nine days, when it's a new moon. How do you think the moon shines so bright during the rest of the lunar cycle without a good polishing?"

I shake my head. "I haven't seen it. Sorry."

Chiara laughs. "Oh, right. It's your first day on board." She rushes around the deck. "If you see the polish, let me know. It's in a giant white glass bottle. My mama makes it herself. Special family formula."

She brings the pails up to the ship's stern and goes back to the closet for more supplies.

"What can I do?" I ask.

Chiara struggles with three extra-long push brooms. "We need to bring these up to the stern."

I take up the back of the brooms and help Chiara up the stairs. The wind picks up on the stern and circles us in an excited dance. Ice collects on the railings and shimmers in the moonlight. Chiara places the front of the brooms on the ground, motioning for me to do the same.

She runs down the stairs one more time and comes back dragging a wooden ladder behind her. "Alessandro likes getting close to the moon when he sweeps," she explains, wiping sweat from her brow. "Now we wait for him to dock."

We stand side by side, staring at the vast dark sky behind us.

The sky is quiet, still.

Not at all like Staten Island, where there's so much light pollution that you can barely see the stars. I've only ever known a silence like this—darkness like this even—when we went to Italy. Standing on the beach in Positano late one night, all I could hear was the whispers of waves crashing against the shore. The only light that night were the lanterns hanging from boats. Here there's hardly even that. The wind has nothing to hold on to. It passes over us, through us, like ghosts. The stars twinkle. There are millions of them, a beauty that's impossible to see from Staten Island. But even with all their glowing, the darkness still overpowers them. It's brilliant in its own way, too. Impossibly big and so, so close.

If I squint hard enough, it's possible to make out the New York City lights glowing far down below. Almost like when you're flying into JFK and all of a sudden the city emerges from behind the plane's wing. It's strange seeing the city from such a far distance.

How small it all feels when looking down on the world. All of my problems seem a little less scary from up here, surrounded by stars and quiet.

Chapter 10

The moon stares directly at us. Her warm light drips over the zeppelin like candle wax. Crags, valleys, and slopes cover the large expanse of her round silvery face. I touch my plastic mask. It's kind of like my burns and scars.

"We're only about half a mile away," Alessandro yells. "Are we ready to dock?"

"Sure are," Chiara calls back. "Start backing her up."

Alessandro spins the wheel and turns the zeppelin parallel to the moon's side. Silver dust motes collect in her light.

I catch some in my hand. It glitters and sparkles, smearing against my palms like my mom's eye shadow. "It's beautiful."

"I think so too," she says. "The moon's especially dusty tonight. Good thing we're here. Scrubbing the moon and stars keeps them healthy. We also collect their dust. Mama and Papa bottle it up."

"What for?"

"Some's used for other parts of our magic, like mixing into cement for building roads and houses. Moon- and stardust can also help you get over a cold or stomach-ache. But the dusts need to be heated up to work. Mama says it's like how the stars are hot—that's how the magic works. So she mixes it into soups or sauces for us. Or heats it up on the stove if she's using it in a balm." She toys with the ribbon at the end of her left braid.

I shake my head. "You're joking, right?"

"Not at all." She grins. "We ship big crates of dust back to Stelle so the other spazzatrici can use it too."

Mom makes minestrone whenever I'm sick, but it never had any star- or moondust in it. Otherwise I would have gotten over colds faster. I wonder if the moon- or stardust could help—if I could get some to add to min-estrone or a chicken parm sandwich. Even just enough until I find a shooting star to catch that would put every-thing back to normal.

"What's the difference between the two?"

"Stardust is smooth and extra glittery. Better for heal-ing. Moondust is still good for healing, but it's grittier and people don't like that texture. Because of that, it's better for building things. Mama uses both in her healing potions. She thinks the moondust adds another level of protection. That makes her medicines extra special."

"Time to drop anchor!" Alessandro yells. He rushes past us in a blur.

Chiara and I chase after him and watch as he turns the crank on the anchor.

"Luna, help me." He motions for me to crank as he takes hold of the heavy steel anchor and its long steel chain.

I stare at it warily. Even drawing for more than fifteen minutes can make my left arm sore and cramp up.

"Keep cranking it," Alessandro says. "I'm gonna hitch it onto that cloud right there." He points off to a sturdy-looking cloud a few feet away. "That should do the trick."

I take hold of the crank, rotating it as hard as I can. Pain throbs in my muscles, the same shaking ache that pulsed through my arm after the accident.

But I'm strong.

I'm a Bianchini.

I push through until a good bit of chain is pooled at our feet.

Alessandro heaves the anchor over the railing with both hands. The chain flies off the deck. It clangs through the air until the anchor hits the cloud with a soft *thud*.

The boat bobs up and down as it levels out. Chiara takes up an old, rickety-looking ladder and leans it against the side of the moon.

"Do you have the timer?" Alessandro picks up one of the brooms and climbs halfway up the ladder until he's only a few feet away from the moon.

Chiara nods and pulls a small brass clock out from her coat pocket. Like the moon tracker, it has little illustrations drawn onto the sides of its face and three hands. She turns the key in its back and presses a little button on top. The clock begins to tick away the seconds with echoing clicks. Chiara places it on the deck before grabbing a broom and hopping on top of a small stepladder.

"We only have so long before the sun rises," she explains. "We need to make sure we don't run out of time when sweeping. The timer's loud, so we can hear it from anywhere."

"Ready?" Alessandro calls down to us.

Chiara nods. Both she and Alessandro get to work, the broom's bristles tickling the bottom of the moon. A soft scratching sound, like sandpaper against a piece of wood, fills the quiet. More moondust falls onto the zeppelin and blankets us in its silvery powder.

I look at the third broom sitting alone on the deck. Sharp pains shoot through my left arm from cranking the machine. I don't think I can lift that broom over my head.

"I want to help you sweep." I keep my eyes on my shoes. "But my arm hurts."

Alessandro looks at me over his shoulder. "You can be in charge of the moondust, then."

"Oh no," Chiara says, pausing her sweeping. "I forgot the jars in the closet."

"Luna, will you grab a few jars out of the closet you got your jacket from?" Alessandro yells from the ladder. "We need to fill them up with dust."

I nod and take off down the stairs. Even as a little kid, I always felt better when I had a task. Some sort of project. That's why Dad never had a problem bringing me to the deli. While some kids might complain about spending Saturday mornings at work with their family, I was proud to be part of a team—even if all I could manage to do was add chocolate chips to the cannoli filling and restock the butcher paper for the deli meat.

By the time I return, Alessandro and Chiara are nearly finished sweeping up this side of the moon. Moondust still tumbles down, and I quickly unlatch the jar's lids and place them underneath the falling dust.

Chiara unscrews the top of a jar filled with a thick, sparkling white paste and scoops half of it into a pail filled with steaming water. She smiles, mixing the paste into the water with her mop. "We've got to get her looking shiny."

Alessandro climbs down and grabs a small brush, dunking it into the pail before heading up the ladder again. Chiara splashes the wet mop against the swept-up side of the moon. The pair scrubs until the light from the zeppelin's lanterns bounce off its side.

"Look at how bright," Chiara says. "Our best job yet."

"We could still do better." Alessandro climbs down the ladder once more and pulls it back into the ship. He puts his hands on his hips. "We need to be the top spazzatrici. I want the other families to know that when the Sapientis do a job, we do it the best."

Chiara rolls her eyes. "Please, you take all the fun out of it. Not everything is a competition."

Alessandro grins. "It's the Sapienti way."

"Well." Chiara lowers her mop back down from the moon and picks up her broom in the other hand. "I'm a Sapienti too, and I'm happy with not being in a race all the time."

Alessandro picks up the pail in one hand, juggling his broom and mop underneath his other arm.

"What's next?" I ask.

"We've got to finish up this section of the moon and then fly around to the next, and so on until we finish each part." Chiara follows after her brother to the middle of the ship. "It takes forever. We still need to check on the stars after this to see if they're adapting."

I follow after Chiara, picking up the ends of her dragging broom and mop. Chiara and Alessandro start sweeping again. I collect the falling dust in jars. I wait until the powder reaches the very top before latching the jars shut and storing them in a wooden crate Alessandro gave me.

The process takes hours and stops every time Alessandro needs to move the zeppelin. Luckily, he doesn't ask me to crank the anchor again. Instead, the cloud follows along with us, keeping us stable rather than locking us into a location.

By the time we get to the last side, my arm starts growing stiffer. The tug of sleep is heavy on my eyelids. At least twenty jars full of moondust sit in the crate by my feet, ready to be turned into magic by the Sapientis.

It's tempting to ask Chiara and Alessandro for a jar of the dust. Asking now, my first night in the stars with them, would be a little rude. They invited me on as a guest, and I don't want to push my luck just yet.

"That'll do it." Chiara hops down from her stepladder. She smiles, giving the moon a little wave. "We need to check on the stars. Alessandro will finish up with the cleaning."

I yawn into the crook of my elbow. It's been a long time since I've felt so exhausted.

This time, Chiara helps me get the goggles on before opening the door to the stars' nursery. Their whines hit us the moment we enter, each one wriggling and stretching for attention.

"Oh no." Chiara shakes her head. "They don't sound too happy."

"What's wrong?"

Chiara moves over to a bassinet and places the back of her hand against one of the stars. "He's burning up. They're still sick. Must be making it too hard for them to acclimate to the atmosphere."

"We can't release them when they're sick." I frown. It's hard watching them suffer, like seeing a sick dog or cat, helpless and confused. "Is there something we can do?"

She shakes her head and spoons a dose of medicine into each star's mouth. "We just need to let them get better. Maybe next time we go up."

I walk between the bassinets. The little stars stare at me with beady eyes.

"They like being tucked in." Chiara smiles. "Just be careful; they can be a little warm. It takes a while getting used to that."

I bend over one of the bassinets and place a tentative hand on the star's head. I flinch at the heat radiating off its tiny body. The little star looks up at me, its cries softening to little gurgles. He looks sad and flushed from being ill. All I want to do is cuddle him. My aunt Therese takes off work when her pug, Bella, isn't feeling well and spends the entire day fussing over the grouchy little thing. That's how I feel about this star. I brace myself for the heat and run my hand across the star's little cheek, its silvery, scaly flesh unexpected but familiar. Similar to salmon or tuna. Maybe stars are the fish of the sky. Or fish are the stars of the ocean.

The star snuggles against my hand like a kitten does when it wants more attention, rubbing its face into my palm. His heat darts up my arm and through the rest of my body like stepping into a shower with scalding-hot water.

I smile, getting used to the warmth.

"It's okay, little baby. You'll be feeling better soon," I whisper.

The star coos and continues to rub against me.

"We should let Alessandro know the stars aren't being released tonight," Chiara says.

I pet the star's head one more time. "Good-bye, little star," I say, before heading back out onto the deck with Chiara.

"Well?" Alessandro calls.

Chiara shakes her head. "Maybe next time."

Alessandro sighs. "Let's head back."

The ship begins to descend as Chiara and I finish sweeping up the remaining dust. We walk up the stairs to the stern and watch as the moon grows smaller. It shines back at us like a lighthouse's beam in the darkness.

I'm not ready to go back. Sadness swells in my stomach. The worries that couldn't catch me as we flew high into the heavens have circled me once more, tethering me back to earth. The endless doctor visits, my parents' constant fighting, everyone looking at me like I'm a monster. I swallow hard. Facing the world again, after everything

I've experienced tonight, feels like the worst kind of punishment.

I clutch my cornicello, rubbing the gold horn between my fingers for comfort.

"What's that?" Alessandro asks.

"Oh." I show it to Alessandro and Chiara. "My dad gave it to me when I was in the hospital."

Alessandro smiles and pulls out a similar gold chain and cornicello from beneath his jacket. "My papa gave me his. It's been in our family for centuries," he says. "Chiara has our mama's. We never take them off, but Mama and Papa always double-check that we have them on when we go flying. You should keep yours on at all times."

"My dad told me the horn will keep me safe."

I stare down at the horn; it looks pretty normal. The cornicello is tiny. Shorter and narrower than my pinky finger. "It doesn't seem very magical."

"Not all magic is big and loud." Alessandro shrugs. He gestures to the zeppelin. "Even this begins as a wooden toy ship. Magic's everywhere. Before flying in this ship, before seeing the stars, you experienced magic. Everyone has. It's just that people don't notice. They're too busy rushing around to see things properly."

I tuck the cornicello beneath my jacket. Seeing the world, *actually* seeing it and not just staring through it, is something I always thought I knew how to do.

We fly in silence. Chiara yawns next to me, and her head lulls to the side. Alessandro pushes the zeppelin through heavy clouds as if they were tissue paper, navigating us gracefully back to earth.

I look down at the glittering Manhattan skyline, at the world sleeping beneath our feet. The city hums with people who live and breathe magic every day and yet never notice it. A magic I'm now trying hard to find and pay attention to. I close my eyes tightly and open them, looking up at the stars twinkling down at us and at the bright, shining moon now no bigger than my thumb.

The sky breaks with the blue-gray haze of dawn, and the sun's light bleeds onto the horizon east of us. The zeppelin lowers between our houses to let us off at our windows. I wave to Alessandro and Chiara from my tree platform. Alessandro tugs at the silver cord tied to the Luna figurehead. Fireflies dance around the zeppelin as it begins to shrink, transforming back into the wooden toy ship.

I climb in through the window and scramble over to my desk. My sketch pad is already open to a fresh sheet of paper, and I grab the first pencil I find. There's no time to be choosy—I need to get it all down. All the visions of shooting stars and magical dust. The big, beautiful moon staring at us. Every moment I spent in the heavens.

I close my eyes, conjuring the round, silver moon. Her

beautiful, craggy face. And the moondust—the shimmering, soft clumps of powder, dancing through the heavens. I push past the pain in my already sore arm and finish the last little peaks and valleys on the moon. I take a step back to look at my drawing in the soft dawn light filtering through my curtains. The moon stares back at me, not exactly the same moon I saw in person, but close enough.

"There will be time to get you looking just right." I smile.

Before dropping me off, Alessandro and Chiara promised another trip. They even let me keep the leather bomber jacket from the closet so I'll be ready for next time.

Birds begin their morning songs, and a soft pattering of snow taps against my window. My clock reads 6:45. Mom and Dad will be waking up soon and the day will begin. Back to life as it was before.

But maybe not entirely. Maybe now it's a little different.

I creep from my room and down the hall, drawing in hand. Dad's door is partially open, and I push my way into his room. His snores echo and bounce off the walls. His hospital bed is squeezed in next to the regular guest bed. I stare at him for a moment, taking in his messy black hair and big nose. My heart twitches. I swallow back the tears pooling in my eyes and place the drawing of the moon on his nightstand. No moondust just yet. No shooting star.

Maybe this tiny bit of magic can make Dad feel a little better.

Chapter 11

Doctor's offices are always cold and stink like those antiseptic wipes. I shift back and forth on the exam table, the sanitary paper crinkling underneath me. The harsh, fluorescent light illuminates every nook and cranny in the tiny white room. There's no place to hide. Mom sits nearby on a black plastic chair. Her knee bounces up and down as we await Dr. Tucker's arrival.

It always seems like we're waiting for something.

I wipe the sleep from my eyes. Mom woke me up an hour after I finally dozed off this morning. But it's not like I would've gotten much sleep anyway. My head is full from my night spent zipping past the stars and all the way up to the moon. It was weird waking up, my adventure burned away by the bright light of morning. I wouldn't have believed any of it really happened if I didn't see the jacket

Chiara and Alessandro let me keep hanging in my closet.

Dr. Tucker opens the door, followed by a woman in a white coat I haven't seen before.

"How are we doing, Luna?" Dr. Tucker asks while checking a clipboard. He looks up, light reflecting off his perfect white smile. His black hair is cut short. A set of bushy eyebrows sits atop his brown eyes, narrowing at the bridge of his nose. His skin is smooth and dark, except for a mole almost the size of a dime right on his jaw, about the same shade of his hair. Sometimes I stare at it when he's talking so he thinks I'm still paying attention. He's kind, and his smile always feels genuine. He doesn't look at me like I'm some wounded kitten.

"My face is still broken," I say. "Not great."

"Luna." Mom shakes her head. "Be nice."

"It's fine, Sofia. Honesty helps us fix problems." He gestures to the tall, blond woman in the lab coat. "This is Dr. Manikowski. She's a radiologist." She smiles, her teeth slightly crooked, red lipstick bleeding from her mouth onto pale white skin.

"Good morning, Luna." She puts her hand out and I shake it. "I'll be taking your X-rays today."

"May I remove your mask?" Dr. Tucker asks.

I nod.

He unstraps it. It feels good when the air hits my clammy skin. The scars itch a little, and I put my hands under my back so I don't accidentally scratch at them. There's a mirror in the room, and I want to ask him to help me up so I can see myself. *Really* see what I look like since there are no mirrors in my house. Not just a distorted view in puddles or a half glance in car mirrors.

A knot forms in my stomach. I think of Nonna Bianchini. If she thought the mask was bad, I can only imagine what she'd think of seeing me without it. It's one thing to wear a mask. It's another to actually see the monster underneath.

"Will the X-rays hurt?" I ask.

"No. Of course not." Dr. Tucker gestures for me to hop down from the table. Mom and I follow after him and Dr. Manikowski into the X-ray room, where Dr. Manikowski helps me lie down on a different table. Above me is the X-ray machine, a white plastic contraption with a camera on the end.

I stare into the camera, its eye cold and unblinking. It's hard to move. I try wriggling, but the machine is only a foot above my body. This must be what it feels like for crickets or worms right before they are devoured by birds. Alone, pinned down, and unable to look anywhere else but into the unfeeling eye of their predator.

I squeeze my eyes shut and think of the heavens. Of the bigness of space. Large, wide, dark, and open. Nothing but the stars and the moon.

"It'll take only about ten minutes," she says. "We just need you to lie still and move your head when I tell you to."

Dr. Manikowski places foam pads on either side of my face to keep it still, her hands small and slightly cold against my warm skin. They place a heavy black vest on my chest.

"Sofia, you'll have to step out while the X-rays are being taken," I hear Dr. Tucker say.

I can't see anyone, only the black camera inside the hulking white machine.

"Okay, Luna, I'll take the X-ray on the count of three. Then I'll reposition you," Dr. Manikowski says. "One, two, three."

She presses a button, moves out of the room, and the machine makes a clicking noise. I wonder what it would be like to be Dr. Manikowski. A bone photographer. Instead of taking pictures of mountain ridges or celebrities, she takes photos of people's skeletons. Do my bones look different to her? Or do we all look the same on the inside?

Dr. Manikowski reenters, her smiling face looming over mine. "Very good, Luna. Now you'll want to tuck your chin closer to your chest and hold that position really still."

After a while the camera feels less cramped. Less like a giant bird waiting to gulp me down. More like my aunt

Therese's pug poking her face against mine when I try to nap on the couch. It isn't comfortable, but more bearable.

She has me tilt my head up, and then I have to lie on my left side. She takes another X-ray of my full face. Dr. Manikowski smiles.

"You're doing really good, Luna," she says. "But we're going to need you to lie down on your right side now so I can get an X-ray of the left portion of your skull. Now, this might hurt a little."

She directs me onto my right side, cradling my head like I was a baby, before gently laying me against the hard exam table. It hurts lying directly on the broken side of my face with no pillow or support. The scars begin to feel even itchier, growing hot and sweaty, sticking to the table like when your legs stick to a car's leather seats in the summer.

The camera clicks, but Dr. Manikowski shakes her head. "You can't move, Luna. You need to do your best to stay still so I can get a good X-ray."

"It really hurts," I say. "I'm getting a headache."

She touches my hand. Her red nail polish matches her lipstick. "I know, but once we get this one, you're done with X-rays."

The camera clicks again, and she reenters to examine the X-ray. "Luna, we really need you to stay still. Dr. Tucker," Dr. Manikowski calls into the hallway. "Will you please hold her still while I take the picture?"

After a few seconds Dr. Tucker's face beams down at me. "Hi, Luna. This'll take only a moment," he says. He holds the foam gently and keeps me still.

My face throbs even more, burning against the exam table. It's not Dr. Tucker's fault, but it feels like being forced under water.

The camera clicks.

"All done," he says, removing his X-ray vest and helping me into a seated position. He calls Mom into the room.

She puts her hand on my knee. "You did a good job, sweetheart."

Dr. Manikowski pulls the X-rays up on the large computer screen. My skull looms white and hazy, like a ghost against the black background. The right side where my fracture happened looks odd, like a puzzle piece being jammed into the wrong spot.

Dr. Tucker shakes his head, looks down at his chart, and back up at the X-rays. "While her cheek fracture is healing nicely because there was no dislocation and the compression mask is holding everything in place, the nasal fracture isn't healing like we thought it would."

"What do you mean?" Mom asks, her voice raised. "I thought everything was on schedule."

"Luna's nasal fracture is healing, just not properly."

He takes a step back, tapping a finger against his lips. He circles the X-ray image of my nose with the same finger. "The skin on her right nostril is still badly burned, and the bones in her nose aren't fitting together. As a result, her nose is deformed. If not addressed, this can cause breathing issues."

The room begins to spin. Everything feels hazy, and my mind travels to the photos of the wolf man in my *Ripley's Believe It or Not* book. He toured with circuses, his face covered in thick patches of hair, his eyes yellow. I think of the Phantom and his mask. How he spent his entire life hidden away in the dark corners of the opera house. My stomach dips.

Deformed. Ugly.

"What can be done?" Mom croaks. "What can you do?"

"There are surgeries," Dr. Tucker explains. He places his clipboard on the table and crosses his arms over his chest.

"And surgery will fix it, right?" she says. "Her face will look like it did before."

"The surgeries will improve her appearance. We can reset the bones into proper alignment. We'd need to take a small skin graft from her abdomen and transplant it onto the right nostril," Dr. Tucker says. "But there's no promise that she'll look the same as she did prior to the accident."

Mom's lips quirk down. Her eyes are wet, but she doesn't let the tears fall. She moves her hand to cover her mouth, her fingers trembling against her cheek.

Her hand moves from her face and over her blond curls. She lets out a shaky breath. "How long is recovery? How much will it cost? We've already spent so much time and money."

I can't look at her anymore. I stare past Dr. Tucker's shoulder at the X-ray of my broken face, unable to pay attention to his response. When I was still in the hospital, Dr. Tucker and the other doctors were so hopeful about everything. The scars would fade. My face would heal smoothly. They all said these things. They all promised life would go back to normal. But going back to before—to *normal*—is no longer an option. Was never an option, I guess.

The X-ray goes blurry as tears fall down my cheeks. A loud, heaving sound moves from my stomach, up my throat, and out into the doctor's office. The tips of my fingers feel numb. My head is cloudy.

I look through the tears at Mom. Her eyes are red, her face wet like mine. I cry even harder. When I was eight her sister, my aunt Marie, died. The same sister we'd visit to drink tea. We were making breakfast in the kitchen when the phone rang. We all knew Aunt Marie was sick. She had cervical cancer and things were progressing fast.

But I remember Mom's movements when she picked up the phone this time: the nod of her head, how she dropped the phone on the counter as if it were a snake that had bitten her. Her face looked the same as it does now: splotchy, red, and twisted in pain. She grabbed me in a hug and we sat on the kitchen floor for what felt like hours, her head on my shoulder. Grief is like a tornado, crushing even the sturdiest buildings.

Mom takes my hand, wrapping her arm around my shoulder.

Dr. Tucker hands us each a tissue.

She blows her nose. "I'm sorry," she says.

"Don't apologize, Sofia," Dr. Tucker says. "It's still a lot to take in."

He looks at me, a weak smile on his lips. "It's going to be fine, Luna," he says. "The surgery will promote a vast improvement over what the X-ray is showing us now."

I wipe the tears from my cheeks. The numbness in my fingers creeps up my hands as the idea of surgery begins to sink in, feeling more like a necessity. It's going to be fine? Who is he trying to reassure?

"It's common for those who have had craniofacial breaks to undergo this type of surgery." Dr. Tucker pats me on the shoulder.

Mom takes a deep breath to steady herself.

He takes up my chart again and looks through the

pages. "Rhinoplasty is a common surgery, so the initial procedure should be very short. But there's always going to be risk with *any* surgery. For example, after we perform the skin grafting, there may be some permanent scarring along the right nostril."

"Luna." Mom looks at me, eyes rimmed red and mascara running down her cheeks. "We need to talk to your dad first, but what do you want to do?"

I don't like having to choose. Mom says I'm indecisive because I was born a Libra, but I think it's because making a decision feels so final. Once it's made, that's the path I'm on. Everything is set in stone.

I think of last night. Of being high up above Staten Island where none of this mattered. Alessandro, Chiara, the baby stars. All of that feels years away now.

"I'm scared." I squeeze my mom's hand and she squeezes back. I'm scared that I'll never be put back together again. That I'll have to take school photos in a compression mask. Or that people will stare at my burns and disfigured nose as I walk across the stage years from now at my high school graduation. That'll I'll be Humpty Dumpty forever.

"If it helps me look normal—even just a little bit—I'll do it," I say, even though it would be so easy to keep hiding behind my mask.

Dr. Tucker nods. "We'll make sure things go as smoothly as possible."

Mom helps me hop down from the table, and Dr. Manikowski assists in putting my mask back on as Mom and Dr. Tucker discuss the surgery. She pulls the strap tight around my head, ripping and adjusting the Velcro, giving me another headache. The numbness begins to fade, replaced by nausea.

I watch Mom's expression slowly relax as Dr. Tucker goes down a list of presurgery requirements. Mom likes lists. She says they keep her mind from floating away.

"It'll be okay, right?" she asks Dr. Tucker.

"Yes," he replies. "Luna's strong."

I *have* to be strong for Mom, Dad, Nonna, and everyone else. But I just want to be a kid again. I want this to all go away.

Chapter 12

"We've got to go to the deli before your therapy appointment," Mom says while pulling out of the parking lot of Dr. Tucker's office. "Uncle Mike needs us. You can do your homework there."

I try not to think about everything Dr. Tucker just told us, doing all I can to push that and Mom crying out of my mind. Exhaustion pulls at my eyelids.

I cross my arms over my chest. "I want to go home. I don't need therapy anyway."

It's almost eleven thirty. Alessandro and Chiara have to be awake by now. They're probably busy with the baby stars. Maybe they're helping their mom make potions from the moondust we collected last night. What if they stopped by to see me?

"Well, the fact that you're so eager to go home and skip out on a trip to the deli makes me think otherwise," Mom says. "You always love going to the deli."

"It's not that."

She arches an eyebrow up at me.

I don't say a word about Chiara and Alessandro.

It takes us a long time to pull out of the parking lot and onto the street. There's more traffic than usual for a Friday morning, with everyone busy rushing around for the best after-Thanksgiving deals. No doubt my cousins are already at the mall, shopping for Christmas presents. Last year Rocco and I ended up buying each other the same gift: a pair of lime-green socks with hamburgers on them. I don't know when I'll do my shopping this year. Or even if we'll be having Christmas with the family. Especially after Mom's fight with Nonna.

Mom adjusts her hands on the steering wheel. My stomach lurches. On her left ring finger is a pale indentation where her wedding band should be.

I look out the window, focused on the passing cars. "This is stupid. I hate this. I've already had to see one doctor today."

"Nowadays you hate everything but being in your room," Mom says. "You're going to the appointment after the deli. Get with the program."

She turns up the radio and we drive the rest of the way in silence. I drum my fingers on my sketch pad. The empty space on Mom's ring finger is harsh in the bright sunshine.

I press my forehead to the window and try to conjure up memories of last night's trip. That nagging thought of whether Alessandro and Chiara will come over to visit nips at me. What if they only brought me up with them in the first place because they felt bad when they saw my dumb mask and broken face? What if they really don't like me at all?

"I need to talk about Dr. Tucker's plan with your father." Mom's voice cuts through my panic.

My head feels heavy. I take a deep breath and squeeze my eyes shut.

The car comes to a stop. "We're here, Luna."

I open my eyes. The big red, green, and white sign for Bianchini's Deli catches the sunlight. Panic rises in my chest. This is my first time here since before the accident.

Mom grabs her purse from the backseat, and I spy the empty space on her ring finger again. I can't believe I didn't notice it before. She could have taken it off at any time, with all the arguing Mom and Dad do and how much she hates him going to the deli when he's not feeling well . . . I can't believe I wasn't paying attention.

We should go home.

I slam my car door shut, lagging behind.

Mom looks back at me and her expression softens. "I know it's hard, Luna." She puts an arm around my shoulders. "But this'll make you feel better. You love it here."

She guides me through the door, and the mingling scents of fresh cookies and fried salami greets me. Deli clerks rush back and forth, filling orders for the long line of customers. Mom and I stand to the side, careful not to get in the way.

I stare at the cookies and pastries behind the glass. My empty stomach grumbles. We didn't have time for breakfast before Dr. Tucker's. And I'd gladly eat a million *sfogliatella* instead of breakfast anyway. My mouth waters at the thought of biting into the flaky pastry.

"Luna!" one of the deli clerks, Matteo, yells. He's been working here with Dad and Uncle Mike since they were all kids. He smiles, and the lines around his blue eyes crinkle. "It's been a while. How've you been, kid?"

"Fine." I stare down at the black-and-white checkered tiles, careful to keep my mask hidden behind my hair. "I thought Uncle Mike completely redid everything."

"Not this side. That's next he says." Matteo laughs. "Your dad isn't too keen on the idea. You should go see the other half though." He lets out a low whistle. "It's something else. People actually stay awhile and enjoy their coffee."

"Let's get you situated over there," Mom says, guiding me toward the large arched entryway to the other side of the deli. "Will you let them know we're here, Matteo?"

He nods and pushes open the door to the kitchen. "Frank! Mike! Family's here."

I stop just shy of the tables and chairs and gasp. When Dad bought the tailor shop next door, he didn't do much with it. It was clean, but looked old. Nothing fancy. Just a few small tables with plastic red-and-white checkered tablecloths and brown cushioned chairs. The only art was a few framed photos of Nonno's parents and their old restaurant in Italy that hung at odd angles on the eggshell-white walls.

But Uncle Mike transformed the room into a Tuscan sunflower field at dusk. A sunset of oranges, pinks, and reds is painted across the ceiling. Beneath the sky are hundreds of cheery yellow sunflower heads popping up from thick, dark-green stems. Their faces all point the same way, searching for the sun. Just like they do out in the real Tuscan sunflower fields.

I stand on my tiptoes and spin around to take it all in at once. Uncle Mike's mural is so real, so vivid, I can almost feel the Tuscan sunset warming my face.

"Mom! It's like being back in Tuscany," I say. "It's magical. Remember all the sunflowers? You took that picture of me in the field with them?" I stretch my arms wide and close my eyes.

"See? I knew you'd love it," Mom says. "They even put in nicer chairs and tables. I think your father's coming around to it."

I open my eyes. They did get rid of the old tables and

tablecloths. Now the chairs are extra cushiony—like the kind you'd find in a fancy coffee shop. There are no tablecloths, but the tables are a pretty dark wood that matches the rest of the room.

"What do you think, Luns?" Uncle Mike leans against the wall, a huge grin on his face. "Nice, isn't it?"

"I love it!"

"The lighting's a little dim," Dad says, wheeling up next to his brother. "But it works for now."

"This guy." Uncle Mike laughs. "He hates change so much that one time it took him two months to replace a lightbulb in the stockroom because the brand he liked went out of business."

"I'm very particular. And you did this without me okaying it first." Dad frowns. "You know I don't like that."

"Oh, come on." Mom crosses her arms over her chest. "It looks great. Don't be such a grump about everything."

"Maybe I wouldn't be so grumpy if I wasn't stuck in this thing." Dad gestures at his chair. "Or stuck at home all the time. It's a miracle I was even allowed to come in today."

A silence falls over the room. I look at the space between my parents, too scared to check my dad's ring finger.

"Thank God you're here, Sofia." Uncle Mike claps Mom on the shoulder. "We need all the help we can get this morning. You'd think the malls would keep people busy, but everyone's filling orders for the holidays."

"Let me know what you need," Mom says. "We've got a couple hours before Luna's next appointment." She looks at me. "Will you be okay on your own?"

I hold up my science textbook and nod.

"We just made a fresh batch of cannoli," Uncle Mike says. "Want one?"

"Can I have a *sfogliatella* too?"

"You're going to make yourself sick," Mom says. "What about some prosciutto and smoked gouda to balance out all the sugar?"

I scowl at her.

"Fine. Fine. At least you're eating," Mom says. "Go sit down for now. I'll be back soon."

She follows Uncle Mike and Dad toward the other half of the deli.

The sitting area is quiet, situated far enough away so that the hustle and bustle from the deli is no louder than a faint hum. I plop down at a table near the thickest section of sunflowers and open my science book to chapter seven: Genes to Traits. I skip ahead to the end and scan the practice quiz. Boring.

I close the book and pull my sketch pad and pencil bag from my backpack, spreading out all my supplies, arranging my pencils from shortest to tallest. Then I pick the shortest pencil in the row.

The details from last night's trip collect like rainwater in a bucket. Drip, drip, drip. Memories of the ship's Luna figurehead, the Amelia Earhart goggles, and Alessandro's moon tracker all come into focus.

I open my sketch pad to a fresh page. There's too much I want to draw. I'm not sure where to even begin. I lean over the table, pencil poised. Start with the basics. That's easiest. First an outline of the actual ship, its belly round and perfectly smooth and the sides slightly curved to fit the large deck. The sets of staircases on either side that lead to the stern and bow. Next comes the Luna figurehead, with long flowing hair and the tiny star resting on her finger. I squint as I try to get her smile just right.

My arm begins to stiffen. I roll my shoulder back, doing one of the exercises I learned in physical therapy. Once the stiffness lessens, I push on to a quick outline of the ship's balloon. The mammoth black balloon that breathes life into the zeppelin. The set of lungs that makes it possible for the ship to fly through the clouds and high into the sky.

Pain shoots through my hand and makes me smear the shading on the balloon. The pencil slips from my fingers as they spasm from overuse. My left hand is bloated and red. I clench it into a fist as more pain courses up my arm.

"Mom?" I yell, walking over to the deli counter. "My hand hurts. Can I have some medicine?"

Mom hands a white box wrapped in red string to a customer before turning toward me. "You know how I feel about painkillers," she says. She looks past me at the table filled with sketches and pencils. "And aren't you supposed to be doing homework?"

"Mom," I groan. "I can do it later."

"Well, I guess you haven't been this active in a while. It's a good sign. Let me grab my purse and a plate of food. I'll be right over."

Mom walks into the back to get the pills out of her purse while I head to the table. I look down at my drawings and sigh. All of the memories from last night swirl around my head, and all I want to do is pluck one of the ideas from my mind and tether it to the paper with my pencil. If only my stupid hand wasn't broken. If only *everything* wasn't broken.

"Breakfast time, Luna." Mom places a hefty *sfogliatella* in front of me. Almond paste pours from its end out onto the plate, and bits of powdered sugar get lost in the little ribbons of pastry. She shakes two white pills from an orange bottle into her hand. "Eat your *sfogliatella*, all of it, before drawing again," she says. "Give these some time to work."

Mom hands me the pills.

"Thank you." I pop them into my mouth and quickly take a large gulp of water to wash down the sharp, chalky taste.

"That's interesting." Mom picks up my sketch pad and holds it out in front of her, head tilted as she takes it in. "Very surreal. Your drawings are usually more realistic."

"Well," I say with a mouthful of pastry, "it *is* realistic. Because it's really real."

Mom arches an eyebrow, looking closer at the drawing. "What do you mean *really real?*"

"I flew on it last night."

She laughs. "My little Luna. Never lose that imagination of yours."

"I told you about this already—twice—and you wouldn't believe me." Heat creeps up my neck. "The new kids next door. They're magical."

"It was probably just a realistic dream." Mom purses her lips. "Dr. Tucker said one of the side effects of your new medication is vivid dreams."

"No." I roll my eyes. "It wasn't a dream. I know what I saw." I look back down at my drawing and the half-eaten pastry in front of me. "It wasn't pretend or my imagination. I was up in a flying zeppelin last night."

"Blimps don't fly that low, Luna. There are flight restrictions."

"It wasn't a blimp." I look up at her, shaking my head. "It's a magical zeppelin. It looks exactly as it does in the picture. I drew it exactly how I saw it. Like the *Argo*, except with a giant bullet-shaped balloon to make it fly.

The Sapienti kids hopped in and flew up to the stars. I went with them."

"You're twelve. You should know magic isn't real." She looks at me warily. "All this time in your room with your thoughts isn't good. I'm glad you're seeing that therapist today."

My face burns. "I know what I saw."

Mom stares at me a moment longer before her eyes drift over to the deli counter. "I can't talk about this now, honey. It's getting busier." She kisses me on the head. "We can talk about the magic and the zeppelin later."

Of course she won't believe me. Mom will never understand. She was the one who told me Santa Claus wasn't real when I was eight years old because she needed help wrapping all the presents for the younger cousins. She's never been one for magic.

I scarf down the rest of my *sfogliatella* while staring at the rough outline of the zeppelin. The pencil smear through the balloon looks like a jagged scar. Even without the scar down the middle, it doesn't feel right. The drawing looks flat and tired. Zapped of all magic. I tear it out of the sketch pad and cast it aside.

My fingers are stiff, but the pain has subsided. I take up a fresh pencil and a clean sheet of paper. I think about what Alessandro said, about people being too busy to see things properly. This time I don't focus on the reality of what I saw. I take a deep breath and draw what I felt.

It's because of magic that Alessandro and Chiara can zoom up to the heavens without the need for space suits. It's because of magic that the baby stars bounce and coo in their little bassinets. It's because of magic that the zeppelin can fly so high.

I touch the plastic mask. Nonna's words about my broken face echo through my mind.

If magic can do all those other things, maybe it can help me heal.

Just as I'm finishing up the bows decorating the balloon, Uncle Mike sits down across from me.

"Working hard, Luna?" he asks.

I look up at the clock. An hour has passed since Mom brought me my *sfogliatella*.

He looks at the mess of drawings on the table. Some good, others not so good. "Looks like you've been busy."

I nod.

"These are stunning." Uncle Mike leafs through the drawings. "How did you come up with this concept? The ship feels so familiar."

"Familiar?" I put down my pencil. "What do you mean?"

"It reminds me of stories I heard when I was your age. Of something that happened way back when. Remember when we were talking about Stelle a couple weeks ago?" he asks.

I stare at my uncle, trying to keep my expression neutral. "I think I remember that."

Uncle Mike hesitates, as if he's about to say something, but then he shrugs his shoulders. "It's silly."

"No!" I bounce up. "What were you going to say? What stories?"

"Well, one of the reasons I went to Stelle was because of those stories your nonno would tell us when we were kids. All those amazing legends about the city and this secret group of *streghe* who used their magic to honor and protect the goddess Luna." He rests his chin on his fist.

"Spazzatrici?" I whisper, my heart in my throat.

Uncle Mike's furry black eyebrows shoot up his forehead. "How do you know about that? Did Nonno tell you?"

I stare hard at the sunflowers poking up behind Uncle Mike's shoulder. "Do you think magic is real?"

Uncle Mike leans forward, his elbows on the table.

Customers filter in and out of the deli, and clerks call orders out over the din.

I swallow the lump forming in my throat.

"I do," he says at last. "But it's a tricky thing to define."

"What do you mean?"

"Magic isn't the same for everyone." He waves his hand at the sunflower mural. "*This* is magic for some people. These sunflowers turn their heads each day to drink up as much of the sun as possible." Uncle Mike smiles at me. "Your talent is magic. The way you see things other people don't and bring life to your art."

"But what about the kind of magic in fairy tales?" I point to one of the zeppelin drawings on the table. "What about the kind of magic that makes ships fly?"

He looks at the picture of the zeppelin again. "How did you know about them?"

I shrug, not wanting to tell him the truth. "I found a book when I was poking around in Dad's stuff. I thought they were neat."

"Mike, your brother needs you." Matteo pops his head around the corner, making my uncle and me jump. "The line's almost out the door."

"Be there in a minute." Uncle Mike takes a deep breath. He looks at me, face weary. "Your drawings are great, Luns. Show me more later?"

"It's a zoo in here, Mike!" Dad yells from the other side of the deli. "Hurry up!"

I nod.

He fixes a shaky smile on his face before heading toward the counter. "Yeah, yeah, yeah. You should be happy we have so many customers."

Their bickering fades into the rest of the chatter filling Bianchini's. I stare down at the zeppelin, and suddenly it feels like just the tip of my spazzatrici investigation. There's so much more to them than I could ever imagine.

Chapter 13

Mom helps me into my coat as we leave for my therapy appointment. "Your father is going to finish up here." She hands me my scarf. "We'll pick him up on the way home."

My arm is still stiff despite the painkillers Mom gave me.

I look over my shoulder for Uncle Mike as we go through the deli door. But he's nowhere to be found. My heart rattles against my rib cage. I need more time to talk to him.

"Luna?" a familiar voice calls.

I look up just in time to see Mrs. Ruiz waving at my mom and me from the parking lot. "Sofia, how are you two?"

My eyes dart down to my shoes. I try opening the car door, but Mom hasn't unlocked it yet. I swallow hard.

Mom smiles and closes the distance between her and Mrs. Ruiz. I stand back, doing my best to hide my face behind my hair. "Janet, what're you doing here?" Mom asks.

"Putting in our dessert order for Christmas. Nobody makes cannoli like Bianchini's." Mrs. Ruiz tosses her car keys into her large purse and runs a hand through her short dark hair. Her bright red lips turn up in a smile. "How are you doing, Luna?" She looks past my mom toward me.

"I'm fine," I say. "Just fine."

Mrs. Ruiz takes off her black sunglasses and looks right at me. She doesn't wince or physically react, but concern flashes in her eyes. The same look my aunts and uncles get when they try to hide their discomfort. Mrs. Ruiz reaches out to give me a hug. The scent of her vanilla perfume fills my nose, a smell that I didn't realize I missed until just now. She's careful not to hug me too tight like she usually does.

"You should stop by for a haircut soon," she says after releasing me. "It's getting so long."

"Yeah, it's been a while." I twirl a frizzy strand between my fingers and look away.

"Tailee misses you, you know. She says you never pick up when she calls." Mrs. Ruiz glances over her shoulder. "She's waiting in the car just now."

"What?" My cheeks grow hot. Sitting in the blue SUV beyond Mrs. Ruiz is Tailee.

I scramble to tug the hair further over my mask. Our eyes meet for a moment before Tailee slumps down. She doesn't wave or smile.

Mom and Mrs. Ruiz continue to chat, but their voices fade far away. I steal glances at Tailee. I spot the black bun she wears on top of her head peeking out of the window as she ducks lower in the back seat.

A knot twists in my stomach. Tailee saw me. It doesn't help that the last time we saw each other, it was so awkward and I could barely talk to her. Did she forget all about the mask? Does she think I look weird?

Mom clamps a hand on my shoulder, jolting me. "Maybe Luna will be up for a visit next time Tailee brings her homework by."

Mrs. Ruiz's eyes flicker between me and the top of Tailee's head. "Tailee said Johnny's going to bring over Luna's homework now."

"Oh," Mom says. "Is there a reason?"

"Just with Tailee's vocal lessons and the auditions for the play coming up, she needs to focus on that."

"Well, then, maybe a sleepover during Christmas break. When there's more time."

Mrs. Ruiz looks over her shoulder at Tailee ducking farther into the seat. "That would be nice, but we'll have to see what Tailee's schedule is like." She shrugs off the idea in that way parents do when they're lying about something. She leans down to kiss me on my left cheek before heading toward Bianchini's. "It was nice seeing you."

"Have a good day." Mom unlocks the car, and I hop in before we see anyone else we know.

I take a deep breath.

Mom starts the car without saying a word. Guilt presses down on my shoulders.

I stare out the window, unable to look at her.

Of course Tailee wouldn't want to see me. It's not like I've tried talking to her. Does she hate me now?

My ugly white mask catches my attention in the side mirror. The scuff mark on the bridge of the nose that won't rub out no matter how hard I try. The scratchy Velcro strap that's yellowing with age. The searing red scars peeking out from behind the mask like cracks in fine china. Mom couldn't get rid of every mirror.

Dr. Miles's office is filled with toys and games. Not at all what I imagined a therapist's office would look like. I sit on a large overstuffed couch in front of a table with colored pencils, charcoals, paints, and stacks of heavy paper.

Therapy is the one thing Mom and Dad agree on these days. They think it will make me feel better. But I don't want to tell people how I'm feeling.

Dr. Miles opens the door and smiles. Her curly red hair is swept back in a low ponytail, and her green eyes twinkle behind her glasses. A smattering of freckles covers her light-brown skin. Some of them pepper her nose, just like mine.

"Good afternoon, Luna," she says. "It's a pleasure to meet you." She walks over to her desk and unlocks a file cabinet, pulling out a manila folder. "You're twelve years old, I see. That means you're in the seventh grade, right? Do you like school?"

"Yeah, but I haven't been there for a few months because of what happened." I shift my attention to the hammock full of stuffed animals in the corner. In the heap of teddy bears, elephants, and rabbits there is a bat. An animal that prefers the moon and stars to the sun. An animal like me.

I think of Alessandro, Chiara, and the tiny stars sleeping in their bassinets. How are they doing now? When will they feel better enough to be released? I can almost see the shimmering city lights below and the bright, fiery stars surrounding us in the darkness. I can almost feel the frosty wind nipping at my face and hands.

"Luna?"

I tear my eyes away from the stuffed bat and look at Dr. Miles. She's sitting on the chair across from the couch, legs crossed, my chart and a yellow legal pad on her lap.

"Do you know why your parents thought it would be good for us to meet?"

"Mom says it's so I can talk about my feelings with someone."

"That's what I'm here for. We can discuss anything you want," she says. "Your mom says you've been having trouble sleeping. Do you agree?"

Dr. Miles wouldn't believe me if I told her about the Sapientis. She'd never guess about the magic and flying up into the sky. I savor this secret like a piece of chocolate.

"I guess so."

"Is it because you can't stay asleep, or do you have trouble falling asleep?"

"Both, really."

"Have you been having nightmares?" Dr. Miles asks, pulling me from my thoughts once more.

The clock on the wall reads 2:15, which means another forty-five minutes of this. "A few, I guess. When I do sleep."

Dr. Miles adjusts her glasses. "Can you describe them for me?"

"I don't want to." I squeeze my eyes shut, trying to keep thoughts of the car wreck away.

"When people go through bad experiences, our brain will sometimes replay the trauma over and over. Oth people completely forget. It's like their brains are wipe

"I wish I could forget," I say. "It's like I can hear the tires screeching and smell the burning rubber. Sometimes I wake up, sweating, because I can feel shards of glass slicing my face." I curl my arms around a pillow and press my face into it. Tears squeeze from my eyes, soaking deep into the pillow's fabric. "Why'd it have to happen right before school started? I could be there with all my friends. Why'd it have to happen at all?"

Dr. Miles's chair creaks. She presses a tissue into my hand.

I look up from the pillow and scrub at my cheeks with the tissue. "I just want to feel normal."

"It's hard feeling happy or normal when you can't forget the bad thing that happened," Dr. Miles says.

"Yeah."

"Do you find it hard to do things you used to enjoy?"

"My favorite thing to do is draw." I cross my arms over my chest. "I still like doing that."

She smiles. "That's wonderful. What do you like to draw?"

"Everything, really," I say. "I've been drawing the sky a lot. The moon and stars."

"That sounds lovely." Dr. Miles scribbles in her notepad. "Your mom says you used to love hanging out with your cousins and friends. How do you feel about seeing them?"

"Used to" hangs in the air between us.

I think of sleeping over at Tailee's house and eating cheeseburgers and corn on the cob her dad grilled. We'd stay up late under the blanket fort we built in her living room, talking about our crushes and playing her brother's video games. Then Tailee would come over after the accident, chatting like nothing was wrong, and I wasn't able to respond. The distance between us as far away as the moon is from earth.

"Are you still with me, Luna?" Dr. Miles asks.

"Can we not talk about it anymore?" I pick up a piece of clean white paper from the stack and sit on the floor in front of the table.

My arm still hurts and there's nothing I really feel like drawing, but I'd rather deal with a sore arm than think any more about how happy I used to be. I start with a regular pencil, one sharp enough to create crisp angles and curves. Some artists begin with color, but that feels backward to me, like putting frosting on the bottom of the baking pan before the cake batter. Mom says I never liked coloring books, even as a little kid. Coloring books feel like living in someone else's story. I'd rather color in my own drawings.

The edge of Dad's jawline takes shape on the page. A little shading on the left side of his face, his curly black hair growing out of the whiteness. That's what I like best about drawing. It makes the thoughts in my head stop for a moment. They race from my brain, down my spinal cord, into my left arm, and shoot out of my fingers into the pencil.

Dr. Miles tries again. "You're a very talented artist."

I draw until I've created a world out of nothingness on the page. Entire worlds, entire little universes of people and places and things live between my head and the empty sheets of paper. It's fun discovering them with my pencil, digging them out of the blankness like an archeologist. Every time I draw, I see something new.

Dr. Miles scoots off her chair and sits down next to me on the floor. "What are you drawing?" She looks over my shoulder. Her perfume smells like lavender.

I don't hide my drawing from her, too intent on getting the width of my dad's eyes right. I add Mom next to Dad. Her long curly hair takes up most of the white space on the right side of the page. Her eyes are like mine, a soft hazel. They're wide, too. She always looks curious or surprised, like there's too much to see and she needs to make sure she doesn't miss anything.

Dr. Miles grabs her own sheet of paper and a green colored pencil and begins to draw next to me. We sit in silence, the clock ticking the seconds away.

Mom's face finally looks the way it should and I begin on my own, focusing most of my time on the ridge of my nose. It's been so long since I've seen it correctly. The Bianchini beak. My nose makes me look like the rest of my family. It's the most important part of my drawing.

I create a sweep of freckles across my cheeks, nose, and forehead before starting on my dark springy curls.

"You got your eyes just right," Dr. Miles says. "You're lucky to have such long eyelashes."

I sketch Mom's left hand draped over my shoulder. Hands are hard to draw, but last summer I spent an entire month practicing them in art class. I carve a dark wedding band into her ring finger and go over it several times until the pencil nearly pierces the heavy, white paper.

"Why is the wedding band so important to you?"

I stare at Dr. Miles, her smile small and hesitant. Behind her, the clock reads 2:45.

I look at the picture of my family, and my cheeks grow hot. It's how I see things, but not how they really are. My dad and I aren't healed. I still have this mask and my nose may never look like the Bianchini beak ever again. And my parents aren't healed either. They're still broken too.

I wasted a perfectly good sheet of paper on a lie. I hold up the drawing and rip it in half. The tearing sound fills the silence. I rip it again and again until it's nothing more than a flurry of tiny pieces.

If only I had a shooting star *now*. Everything could be wished back to how things were.

"I'm sorry, Luna." Dr. Miles shakes her head. She picks up her own drawing and tosses it into the trash. "Before we end for the day, let's talk about your therapy goals. This is your time, so what can we do that will be useful for you?"

The pieces of my drawing sit uselessly on the table in front of us. "I want to see my friends and not feel like I can't talk. I want to sleep without having nightmares. I want my family to stop treating me like I'll break." My voice cracks, and I swallow the lump forming in my throat. "Can therapy help with all of that?"

Dr. Miles stares at me, head tilted. "Those are all very good ideas. We can certainly try figuring those out."

"But it's not a sure thing, is it?"

"It'll take time, but with some work and patience, therapy can help you develop skills to achieve your goals."

"We'll see." I stand, collecting the pieces of my drawing and tucking them into my coat pocket.

Snow falls steadily late into the night. So thick that it feels as if the entire house is being folded into giant bedsheets. All of New York, silent and still, snuggled up in fluffy white blankets of snow.

I sit on the window bench, listening to the quiet and watching for Chiara and Alessandro. The torn-up picture from Dr. Miles's office is in front of me.

After my appointment, Mom and Dr. Miles had a conversation. Mom wasn't too happy afterward. I don't know what was said, but when we got home Mom kissed me on the forehead and didn't make me come down when it was time for dinner.

My eyes move from the window and down to the torn-up drawing. I pick up one of the pieces—what looks like Dad's left eye—and find the piece that fits next to it. Sometimes even Mom doesn't know what to do to make me feel better. So she just lets me be until the sadness passes. But that's been taking longer than it used to.

I find a piece that shows half my smile and dig through the pile of scraps for the other half. Putting together the puzzle that is my family's happy ending.

A soft tapping at my window makes me jump. Chiara's face is pressed against the glass. She waves. Her breath fogs the glass.

I lift the window.

"Are you coming tonight?" she asks.

"I thought you might've forgotten about me." I scramble to my knees as a warm blast rushes in. Alessandro waves from the zeppelin's wheel.

"Forget about you?" Chiara shakes her head. "You're the only non-spazzatrici in the history of the world that we've taken up to the heavens with us. You're pretty important."

"Well, when you put it that way . . ."

"So, are you coming or what?"

Before I think to say yes, I leap from the window bench and grab the coat Chiara and Alessandro let me keep.

"What's on the agenda tonight? More moon sweeping?" I quickly tug on a pair of jeans and lace up some heavy snow boots.

Chiara grins. "Tonight you'll meet the stars."

Chapter 14

Alessandro abandons the wheel and runs to help me jump down from my tree platform. Salt crunches under my boots.

"Should keep the snow from piling up," Alessandro says.

A sharp gust of wind kicks up around us, and flurries of snow pelt our faces. Chiara hands me a pair of mittens and a heavy knit hat. Though it's not as cold as it could be because of the zeppelin's magic, it's still much colder than last night.

"Storm's getting worse." Alessandro hurries back to his station. "We need to get past the snow clouds fast. Start helping Chiara store the buckets and brooms in the closet."

There's no time to chat as Chiara and I rush to secure equipment for takeoff. Alessandro spins the wheel slowly and carefully to ensure we don't get stuck between the two houses.

"Get ready. We're leaving," Alessandro calls out.

The zeppelin wobbles in the air like a top just about to fall. The lanterns flicker. The *Stella Cadente* stalls.

My stomach drops. "What's going on?"

"Hold on!" Alessandro yells.

The ship could crash to the ground and leave smoldering wreckage.

I swallow hard. Like the car accident.

"We need more power," Chiara says.

She continues to float between our houses, unmoving.

Alessandro pulls a lever by the wheel. A mechanical noise booms over the storm. Chiara tugs at my arm and leads me to the back of the ship. A large brass propeller slides out from underneath and hooks itself to the back, replacing a smaller propeller. It kicks up and cuts through the air like knives, its whir low and fast. A consistent hum competes with the whistling, twisting wind.

"It's the only way we'll push through the storm clouds." Chiara holds tight to the railing. "Grab on to something. It's going to be bumpy for a while."

I grip the railing and hold my breath to keep from vomiting over the side of the *Stella Cadente*.

Chiara grabs my hand. "Don't worry," she says. "Alessandro's one of the best captains around. He'll get us out of this safely. Do you have your cornicello?"

I nod.

"Then there's nothing to worry about. I promise." She squeezes my hand.

The ship dips again. I clamp my eyes shut. That terrible Wednesday before Labor Day fills the darkness. Dad slamming on the brakes, his arm flung across my chest. The huge SUV ramming into us from the side. Our car flipping through the air like a tin can. The airbag colliding with my face and shards of glass cutting up my arms. Fire. Pain. Blackness.

The burns on my face start to throb. My hands and head start feeling cramped and sweaty in the wool hat and mittens.

I take deep, shaking breaths, trying to steady myself.

"What's wrong?" Chiara asks, wrapping her other arm around my shoulders. "You look sick. What's the matter?"

"I'm scared of falling out of the sky." My voice quivers and sounds so small, so far away. Unlike my real voice at all. "I don't want to die."

"You're not gonna die," Chiara says. "This is normal during a storm." She pats me on the back. "It's all gonna be great. We'll be up with the stars soon. Hey! I bet I can catch more snowflakes on my tongue than you can."

Chiara tilts her head back, her scarf whipping behind her in the wind. She sticks out her tongue as snowflakes cling to her hair and eyelashes. "There, I got one. Now two . . . three . . . four." She counts all the snowflakes, her voice sounding silly as she counts with her tongue out.

I laugh. "I can't even tell what you're saying."

Chiara stops and smiles at me. "It's harder than it looks. You try."

She grabs my hand and holds tight. "Do it like this!" She sticks out her tongue again as several snowflakes fall onto her cheeks and chin. "See?" I tilt my head back, doing my best to stick out my tongue. My jawbone on the right side of my face is still sore, and the part of my mask keeping it in place makes it hard to push my tongue past my lips.

"I'm not very good at this," I say, frustrated. What used to come so easy for me is now a struggle, even things as simple as brushing my hair and teeth.

"Keep trying," Chiara says. "You can do it."

I push through the pain and can finally stick out half of my tongue. Chiara dances me away from the railing and around the deck, our tongues out and heads back. She sings a song in Italian as she bounces us up and down. Wind lashes at our cheeks and salt crunches under our boots.

I look up and watch the snow drift underneath the balloon. One tiny snowflake lands on the very tip of my tongue, melting instantly and sending a chill down my spine.

My eyes widen and I jump. "I did it!"

Chiara giggles. "You caught one."

Another lands on my tongue and then another. I laugh, spinning and giggling along with Chiara until my stomach aches. This is the most normal I've felt since the accident. Twirling on a flying ship with a little girl who sweeps the moon and can make doll furniture big with the snap of her fingers. Catching snowflakes on our tongues. I feel okay.

"Are you two going to help, or are you just gonna play all night?" Alessandro stands behind the wheel, hands on his hips.

Chiara and I stop spinning and look around. The *Stella Cadente* has stopped rocking. Darkness. Stars. The moon hangs above our heads, silver and smiling. Only a few clouds float around us. Snow drifts in sprinkles of white. Far, far beneath us is a thick layer of snow clouds.

We made it through the worst of the storm.

Chiara claps her hands. "See?" A large smile stretches across her face. "We're safe. We made it."

I laugh again and toss my head back in relief. "You were right, Chiara."

"Well?" Alessandro taps his foot on the deck, glaring at Chiara and me. "Grab the ladles. We're almost to Lynx."

"We're not going to the moon at all tonight?" I ask.

Alessandro shakes his head. "No. Tonight we help the stars. They like to move around every so often, so we lend them a hand. We need to collect some stardust too."

Chiara runs toward the supply closet and gathers some jars and three shiny silver ladles as big as my head.

"What are those for?" I ask.

Chiara hands me one of the ladles. It's a lot lighter than it looks. "They're for scooping up the stars. They can move a little on their own, but not super far. Plus, the silver feels cool against their little bodies. It's like a ride for them." She shrugs. "But sometimes we just use our arms to carry them around. They can sometimes get too warm, though, so we wear jackets."

"How do you know when they're a baby or adult or whatever?" I ask.

"You sure love asking questions." Alessandro laughs. "You can tell a star's age by how long they go between blinks. The longer they shine without flickering, the older they are."

Alessandro spins the wheel to the left, looking at his moon tracker to confirm our course to Lynx, when his eyebrows disappear under his messy dark hair. "Whoa!"

"What?" Chiara asks, leaning on her ladle like a cane.

"According to this, there's a shooting star only five miles away."

"A shooting star!" I yell. My wish buzzes through my mind like a honeybee that just found its flower. I drop the ladle and rush to the bow of the ship. "We need to catch him! I've got a wish to ask."

"We'd be off schedule if we did." Alessandro scratches his chin. "It's kind of dangerous to chase a shooting star. Usually it's better to wait to cross paths with one."

"Come on, Alessandro. It'll only take a minute if it's that close by," Chiara says.

He looks down at his moon device and back at Chiara and me. A grin creeps up his face. "It *would* be fun."

"Yes!" Chiara pumps her fist in the air. "Help me with these, Luna. We're gonna catch that shooting star for you."

We move at a breakneck speed, the propeller catapulting us through the darkness. I grip tight to the railing, nausea roiling around in my belly once more. Alessandro stands firm at the wheel, guiding us expertly between stars.

"Watch out for that old satellite," Chiara calls, looking up at the big balloon with concern. Alessandro spins the wheel, and the ship rocks violently to the left—narrowly missing the old, eroded space debris.

Fiery metal and burning tires flash through my head again. I take hold of my cornicello, pushing away thoughts of the wreck and the trouble we had getting up into the sky earlier. *Alessandro knows what he's doing.*

"Look, Luna! He's right there!" Chiara tugs at my sleeve.

I gasp. About half a mile away is a bright, fiery burst of light with a red and orange tail as long as a football field.

It's faster than anything I've ever seen. Like one of those bullet-shaped cars breaking the sound barrier.

"Chiara, get the net! Luna needs to catch him," Alessandro yells. He hunches over the wheel, eyes focused on the star's whiplike tail. "He's moving fast."

The *Stella Cadente* hitches a bit as Alessandro pushes her faster. Chiara and I tumble forward, gripping on to each other for support.

"Alessandro, watch it!" Chiara screams.

A craggy meteor collides with the ship's side, jostling all three of us off our feet. I land on one of the ladles. It digs into my side and knocks the wind from me. Pain radiates in my arm and stomach. I cough, struggling to my knees.

"Are you guys okay?" I ask, my voice a wheeze. "Oh no! The ship. Are we going to sink?"

"Sink? We can't sink if we're in the sky!" Alessandro stands on wobbly legs and shakes his head. "But she'll need repairs." He presses his lips in a straight line, rubbing the bruise forming on his forehead. "We've got to abandon our mission and hurry up with the constellations before it breaks down worse. That shooting star was just too fast."

The shooting star's tail slaps against the darkness as it hurtles farther away into the night sky. I bite my lip, wanting to urge Alessandro forward, but I don't want the *Stella Cadente* to get even more damaged.

My wish flickers out of view, swallowed up by space.

Chiara looks over the side of the ship at the four boards that broke off and the small hole left behind by the meteor. "It doesn't look too bad."

"Not yet," Alessandro says. "Papa's going to be upset."

Chiara picks up the ladles. "We'll tell him it was an accident."

"Just don't tell him we were chasing a shooting star. Then he'll be really mad."

"On to Lynx?" Chiara asks.

He nods. "It's only a half hour from here."

We ride to Lynx in silence, the *Stella Cadente* creaking every so often. I peek over at the crack in her side, guilt blossoming in my chest. If it weren't for my wish, the ship would be fine. My eyes drift to the darkness, looking past the stars for any remaining sign of that bright flame of a tail.

So, so close.

"We'll find another," Chiara whispers. "Just not tonight."

"We've got to."

She pats my hand and tilts her head toward the other side of the ship. "Look over there."

The constellation takes shape the same way tiny houses and buildings do when touching down in an airplane. No longer are the stars pinpricks in the night sky.

They're actual, glowing orbs of light. Bigger than the baby stars in their bassinets, but not by much. It seems that, aside from the sun, stars are a lot smaller than I imagined.

"Wow," I whisper, hearing my history teacher's lecture about the ancient Greeks' and Romans' beliefs that the stars were the eyes of the gods and goddesses watching down on them, guiding their futures, and looking into their souls. Oceans were crossed and wars were fought all in the name of these stars.

And here we are, just a bunch of kids in a zeppelin, flying among the constellations—collecting their stardust and moving them around like chess pieces.

Alessandro pulls the ship up next to a cluster of stars, each one twinkling and blinking like a flashing traffic light. He hurries to the stern, cranks out the anchor, and tosses it onto a nearby cloud. Chiara and I follow, and she hands Alessandro one of the ladles.

A star the shape of a pearl but the size of my aunt Therese's pug, with a quick blinking light, sits just on the edge of the constellation. She doesn't even look up when Alessandro anchors the ship nearby.

"Ellie?" Chiara says.

The little star's eyes are filled with tears. She sniffles.

"Ellie, what's wrong?"

"I miss my mommy." She floats closer, and the air

around her feels like it does on the first day of summer vacation. Almost warm enough to wear shorts.

"What happened to her mom?" I frown.

"There was a fire when Ellie was little. She and her mother were trapped in their apartment and never made it out," Alessandro whispers. "We've tried searching all over for her mother, but sometimes stars don't remember much from their human lives and it's hard reminding them. Ellie and her mother died in the 1920s."

"That's terrible," I say.

Chiara pets the star on her head. "We'll find her someday. We won't stop looking," she says.

Ellie wriggles around a bit. "It's lonely up here."

"We can come visit again soon," Chiara says. "How are the rest of the stars in Lynx?"

"They're fine. Martha is nice, but she fusses over me a lot. Always making sure I'm shining bright enough and getting plenty of sleep." A little smile tugs at her lips. "Arturo tried to cheer me up the other day. He showed me what his great-great-grandbabies are up to. We watched them play outside in the snow. They were chasing after their puppy." She starts to giggle. "I want a puppy."

"We have hermit crabs," Alessandro says. "They're easier to travel with."

"I wish I had hermit crabs." Ellie giggles again, brightening a bit.

"I don't think they'd like it in space." Alessandro smiles.

Chiara grabs a brush and a jar from the supply closet and brushes Ellie until she's sparkling much brighter than before. She passes the jar to Alessandro and pats Ellie on the head again. Chiara was right—the stardust does look smoother than the moondust. It's also a little less silver and more of a blinding white. The stardust shimmers like the glitter in art class.

"We have to brush the other Lynx stars now. But we'll see you soon, all right?"

Ellie nods. "I miss you already."

"Miss you too, Ellie."

Alessandro and Chiara set to work brushing the other stars, making sure to gather the stardust. After having me watch for a while, Chiara teaches me the proper way to brush a star. It's much more delicate work than scrubbing at the moon. Light strokes and gentle motions to not tickle them.

We move on to Hercules and have fallen into a rhythm, brushing stars and quickly collecting their dust so we can hurry to the next constellations as fast as possible.

Some stars wriggle around when being brushed, while others love it. Each one is unique. A glowing soul with its own likes and dislikes.

We finish working with the last remaining stars of Sagittarius. Alessandro and Chiara scoop up a few more and give them new spots in the constellation until the big move in late winter.

Chiara's timer goes off, the shrill ring echoing throughout the sky.

"Oh no," she says. "We didn't make it to Pegasus."

Alessandro frowns, glancing over at the *Stella Cadente*'s damage. More boards broke off in our travels between constellations. He shakes his head. "We'll have come back tomorrow night. Got to get the ship fixed up."

He runs to the wheel and pulls the lever to start up the propeller. Chiara and I organize the jars of shimmering stardust. The ride home is smooth, aside from worrying creaks and groans from our collision. But the storm from earlier has mostly cleared up.

Chiara and I sit on the steps leading up to the back of the ship. She rests her head on my shoulder and yawns. "It's been so busy."

"I'm definitely going to sleep tonight," I say.

"I'm glad you came up with us," Chiara says. "It gets boring with just Alessandro. He's nicer when you're around."

I smile. The heaviness of sleep presses down on my shoulders. "I'm glad too."

The wind tangles our hair, whistling in our ears. Snow begins to fall again, but it's not the same blizzard as it was earlier. It falls in peaceful, soft clumps and looks like white flowers in our dark hair. Chiara begins to hum a lullaby, and the sound travels on the wind.

I lean my head onto Chiara's. I don't even flinch when her face touches my mask.

I think of Nonna Bianchini and how she cried over my burns, her blotchy red cheeks and eyes filled with fear. My heart squeezes like a fist. Chiara and Alessandro haven't even asked about my face. I've never even caught them staring. I wish my family would treat me like they used to. If only they weren't so worried about how I was feeling or what I looked like.

"Hey, Chiara?" I mutter, stifling a yawn. "If we can't catch a shooting star, do you think your magic could fix the bones in my face?"

Chiara's humming is replaced by soft snores.

I snuggle deeper into my coat. Alessandro takes up Chiara's tune. He whistles her lullaby to the stars and the moon as he navigates us back to earth. I close my eyes, unable to open them again, and let the gentle rocking of the ship send me off to sleep.

Chapter 15

The doorbell rings throughout the house like a mosquito buzzing in my ears.

It's three forty-five on Thursday. Tailee isn't coming around to drop off my homework or pick up the stuff I've already done.

"Luna, please answer the door." Mom pounds sugar cookie dough into the counter with her palms. "Please."

"Why can't you do it?"

Mom rolls out the dough and sighs. "Because you can't hide all the time."

"I'm not hiding," I say.

"Go." Mom returns to the cookie dough.

I groan and drag myself toward the front door, doing my best to cover my mask with my thick, curly hair.

The doorbell rings again.

I look out the peephole and frown. Johnny Roma

stands on the front porch. Uniform shirt untucked, backpack slung over one shoulder, and freckled white face flushed with the cold. He has a bright purple binder under his arm. The same one Tailee carries my homework in. "Johnny?" I say, ducking back behind the door a little.

"Hey, Luna." He looks down at his shoes. "How're you feeling?"

"Fine."

Johnny holds the binder out to me. "Mrs. O'Neil said you can e-mail her if you have any questions about the history project. We have to create a family tree."

"Okay," I say. "Here's my math and English homework." I hand him two different binders to take back to school. Mr. Gonzalez isn't going to be happy with my sloppy book report on *The Outsiders*, but it was written late last night. Math was easier. I'm good at negative numbers. It's just been hard getting homework done. Not because the subjects are challenging. I just don't feel up to it.

"Everyone misses you," Johnny says.

"Thanks."

He runs a hand through his dark-brown hair. "I'll see you later."

"Wait." My grip on the door tightens. "Have you seen Tailee?"

"Yeah. I forgot. She says hi."

"Okay."

"Bye, Luna."

I close the door and lean against it. Tailee said hi. My face heats up; the burns under my mask throb. I've been terrible. My stomach rises into my throat. No wonder she doesn't want to be my friend.

"Luna?" Mom calls from the kitchen.

"What?" I say, my voice sharp.

"Luna? What's wrong?"

"Nothing's wrong." I wipe away tears. "I'm fine."

Mom stands in the doorway to the kitchen, wiping her dough-covered hands on a dish towel. "Did something happen with Tailee?"

"It wasn't Tailee," I say. "It was Johnny Roma."

"Oh."

"Remember? Mrs. Ruiz said Tailee wouldn't be coming anymore." I push away from the door and sigh.

"Are you sure you're all right?"

"Yep." I wave my homework binder in the air. "Got a lot to catch up on this week."

The doorbell rings again.

"That must be your uncle. Can you get it?" Mom asks. "He's bringing the old Bianchini tree over. I need to find the Christmas cookie cutters." She disappears back into the kitchen to rummage through the cabinets for the big plastic bag with all our cookie cutters. A task that's much easier than searching for the once happy and friendly Luna.

Uncle Mike smiles when I open the door, his eyes resting on my mask for only a moment. He's gotten better at hiding his glances, but every now and then one slips through.

"How've you been, sweetheart?" he asks. "Have you started baking cookies yet?" Uncle Mike picks up the giant old cardboard box that holds the Bianchini Christmas tree and follows me into the house.

"Mom just started this morning," I say. "We already made chocolate chip. She's working on sugar cookies right now."

"My favorite." Uncle Mike takes off his coat and shoes and carries the cardboard box toward the living room. "Sorry I haven't been able to come over sooner, Luns." He lowers his voice. "I haven't forgotten about our talk. I brought something I think you'd like to see."

It's been a few days since Uncle Mike and I discussed the spazzatrici. Since then it's been all hands on deck at the deli as the holiday orders pour in and need prepping. Dad said Uncle Mike barely has time to go home and sleep.

"What is it?" Excitement bubbles up in my chest.

"My old sketch pad. The one I had when your nonno started telling us the spazzatrici stories." His grin widens. "I'll show you later. First, Christmas decorations."

"Christmas can wait!" I bounce up on my toes. "I want to see it now."

"You know Christmas *can't* wait. Not with this family," says Uncle Mike. "Grab that other box, will ya?" He gestures to the squatter box by his feet.

The excitement growing in my chest is squashed like a bug against a windshield. After what happened at Thanksgiving, you'd think Mom wouldn't want to host both Christmas Eve and Christmas. But now it's like she wants to prove to Nonna Bianchini that she can host a family gathering where everything is normal. Obviously, Dad and I weren't happy.

"Victoria offered to host," Dad mentioned two nights after Thanksgiving. "Your sister's house is bigger. It would be easier for her to have everyone over."

"She has her hands full preparing for Gloria and Rocco's Christmas pageant." Mom shook her head, as if she knew this argument was on its way. "And besides, your family wouldn't come over to my sister's. Your ma would have a fit. We don't want to upset her even more."

Dad sighed but said nothing. The only thing worse than having Christmas Eve and Christmas at our house would be to provoke the wrath of Nonna Bianchini.

Uncle Mike lugs the box into the living room, where Dad's reading the paper. He looks up and laughs. "Where are we putting that ugly thing this year?"

"Right next to your bed so you can stare at it all night." Uncle Mike places the box in the far-right corner near the bookcase.

"Very funny." Dad grins. "Just remember that next year's your turn to host."

I smile. Dad's laughter comes easier with Uncle Mike. The jokes come quicker, and even his body takes a different shape. His shoulders loosen, his back straightens, and there's a spark in his eyes. It's as if his soul is puffing up to fill him out rather than hiding far away.

"Are you going to help us decorate the tree, Luns?" Uncle Mike asks. "I brought plenty of silver tinsel."

"Even more than the boxful Mom and I pulled out of the attic yesterday?" I drop the cardboard box of decorations next to the Christmas tree. "That stuff sticks to everything."

"It pretties this ugly old tree up. Thing's been around since before I was born," says Uncle Mike. "It needs a little something to give it some life."

The Bianchini Christmas tree is a sight to behold. Nonna and Nonno Bianchini bought it in a grocery store parking lot the year after they got married. They never believed in using a real tree because of the mess it left behind. Instead, they purchased a seven-foot frosted pink monster that rotates with the help of an incessantly buzzing motor that's seen better days. The tree has survived more than forty Christmases and has been knocked down on Christmas morning at least three times. My cousin Tina says she remembers it catching fire one year, but I haven't seen enough evidence to believe her.

We always do our best to gussy it up with ornaments, electric candles, strands of popcorn, and at least five pounds of tinsel—nothing really helps. But as hideous as it is, Christmas wouldn't feel right without it.

Uncle Mike rips the loud, sticky piece of packing tape from the box. Bits of frosted pink tree poke out, the cotton-candy hue in stark contrast to the dull brown of the cardboard.

I help Uncle Mike set up the stand and bottom half of the tree, bending and fluffing up the branches while he works on freeing the rest of it. The thing about fake trees is that they're built to be malleable, like a bunch of pipe cleaners all stuck together. A real tree branch would snap if you fussed over it, but fake ones are made to withstand the poking and prodding of Christmas decorating.

Uncle Mike screws in the middle part of the tree and then attaches the top. He plugs in the stand and presses the button to make it rotate. The motor kicks up with a rusty groan, whirring at a slow and choking pace.

We take a step back to stand by Dad for inspection. The tree reaches just about the same height as the book-shelf, but stands at a crooked angle, leaning a little more to the left like a broken spinning top. Its pinkness is loud against the eggshell living room walls and brown hardwood floors. Even our blue couches feel too quiet next to it.

"What do you think, Frank?" he asks, trying to keep the smile from his face.

"We're going to need more ornaments this year." Dad laughs.

I squint at the tree, taking in all its imperfections. Its broken branches, crooked angles, and rusty motor. The tree reminds me of visiting the moon with Alessandro and Chiara. Of seeing all its valleys and craters up close. It may not be the prettiest tree in Staten Island, but there's something about the Bianchini Christmas tree that's magnificent.

"I think it looks nice." I take a step forward and brush my fingertips against one of the pink tree branches. "Not everything has to be perfect."

"It's just right for us." Dad smiles. The scars on his face are a lot less noticeable than mine. The accident affected us differently. We carry our physical scars in different ways—his more prominent on his legs and arms, mine in my face and left hand. We carry the emotions the same. Slumped shoulders and wary eyes. But every now and then a real smile slips through.

Dad, me, and the Christmas tree—a trio of imperfect Bianchinis.

Uncle Mike claps his hands. "Let's get decorating."

I poke my head around the wall to look out the window. The sun bleeds yellows, reds, and pinks across the gray winter sky. Soon the stars and moon will be out. And a few hours after them, so will Alessandro and Chiara.

I lean forward to get a better look out the window. I'll be out with them.

"Bring that box over here, Luns?" Uncle Mike asks while unknotting a set of green and red Christmas lights. He hands Dad another tangled-up bunch of lights to straighten out.

I take one more glance outside before picking up the box of tinsel Uncle Mike brought with him. I rip the worn piece of tape off the top and push my hands underneath the shimmery waves, pulling out two large handfuls, letting them drip from my fingertips. The strands catch in the lamplight, sparkling almost as bright as stardust.

It reminds me of the baby stars. Are they coming up with us tonight?

I stare at the clock on the cable box. Only four o'clock. It's going to be more than a few hours before we can go up to the sky. Days are supposed to feel shorter in the winter. But when all I want is for it to be nighttime, they feel three times as long.

"First batch of sugar cookies is ready!" Mom places a

plate overflowing with sugar cookies shaped like colorful ornaments, spiky trees, and fat Santas on the coffee table.

I breathe in the sugary, buttery smells of Christmas.

Mom hands me one of the ornament cookies. The frosting is a pearly blue and decorated with intricately drawn silver and dark-blue stars. Her cookies are the best-looking ones in our neighborhood. Every Christmas Eve, before Mass, we bring over boxes of cookies and homemade hot chocolate mix to the houses on our street. I wonder if Mom will keep that tradition this year.

"It's beautiful," I say. The star cookies glitter with the faintest bit of pearl dust, twinkling almost like the real ones. Alessandro and Chiara would love these.

"Well, you know how much I get into my baking." She bites into one of the trees and wipes some crumbs from the corner of her mouth. "And you've been drawing so many celestial pictures lately. You inspired me."

I bite into one and close my eyes. Sweetness spreads through my body and reaches the ends of my fingers and toes. Every part of me feels warm, cheerful, as if Mom mixed Christmas into the dough. They're not as fantastical as a flying ship or as bright as the moon. But maybe her cookies are that small, everyday magic. The kind Uncle Mike talked about in the deli. Maybe he's right. Maybe that magic is just as important.

"I've got a batch of Florentines in the oven," Mom

says. "Want to help me frost the rest of the sugar cookies while those bake?"

"I'm not the best at decorating cookies." I shrug.

"You don't have to be the best at it."

"You could set up the nativity scene while your Dad and I figure out these damn lights," Uncle Mike says.

Everyone looks at me, trying to gauge my mood. To get me into the Christmas spirit. But even Christmas can't keep me from longing for nighttime.

"Or you could work on your history project," Mom adds.

I glance out the window again. The sky is almost completely dark. My left hand tingles with that need to get my thoughts on paper.

"Maybe later." I grab my sketch pad off the coffee table. "Is it okay if I draw for now?"

"Do it in the living room though, so you can spend time with everyone." Mom brushes the hair from my face and kisses me on the forehead. "We like having you around."

Mom makes her way back into the kitchen while Dad and Uncle Mike continue to untangle all the Christmas lights.

I snuggle deeper into the couch and rest the sketch pad on my knees. Mom and Dad have been strict about keeping me out of my room and spending time with them. Dr. Miles recommended that I spend a few more hours a day with my parents rather than running off to my room after doctors' appointments and our morning walks. "Family bonding is important," Mom said. But it seems like they're scared to let me be alone. Worried I'm growing sadder. That I'm becoming more like the lonely Phantom with each passing day.

My stomach tightens as I think of Tailee not bringing my homework this afternoon. But I'm not a shut-in. Not really. You can't be alone when surrounded by the stars. And I have Alessandro and Chiara. Two of the only people who don't make me feel like I'm broken.

The charcoal feels like a natural extension of my hand, a sixth finger. Small stars appear on the white piece of paper. Little dots lined up in rows. Rows that build constellations. Constellations that light up the night sky.

How far away was the Lynx constellation from the moon? How bright did Ellie glow when she talked about wanting a puppy? It's only been two nights but already I'm forgetting.

The shading isn't right. *None* of it is. Drawing the heavens from memory is difficult when they slip through the cracks and fall away before I can capture them on the page.

I tear the drawing out of my sketch pad and roll it up. Uncle Mike winds a strand of lights around the tree while

Dad sorts through the box of ornaments. Christmas music accompanies the scene. One of them must have turned it on when I wasn't paying attention. The sugary chocolate smell of Mom's Florentines fills the room.

Uncle Mike's black boots sit next to the front door and are caked with white sidewalk salt. I tuck the drawing into one of them. It's still a good drawing, even if it isn't completely accurate. Maybe it'll make him think about the spazzatrici.

Darkness sweeps across the sky and leaves no trace of the sun. Snow gently falls in soft little clumps. Not at all like Friday's bad storm.

I press my head against the window, trying to see through the fat snow clouds and to form constellations out of the tiny, pinprick stars. But the clouds are too thick and the stars too far away to form any sort of patterns. Tonight it'll be different. Once we push through the clouds, the night will be clear and the stars will be bigger. I'll take my sketch pad and draw exactly what I see. And I won't be stuck drawing magic from memory.

Dad's cornicello sits under the lamp on a worn felt coaster. Capturing its curves and angles from sight is much easier than trying to pin down flying through the night sky. I squint at the drawing to capture the glint of lamplight bouncing off the tip of the cornicello just right.

Drawing with a model is always easier than drawing from a memory. Memories become feelings. Faint, intangible moments that change over time and are altered by emotions. But is that how it will always be when trying to capture something magical in a drawing? Maybe the night sky won't ever look the way it really is. It's always going to be influenced by feeling. It's fluid and undefinable. Trying to explain magic is like trying to nail your shadow to the wall.

Pain throbs in my left temple. I put down my charcoal to rub my head. At least a dozen drawings litter the coffee table and couch. Magic might not have a definition, but that's not going to stop me from trying to bottle it up in my drawings like stardust.

I hop off the couch and rotate my left wrist to get rid of some of the stiffness. Dad and Uncle Mike have buried the pink tree under gobs of silver tinsel. Old family ornaments and strands of red and green lights twinkle on the tree from underneath it . The tree struggles to stand under all the Christmas decorations, threatening to topple over. But the Bianchini Christmas tree is stronger than that. If it's lasted decades of holiday cheer with my family, it'll withstand a few pounds of tinsel and ornaments.

"What do you think?" Uncle Mike asks, eyebrows raised.

"It's a lot," I say. "Santa won't have trouble finding it."

"It looks like the Christmas spirit threw up," Dad says. Both him and Uncle Mike laugh.

Jokes are good. He's happy.

The smells of pesto and chicken overpower those of cookies, and my stomach grumbles. I wander into the kitchen to see Mom chopping up zucchini and adding it to a pan of sizzling oil and garlic.

"Dinner will be ready in a few minutes," she says. "Why don't you wash the charcoal off your hands and set the table? Remember, Uncle Mike is staying for dinner."

"I just have to put my sketch pad upstairs."

I run up the stairs and toss my sketch pad onto the desk. The window is covered in fog and ice. My heart sinks. Written on the glass in small, loopy handwriting is a note.

No spazzatrici trips tonight. Papa's still repairing the Stella Cadente.—*Chiara*

I open the window, and a cool breeze ruffles the curtains, wrapping itself around me. Alessandro's window is dark. There are no fireflies floating by the window. The Sapientis' house looks quiet and cozy, a hibernating rabbit in the middle of winter. I sigh, scrubbing Chiara's note off the glass with my sleeve and closing my window once more.

"Luns?" Uncle Mike knocks softly on my door.

"Come in."

He opens the door and sits beside me on the window bench, a leather-bound sketch pad in his lap. "What's wrong?"

I shrug. "Just tired."

"After our talk in the deli, I went looking through some old boxes." Uncle Mike opens his sketch pad and leafs through the pages. "Look." He taps his finger against the page.

Drawn in pencil on the yellowing page of his sketch pad is a zeppelin like the Sapientis'. "It looks just the same."

Uncle Mike smiles. "I'd draw and draw when my pa would tell us stories of Stelle. I knew your sketch was familiar."

The big bullet-shaped balloon, the rows of ribbon flowing from the carriage, and the gold-rimmed portholes on its sides. I grab the sketch pad from my uncle and turn through pages and pages of the zeppelin, each one slightly different. "These are incredible."

Uncle Mike closes his sketch pad and leans back on the window bench. "I grew up different from your dad and the others. I always had my head in the clouds. Thinking no one understood me or my passion for art. I thought my pa hated my drawings. But when he gave me that plane ticket to Italy before I started college, he told me it was because of how proud my art made him. That was magic to me." He ruffles my hair. "People can surprise you. They might see better than you think."

Snow beats against the window. I touch my mask, the hard plastic warm against my fingers. It would be nice if people saw beyond my ugly mask and scars. Uncle Mike is wrong. It's not a matter of seeing better; it's a matter of seeing the truth. And to most people the truth is that I'm different. I take a deep breath, feeling the sadness well up inside my throat. If we could catch a shooting star, or if Alessandro and Chiara could somehow use their magic to fix my face, then maybe things could be normal again.

I could be normal again.

"Luna? Mike?" Mom calls up the stairs, her voice just loud enough to hear over the Christmas music. "Dinner's almost ready. Time to set the table."

Uncle Mike gets up from the window bench, and I follow. We walk downstairs in silence, my thoughts swirling with magic.

Angela Bellantuono
310 Rose Lane
Staten Island, NY 10301

Hi Luna,

Thank you for sending me this drawing. I was surprised to find it in my mailbox. It was nice receiving something other than bills and junk mail for a change. People don't take the time to write letters anymore. Yours made my day just a bit brighter.

I have your drawing sitting next to the mirror on my dresser so I see it every morning while getting ready for work. Your depiction of the moon is beautiful. It's rare that we get to see every little bit of it. Your drawing got me thinking about the man in the moon. How lonely it must be up there, staring down on earth without anyone around to talk to. That's what I thought at first at least. It took me a day to even see the small shadow on the left corner of the moon.

Maybe I was too preoccupied with getting ready in the mornings, or maybe it really did take time for your drawing to sink in. But seeing the flying ship's shadow bouncing off the side of the moon was a surprise.

I stared at it for a long time. The moon wasn't so lonely after all.

With love,
Angela

Protector

Chapter 16

Mom hands me two aspirin with a tall glass of water and sits down at the kitchen table opposite me. "I wish your head felt better," she says.

At our last doctor's visit, Dr. Tucker gave me a tighter compression mask to wear since my face wasn't healing properly. Ever since, I've been in a constant state of pain. The old mask was uncomfortable, sweaty, and a little snug. This one feels like a snake has wrapped itself around my head and won't stop squeezing. Sleeping with it on isn't an option. After my mom heard me pacing and groaning at four thirty in the morning, she came in and said I could sleep with the old, looser mask.

But now the new mask is back on, suffocating me.

"I wish it did too." I pop the aspirin into my mouth and take a long drink of water.

"That should help." Mom smiles. "You should come

Christmas shopping with me. Getting out and walking around might help make you feel better too."

"I don't think so."

"Oh, c'mon. It'll be fun. We don't spend enough mom and daughter time together."

"I see you all day, every day." I finish the water in my glass and bring it to the kitchen sink.

Mom sighs. "You know what I mean."

I walk into the living room and plop down on the couch near Dad's recliner. Mom follows after me. Her arms are crossed over her chest, the Bianchini Christmas tree a ridiculous backdrop. "It would be fun," Mom repeats, this time in a singsong voice. The tree spins behind her. Its motor rasps like a man who spent days in the desert without water.

"Fun?" I picture the crowds of people staring at me. Some with a pitying shake of their heads, others laughing behind their hands. "Nope."

"What's the problem?" Dad asks, turning away from the weather forecast.

"Mom wants me to go Christmas shopping with her."

He looks between Mom and me and shrugs. "You should go."

My eyes widen. I catch a glimpse of Mom's equally surprised face before looking back at Dad. "Really?" I say. "But *you* never want to go anywhere except for the deli."

"I'm not the one going." He smiles. "It'll do you some good. And I could use some peace and quiet."

"I know things have been tough for you and Tailee, but maybe you could find a present and bring it over to her?" Mom says. She rests a hand on the back of Dad's recliner.

My stomach aches. It would be nice to be friends with Tailee again, but even the idea of trying to talk to her makes me nervous. Maybe if I get Tailee something really good for Christmas, she'll want to be friends again. I lean forward on the couch. Christmas Eve is only three weeks away, so time is running out for the perfect gift. I should find presents for Alessandro and Chiara, too. We haven't gone up to the sky all week because repairs are taking longer than expected. But I've helped them with the baby stars a couple of times. What kinds of gifts can you get spazzatrici at the mall?

"Fine. I guess you're right." I slide off the couch and head upstairs to grab my purse.

"See what happens when we parent together?" Mom says when she thinks I'm out of earshot.

"The kid actually listens." Dad laughs. "We're a persuasive team."

I pause on the stairs, a smile tugging at my lips. They're actually agreeing. Talking instead of yelling. Maybe there's room to be hopeful. Maybe everything—my parents, my best friend, my family—isn't such a lost cause.

. . .

Coming to the mall on the Saturday three weeks before Christmas wasn't one of my Mom's better thought out plans. After circling the parking lot for twenty minutes, we finally squeezed into a spot between two poorly parked SUVs. Mom said it was lucky it only took us that long to find parking.

She takes hold of my hand, grinning down at me as if she were one of the Three Wise Men who got to see the baby Jesus. "Are you having fun?"

I look at the entrance to the mall. People spill out of the doors by the dozen. "Mom, we haven't even gotten inside yet."

"Just checking. We can leave if you start to feel uncomfortable."

"It'll be fine," I say, trying to convince myself as much as I am her. My face is clammy underneath my plastic mask and grows warmer every time someone glances our way.

"I only have a few stops to make this trip anyway." Mom consults the shopping list on her phone. "We need perfume for your grandmother, a shaving kit for Rocco, and a picture book for Giovanna's baby."

"The baby hasn't even been born yet," I say. "It can't read."

"A baby can still enjoy a good book, just like everyone else."

We make our way through the entrance and are greeted by the cavernous halls of the Staten Island Mall. Giant gold ornaments tied off with red ribbons and sprigs of comically large holly hang from the ceilings. Store windows display large snowflakes and fireplace setups that showcase their holiday gadgets and clothes. Christmas music echoes throughout, just loud enough to be heard above the hundreds of excited shoppers. Last year, as a holiday treat, Mom took me Christmas shopping in the city—where every block was jam-packed with people. We stopped and posed in front of the tree, then got frozen hot chocolate at Serendipity. I haven't been back there in a while. I haven't been anywhere, and neither has Mom. She looks so content just to be bustling from one shop to the next, taking in the crowds and the decorations.

So far being in the mall doesn't seem as bad as I thought it would. No one's stopping to gape. People are too busy finishing up their Christmas shopping and shoving their way through the crowds to pay attention to me. It's a relief not being at the center of all the stares and whispers for a change. Mom looks my way every couple of minutes to make sure no one's bumping into me or my mask too hard, but soon we settle into the mall's chaotic pace.

Mom and I follow the flow of shoppers past a couple of kiosks selling hair straighteners and remote control helicopters and a delicious-smelling pretzel stand, cinnamon and salt wafting within a twenty-foot radius. A humongous Christmas tree decked out with lights, strands of silver beads, and tiny crystals sits right in the center of everything. Beneath it is an old man in a Santa suit, taking pictures with kids and handing out candy canes.

Mom squeezes my hand, and I squeeze back. "Are you having fun now?"

I nod. Our trip to the mall almost seems normal. After Halloween, Christmas is my favorite holiday. It's been hard feeling any holiday cheer. So far, only our living room is decorated. Dad usually puts up the lights outside, but he can't this year. As cheesy as the mall's decorations and music are, they feel right. Even the crowds of people pushing by and hurrying from store to store make it feel like Christmas.

"Let's buy caramel corn on the way out," Mom says. "Dad will like that."

We reach the department store on the other side of the mall. Mom weaves us through the maze of people and makeup counters until we find the one that makes Granny Ranieri's favorite perfume.

"Your grandmother has smelled like lily of the valley ever since I can remember." Mom smiles. "Sometimes vanilla when she was baking or gravy when she was making dinner, but I'd always smell her lily of the valley perfume when she'd tuck me in at night. She even sprays it on the clean sheets."

I close my eyes, conjuring Mom's perfume. A bold smell—woody and strong. When I was little, I fixated on the squat dark-purple bottle of spicy-smelling water on her vanity. One day I knocked it over and the musky scent exploded in my parents' bedroom—so pungent it made my eyes water. Too much of a good thing. The perfume left a stain on the wooden floor and permeated so deeply that you can catch a faint whiff of it if you breathe deep enough.

She still wears that same kind. One dab behind each ear, a dab to the pulse point on her neck, and two for each wrist. A ritual as sacred as star sweeping.

The woman behind the counter wraps Granny Ranieri's perfume in a silver piece of tissue paper before placing it in a shimmery silver bag and tying it off with a dark-blue velvet ribbon. She hands the bag to Mom, and as we turn to leave a voice rings out from the shoe department on the left side of the store.

"Sofia? Luna? What a surprise," Mrs. Whitmore shouts, running over to us with shopping bags dangling from her arms. Mom squeezes my hand and I squeeze back. Behind Mrs. Whitmore are Emily Whitmore, Isabella Mantoni, and Aubrey O'Connor—three girls from my grade. They're popular. Nice in that way that wool socks from your nonna are nice—prickly, but you're forced to like them or else you'll get in trouble. One time Isabella let me borrow a pencil in math class. She's nicer than Emily or Aubrey. Aubrey made fun of me about my face being too greasy in front of the entire cafeteria, and Emily is always trying to one-up Tailee's science grades. They've all made sure we're on a list of the few girls never invited to their sleepovers or birthday parties. It's safe to say we don't talk much.

My legs feel wobbly. I dig my nails into Mom's hand.

The group stops a few feet short of us like the mere sight of my disfigured face can cause complete immobility. "Oh, dear. Your face." Mrs. Whitmore touches her own cheek as if to double-check that she's not the one wearing a plastic compression mask. She's a tall woman with smooth white skin. Her hair is the kind of natural, golden blond women like my mom pay good money to replicate in salons. And she's got a tiny nose that slopes in that pretty way models' noses slope. A tiny little button of a nose. No beak for her. There's no need for her to fear that my scars and burns have leapt onto her normal, unblemished face. "You're too pretty for a mask like that," she says.

Emily whispers in Aubrey's ear, and they both giggle.

My shoulders slump forward, and I curl lower into my jacket. I let my frizzy curls fall over my face. My whole body shrinks. Everything inside me shifts in an attempt to take up less space. To make myself smaller. The incredible shrinking girl, withering away from the embarrassment of a single comment.

Mom's eyes narrow, her lips pressed tightly together as she weighs the pros and cons of making a scene. Her anger registers in the twitch of her right cheek and the tightness of her hand in mine.

"Hello, Jessica." Mom's voice is low, a voice I've only ever heard once before, when a boy ran over my foot with his bike and his mother blamed me for being in his way.

"Sofia, it's been *so* long. We heard about the accident. Emily was so upset, weren't you, hon?" Mrs. Whitmore nudges Emily, her smooth and straight, equally golden-blond hair bouncing as she nods.

My legs start to shake, and a lump forms in my throat. I swallow, but it won't go away.

"Thanks for your concern." Mom's voice is even, unshakable. She squares her shoulders. "But we'll be fine."

"We haven't seen you in church." Mrs. Whitmore tilts her head to the side, her perfectly plucked eyebrows scrunched together. "Why is that?"

"It's been hard getting there."

"Now's not the time to stop going." She smiles, revealing a smear of lipstick on her teeth. "We've been praying for you. We all pray every Sunday."

The girls giggle again. Aubrey winces as she stares at me, like she's daring herself to look at a house fire.

We're standing in the middle of the walkway, and as more people push past, more begin to stare. A man slows down a bit to eavesdrop, and I swear he squints at me to get a better view of my face, elbowing his wife to take a look.

Emily pokes at her nose and points at me. She whispers something to the other girls. The word "ugly" slices through the space between us.

Ugly.

A dull, heavy feeling hits me in the chest. The word Mom and Dad have tried to protect me from. The reason Mom hid all the mirrors in the house.

Ugly, ugly, ugly.

"Excuse me?" Mom snaps, her face stop-sign red, "All that praying and not an ounce of compassion? Real nice."

"Mom, stop," I plead.

People within earshot stop to gawk. My throat tightens. Before she can start yelling again, I wrench free from my mom's grip and push my way through the crowds, zigzagging between the makeup counters and out into the mall.

The mask feels too tight. My coat is too hot. "Jingle Bell Rock" blares around me, but it is no match for the booming sound of my heartbeat in my ears.

Ugly. It's the word that I always thought bubbled up in people's heads when they saw me. The one they quickly tamp down with forced smiles. It's why Nonna Bianchini started to cry at Thanksgiving. The fear that I'm ugly. That the world will be tough and mean now that I'm no longer normal looking.

My face is numb. So are my hands and feet.

I kneel in the corner by a potted plant and try to catch my breath. I try to hold on to the air. A heaviness pushes down on me, and it feels like I'm being buried alive. My throat still feels tense, making it hard to breathe. All the air in my lungs is stuck and pushing against my ribs. Each nerve in my body is on fire.

Everything's a blur.

The world is dizzying and bright and loud. "Luna?" Mom's voice calls out, sounding far away. She scoops me up under my armpits and brings me to my feet. "Luna, honey."

Mom pulls me into a hug and rubs her hand on my back in big circles. "Oh, my Luna. I'm sorry," she whispers. "I'm so sorry."

After a few moments my heartbeat steadies and I'm able to catch my breath. Feeling slowly comes back to my body. The world stops spinning. Mom's pulled me back from inside myself, grounding me.

"Why'd you have to yell?" I ask, my voice muffled

against her shoulder. "Now everyone in class is going to find out and make fun of me."

It'll catch like some sort of viral disease, and after my first day back in school everyone will know. Not only will I be the ugly one, but I'll be the ugly one with a loud, angry mom.

"I'm not going to let people treat you that way," she says. "You deserve respect."

"I'm *ugly* now." The word sticks in my throat like a splinter digging deeper into my flesh. "I don't deserve respect or anything else."

Mom holds me out at arm's length and wipes the tears and snot from my face with the end of her sweater. "You're *not* ugly." She shakes her head. "And you absolutely deserve respect, Luna." She's got tears in her eyes too, and her face is still that brilliant red. "I'm so sorry you got in that wreck, that you had to start dealing with horrible things like this at such a young age. The world isn't always kind, especially to those who don't look or behave the way others think they should." Mom takes a deep breath. She looks tired, fed up. Her dark-brown eyes meet mine. "I wish you could see what your Dad and I see." Her eyes soften, and she squeezes my shoulders. "We can go home now if you want. Let's go?"

"But my present for Tailee," I whisper. The present that could make things right between us.

"There's still time," she says.

I look around the mall. At the throngs of people fighting to get through to stores or to see Santa. It's too much. I'm not ready for another encounter.

I take Mom's hand and we walk through the crowds. Santa waves and shouts from a plywood North Pole as "Carol of the Bells" provides background music for the holiday-shopping festivities and our exit. Mom squeezes my hand, and I squeeze back. We exit through the revolving doors, and I breathe in the cold winter air, letting it dry up the remaining tears on my cheeks.

Francis Andrews
187 Marigold Court
Staten Island, NY 10301

Hi Luna,

My name is Francis Andrews, but my
friends call me Fran. My dad opened your
picture, but he thought I'd like it so he
left it on my bed and I saw it after
getting home from school. You sent us the
one of tiny little stars being tossed into
the air by some kids in their backyard.
It reminded me of the illustrations in
picture books, except it didn't feel like
a cartoon. It all felt so real. Like the
drawings in Jumanji. Magic happening in
an ordinary place, not on some faraway
snowy mountain or in a world you get to
through a wardrobe.

I want to know more about the kids
in your drawing. And the stars. Why did
they fly all the way down from the sky
for them? Why not fly to a castle or
a skyscraper or a navy ship? Something
exciting? The kids look pretty ordinary.

Like they could live right here on our block. It's weird, but I guess magic like that can exist anywhere, even in a small Staten Island backyard.

—Fran

Chapter 17

After the mall, Mom promised not to tell Dad what happened. We both thought it would be better he not know. She spent the rest of the afternoon trying to keep my mind off Emily and the others. We baked more cookies, and she taught me how to decorate her way with the different-colored frostings. Dad was busy adding finishing touches to the decorations. Snow slapped at the house, knocking on the windows and doors as if it wanted to come in and help us get ready for Christmas.

But Mom and Dad didn't argue once. They even laughed and made jokes. No one shouted. No one cried. And as the snow kept falling around us, we remained steady. When we finished the last batch of rainbow cookies, Mom helped Dad onto the stair lift and both of them went upstairs into the guest room, where Dad's hospital bed is set up. They've been in there for a while, door closed, their voices only whispers. A good sign. Both of them are loud when they get angry. Whispers mean conversation. They mean calmness. And maybe with enough calmness Mom will put her wedding ring back on.

Staying busy almost helped me forget the way everyone stared like I was some sort of sideshow act. And the way Emily spit out the word "ugly" like it was something rancid. Almost. I nestle deeper into my comforter, my sketch pad balanced on my knees and a hot cup of tea resting on the windowsill.

Ugly, ugly, ugly.

My chest starts feeling heavy again. That same heat moves up my neck and over my face. I take a deep breath and rub the tears from my eyes. That's the one thing I don't like about the nighttime. Sometimes it's so quiet, too quiet, that all you can hear are the painful little thoughts calling from the darkest corners of your mind.

I shake my head until Emily is erased from my brain, like a drawing on an Etch A Sketch, and move the curtains farther back to look out into the storm. It's only ten o'clock and Alessandro's window is barely visible. After what happened last time—and with the ship probably still needing some repairs—it would be impossible to take off in the blinding white of all this snow. No flying tonight. Once again I'm grounded, tethered to the earth like a penguin—all the aspirations to fly but not the right set of wings.

I sketch a group of little penguins at the bottom of the paper. Just like the ones in the Central Park Zoo, all of them playing under a big moon. And snow drifting onto their heads, freckling their oily black feathers with white specks.

Ugly, ugly, ugly.

A faint light catches the corner of my eye. I put my sketch pad aside and press my face to the glass, straining to see the foggy glow emanating from Alessandro's window. The light swings back and forth and bounces off my window. It must be a flashlight.

I open my window, and a gust of wind throws wet snow onto my comforter and into my tea. "Gross." I look into the cup at the wet clumps slowly melting into what was once a warm, milky cup of chamomile.

"Luna!" Chiara yells. Her voice sounds far away, drowned out by the wind howling through the trees. "Luna, wanna come over?"

It takes me a moment to see them through the heavy snow. Finally, I spy Alessandro and Chiara framed by a halo of light pooling from the window.

"Come over?" I yell.

"Yes!" Chiara waves her arms in a windmill motion. "Come for a sleepover."

The last time I went to a sleepover was the weekend before that awful Wednesday. I spent the night at Tailee's house. We swam in her pool all day and then stayed up eating s'mores and watching horror movies, even though Tailee's afraid of everything. "I like when the monster is just out of view and then pops right up in front of the main character," she said between bites of gooey marshmallow and melted chocolate. "Jump-scares like that make me feel like I just got off the biggest, wildest roller coaster." At one point in the middle of the night we played with her mom's old makeup. Tailee used it to make herself look like a zombie and scared her little brother. We laughed so hard our stomachs started to hurt.

Somehow I doubt a spazzatrici sleepover will involve makeup and horror movies.

I listen for my parents. The whispers have stopped. Quiet. They must have already gone to bed. I'll be back before they even know I'm gone. And it's not like I've told them about the times when I've left earth. Going to the neighbors' for a sleepover is a lot safer and seems like less of a punishable offense.

I grab my watch off my desk and zip a hoodie over my pajamas.

"I'll be over in a bit!" I yell out the window. "Do you want me to come through the front or back door?"

"Door?" Alessandro yells. "We're tossing you a bridge."

"Bridge? What are you talking about?"

Chiara's loud laughter whips up in the wind and travels between our houses. "You'll see."

She tosses one glowing strand of rope between our windows and then another. Both latch on to the wooden platform in my tree with little crescent-moon-shaped fasteners. Chiara bolts the other two onto their window. Lighted threads weave together between the ropes and form a walkway. The bridge illuminates the space between our houses, making a clear path through the whiteness. I scurry out onto my tree and press my palm against the glowing bridge. It has the same sturdy resistance as any bridge found on a playground. I can't quite believe my eyes. My stomach flutters like it's full of baby stars, squirmy and wiggly.

"It's safe!" Alessandro yells. "Don't worry about it."

I unknot the worry in my stomach and tuck my sketch pad under my arm. Alessandro and Chiara wave at me to hurry. I've never done anything like this. The closest I've come is the treetop ropes course Gloria and I did at summer camp. I take deep breath and grab hold of the railings. Snow collects on the lighted path and quickly melts into the rope. Wind lashes at my face, but the bridge remains steady and the light makes it easy to see through the storm.

"Don't look down. Don't look down," I whisper,

pushing through the snow. I block out the rushing sounds of wind and the ice cold seeping under my skin and instead focus on Alessandro, Chiara, and the warm light pouring from behind them.

Chiara and Alessandro reach outside and help me into the room, shutting the window. "It's chilly out," I say, rubbing the warmth back into my arms.

Alessandro hands me a dark-blue star-patterned blanket, and I toss it over my shoulders. "Of course it is." He smiles. "You just ran through a snowstorm in only a sweatshirt and pajamas."

"That bridge is so awesome." I look out the window. The glowing bridge remains steady in the storm.

"Thanks," Alessandro says, running a hand through his curly dark hair. "We build them ourselves. Spider silk and spun silver."

"And a little bit of moondust?" I ask.

"Obviously." Chiara laughs. "Couldn't do it without that."

I tighten the blanket around my body, looking around the room. It has to be Alessandro's bedroom. His walls are painted the same dark blue as the blanket, the floors a rich dark wood. The bed, dresser, and nightstands all look heavy and well crafted—as if they were made centuries ago. On his bed are crisp white sheets pulled tight and a fluffy gray comforter. Movie posters with titles scrawled in Italian hang in frames on his walls. Shelves of fantastically bizarre trinkets and models of flying machines hang over his bed and desk. A full-length mirror sits next to his dresser. I resist the impulse to peer into it.

Everything is neat and tidy. Even the books in his bookcase are organized by color, and not a single paper is out of place on his desk. I think about my room: the mugs of half-drunk tea, my wrinkled comforter spilling over my window bench, crumpled-up drawings scattered across my floor like tumbleweeds in an old Western film, and books stacked high on every available surface. "It's like a tornado touched down in here," my mom often says with a look of exhaustion. Usually I tell her a messy room is a sign of creativity, but then she just stares at me until I start cleaning.

"Your room is so organized." I run a hand over his dust-free desk. "Everything's so precise."

"He's weird about messes." Chiara rolls her eyes. "One time I spilled water on his rug and he ran for the paper towels he keeps in his bottom dresser drawer to clean it up." She shrugs. "It would've dried clean."

"You have no concept of mold, Chiara." Alessandro glares at his sister. He looks at me and straightens his shoulders. "I like things in order. An uncluttered room lets you live an uncluttered life."

"Come on." Chiara tugs at my hand. "I wanna show

you my room. That's where the sleepover is gonna be anyway."

"Do your parents know I'm here?" I pause, thinking about our trips to the sky. "Do they know I've been going up to the stars with you guys?"

"Our mama knows," Alessandro says. "She saw us dropping you off the first night. She said we should invite you over."

"Papa doesn't know." Chiara looks at her purple-painted toenails. "He gets nervous about keeping the oath, but he'll be fine."

"But we're not going to tell him," Alessandro says.

"He won't mind if he finds out." Chiara smiles with the confidence of a girl who knows she'll be able to convince her dad that she didn't break any rules.

"Is your mom a spazzatrici?" I ask. "I mean, if she's not part of the Order, then how does that work?" My eyebrows knit together while I envision different threads coming from the spazzatrici and tying together Alessandro, Chiara, and their parents. I had never really thought about the history of the spazzatrici or how their magic works.

Alessandro shakes his head. "The people of Stelle, our home, know the spazzatrici and the order of families are real. But they're the only people who are supposed to." Chiara pulls me through Alessandro's door and down the hall.

"We're famous there, which can be very hectic. That's why we pop up in empty houses in big cities across the entire world. It's safer for us. We can get up to the sky with no one really paying attention. Things are quieter," Chiara says.

"The light pollution from cities helps too. When you can't see the stars, you're not really looking up. Plus, if anyone *did* see us, they'd mistake us for a blimp and we'd simply move to a new city," Alessandro adds.

"Spazzatrici must have been coming here a long time," I say.

"For a while. We started traveling to America in the twenties, when it became too hectic to go to the sky from Stelle and when places like New York City, Philadelphia, and Chicago became *big cities*—especially for Italians like us."

Chiara pushes open her bedroom door. "I cleaned up a bit before we invited you over, but it'll never be as neat as Alessandro's."

She's not wrong. Chiara's bedroom is the near opposite of her brother's. Her dark wooden floor is covered with a fluffy white rug that looks perfect for a long nap. The walls are a deep yellow and bordered with hand-painted green ivy.

"We use magic to make our rooms look like they do back in Stelle," Alessandro explains, noticing my eyes linger on the intricately painted walls.

A white cast-iron bed sits in the center of the room, a gold canopy covered with butterflies hanging from its sides. Her dresser is cluttered with notepads and colored pencils and books about insects and flowers. Unlike her brother's room, Chiara's feels lived in. Comfy.

Chiara dances into the center of her room and falls backward into an orange beanbag chair near the foot of her bed. "Mama said she'd make us snacks." She gestures toward a purple beanbag chair a few feet from hers. "Sit down. Take off your shoes and relax."

I remove my shoes by the door and carefully sit down across from Chiara, sinking into the beanbag chair like a stone in wet sand. "Your room is so bright," I say.

She smiles, toying with the end of her long black braid. "Thank you. It's warm, isn't it? Like the sun is always out."

"I would've expected stars."

Chiara scrunches her nose. "I like stars, but I see them all the time. Even more than the sunshine."

Alessandro grabs one of the hundreds of pillows on Chiara's unmade bed and lies down on the fluffy carpet by our feet. "I'm surprised she's never drowned in all her pillows and blankets. I could never leave my bed so messy."

"Good thing my bed isn't *your* bed, then." Chiara pokes at my ladybug-speckled bright-green socks. "These are neat."

"Thanks, they're my favorites." I wriggle my toes, making the ladybugs dance.

There's so much to their world that I don't know. I stare down at the little ladybugs and take a deep breath. "Tell me more about the spazzatrici."

Chapter 18

Chiara looks at Alessandro. "Like what?" she asks. "What would you like to know?"

"Everything," I say. "I've been up in the flying ship. I've gathered moon- and stardust. I've sung lullabies to baby stars. But why? Why do the spazzatrici exist? Who gets to be one?"

Alessandro laughs. "Slow down. We've got a lot to cover."

"But we can answer your questions." Chiara shoots up from the beanbag chair and pulls several books from her bookcase. "Mama and Papa make us learn all about the history. We have to study almost every day. It gets boring."

"It's not boring." Alessandro sits up. "It's important that we know what the Order and our family have accomplished. We need to learn if we want to be great spazzatrici."

"But I don't want to be an official spazzatrici, remember?" Chiara says.

"You know Papa doesn't like when you say that." Alessandro crosses his arms over his chest.

"It's not his decision."

Chiara places a stack of leather-bound books in front of us. Each one looks older than the last, dust permanently trapped in the cracks and crevices and loose pieces of paper sticking out from their sides.

She opens the largest book, handling the moth-wing-thin pages with care. "This is my favorite one. It's got spazzatrici fairy tales." Chiara points to a drawing of a beautiful woman with dark braided hair like hers, sitting atop the crescent moon—a band of silver stars circling her head.

"Is that Luna?" I ask.

"Yep! The moon goddess herself. We sweep for her."

"My uncle says you get your powers from her."

Chiara and Alessandro share a look. "Your uncle?" Alessandro says.

"Oh, well, my uncle Mike saw a drawing of mine," I say. "Of your zeppelin." My face burns up. Maybe I shouldn't have mentioned my uncle, but it's too late now. "His dad told him all the stories of the spazzatrici. Except he called them *streghe*."

"Legends of the spazzatrici travel far and wide. Though

most people think of our magic as just that. Legends." Alessandro turns through pages in the book. "It's remarkable that he has held on to believing we exist."

"He said the stories stuck with him all these years. I think we—my uncle Mike and me—have an eye for these things," I say.

"You wouldn't be the first. But it's not typical outside of Stelle, at least," Alessandro says. "Most people's eyes glaze over when they see us. People need to be willing to believe and not try to use logic to explain away magic."

"My uncle also said that in my nonno's stories, Luna blessed the spazzatrici with their powers."

Alessandro shakes his head. "Not exactly. Your nonno's not wrong. He also wasn't wrong when he said we're *streghe*. We're just a different kind. Our magic's older than Luna's blessing and stronger because the spazzatrici devoted their lives to helping her. Our magic is handy."

"Handy?" I say.

"Useful, practical. We're not focused on making things look nice," he says. "Our magic's not fancy or pretty like *streghe* who use theirs to transform into animals and cast good luck spells or those that can conjure up fields of flowers and lush forests from dry earth. But it is special." He smiles, leaning closer. "We don't make things like love potions and charms—that's not our trade. But utilitarian *streghe*, like us, did help build the Colosseum. Our kind of magic is stuff even ordinary people can comprehend."

"You built the Colosseum?" I ask.

"We sure did," Chiara says. "Well, our ancestors did."

There's a knock on the bedroom door. "Chiara, Alessandro," a soft voice calls, one with an Italian accent as rich as my nonna's. "Midnight snacks?"

Alessandro jumps up and opens the door for his mom.

Mrs. Sapienti walks into the room carrying a tray of hot chocolate with snow-pile mounds of whipped cream and a plate of fresh chocolate chip cookies with sea salt sprinkled on top.

"You must be the famous Luna." Mrs. Sapienti's warm, dark-brown eyes land on me. She's a short woman, only a few inches taller than Alessandro. Her hair is thick and falls down her back in large black curls. Mrs. Sapienti's skin is the familiar olive tone of my Granny Ranieri. She grins, an easy smile, and puts the tray on the desk nearby.

"Nice to meet you," I say. "Thank you for letting me come over. And for the cookies and hot chocolate."

"Of course." She ruffles Chiara's hair, patting me on the shoulder. "Alessandro, it's getting much colder out there. Your papa wants your help moving the stars into the house."

"Now?" Alessandro groans.

"Yes, now. He's waiting for you downstairs. It'll only take a moment."

Alessandro shakes his head, but hurries out of Chiara's

bedroom. Mrs. Sapienti watches him go before handing Chiara and me mugs of hot chocolate and placing the plate of cookies between us.

Chiara dunks a cookie into her hot chocolate and shoves it into her mouth. "Mama makes the best hot chocolate."

Atop the fluffy whipped cream is a small sprinkling of what looks like stardust. "Just a touch," Mrs. Sapienti says. "To keep you all well."

I slurp from the mug. The chocolate is rich and milky, hot but not too hot, warming me from the inside out. "It's delicious."

Chiara takes a long drink from her mug, getting a glob of whipped cream on her nose.

"You got it all over you," I say.

Chiara laughs while trying to lick it away.

"Chiara says you're a Bianchini." Mrs. Sapienti looks at me over the whipped cream bobbing up and down in her cup of hot chocolate.

"I am," I say.

"Very good. Very good." She grins. "I've known many Bianchini in my life. Good people. I see you've got the nose."

My cheeks heat up. I touch the spot where my mask meets my nose. It doesn't really look the same. "I don't know about that."

"Well, I certainly see it."

I smile, happy she can see the nose I'm still struggling to remember.

"What are you two looking at?" Mrs. Sapienti eyes the book between Chiara and me.

"We're teaching Luna about Stelle."

Mrs. Sapienti places her mug of hot chocolate on the floor and kneels next to us. She turns to a page in the book of men and women holding their hands out in a gesture that reminds me of the way Chiara held her hands out when she was making the furniture in their home grow big that night they moved in. Before the men and women in the picture is a large ship like the *Stella Cadente*. "This"—she taps the page—"is the first flying ship. Built in 1832. The four families came together and crafted it to honor their foremothers. Before the ships, star sweeping was much too dangerous and done in rickety single-person flying machines. But the spazzatrici did it anyway. They always had a love for the moon. That love began all the way back with the Four Sisters—the Quattro Sorelle," Mrs. Sapienti says. "The founders of Stelle."

"Oh! That one's my absolute *favorite* fairy tale ever." Chiara clutches a heart-shaped pillow to her chest, eyes wide. "Mama tells it the best."

"It's my favorite too." Mrs. Sapienti smiles. She flips through the book to a page featuring a drawing of four women standing in an open field, their heads tilted toward the night sky. Each woman is draped in a dark-blue cloak, stars dotting their hems. "These are the Four Sisters: Augusta, Alba, Aurelia, and Aelia."

Chiara taps the image of the shortest sister. "Aelia is our great-great-great-times-a-hundred-grandmother."

"Plus or minus a few of those *greats*, but yes." Mrs. Sapienti takes a sip from her mug. "The Four Sisters escaped Rome during an angry feud between the gods. Legend says they traveled all the way south and took refuge on a hill by the sea. No food, no clean water. Their magic was weakening and the sisters were ready to give up. Except for Aelia.

"Aelia began to shape a tall tower from the earth. She worked through the night since the days were too hot for work. Using the moonlight as her guide, she built the tallest, sturdiest tower in all of Italy."

"The moon liked that, right, Mama?" Chiara asks while nibbling on another cookie.

"She did. The stars did too. They peeked down from the heavens to watch Aelia build her tower. Luna, the goddess, whispered to Aelia. She told her to keep building, and if the tower kissed the belly of the sky, she would bless her and her sisters with rivers flowing with fresh water, a sea full of fat fish, and endless fields of golden grain."

Mrs. Sapienti turns the page to an illustration of the

Four Sisters using their magic to build the tower higher, the stars, the moon, and Luna looking on from the sky. Fireflies circle the sisters as they work. It's beautiful—I can almost imagine the sisters leaping from the page and actually dancing together in the moonlight. "Aelia got her sisters to help build, and together they completed the tower in three nights—the moon and stars keeping them company. It would have taken decades without magic.

"Luna was impressed by the sisters and kept her word, blessing them and their city," Mrs. Sapienti says. "In return, the sisters named the city after the stars and pledged allegiance—and their magic—to Luna. And soon others fleeing from war-stricken cities found safety in Stelle."

"That is how the Order of Spazzatrici formed," Chiara adds.

"That's right. The sisters had Stelle's finest artist create the first tools to sweep the moon and stars. Including that rudimentary flying machine to fly to the heavens. Flights in that were quite harrowing. The one you and Alessandro use today is much more secure.

"Soon the Four Sisters got married and grew into the Four Families—each family able to trace their bloodlines all the way back." Mrs. Sapienti turns the page to a map of Stelle. It's nestled in a valley with high mountains on three sides, open to the Mediterranean on its fourth. "Stelle is a small city, but it's proud. We honor Luna with a huge festival each year, and the city has great respect for the families."

"The Cielo Stellato!" I say. "My uncle said there were tons of fireflies. Like the ones that come out every time the ship flies into the sky."

"I love the little fireflies." Chiara claps her hands together.

I try to remember any stories Uncle Mike or Nonno Bianchini might have told. Did Uncle Mike ever talk about Stelle before and I just wasn't paying attention? Did Nonno Bianchini tell me about the Four Sisters? It's possible, but I just didn't see things like I do now. I could've explained it away, just as Alessandro had said.

"I should have known about you sooner."

"Sometimes it takes a while," Mrs. Sapienti says. "Sometimes people never see it."

I let the information sink into my bones. It all seems so strange yet so familiar. Like an old journal from years ago or a musty old blanket your nonna knitted for you before you were born. The legend of the Four Sisters answers many questions. They are why the spazzatrici exist. They are why Stelle was founded. But it's as if one answer breaks off into hundreds of questions. I try to latch on to them. To catch all the things I still need to ask in order to make the magic puzzle easier to put together.

But the questions move through my head before I can

collect them all. I stare down at the chipped polish on my fingernails. It's dizzying, trying to figure out how this magical history fits into the world I know. My brain feels light and is threatening to float out of my skull. I try to steady myself and look up at Mrs. Sapienti and Chiara. "It's just a lot," I say.

"You'll figure it out. It sounds like you're already understanding the most important parts. Like how spazzatrici navigate through space and take care of the heavens." Mrs. Sapienti takes another sip of hot chocolate. "Are you enjoying your time up there?"

"Oh, it's been one of the most amazing things in my entire life!"

Her smile grows. "I remember my first time up. Their papa is one of the most skilled spazzatrici."

"Papa says you got sick and threw up over the side of the ship," Chiara says.

Mrs. Sapienti purses her lips. "Ah, I remember it differently. I remember your papa being a bit of a showboat and accidentally conking himself on the head with one of the moon brooms."

Chiara laughs.

"Though we did see a shooting star that night. Very lucky," she says. "He tried to catch it, but the little fella zipped away."

"I've heard about them." My heart thrums in my chest. "They're not like the other stars."

"Much, much older. They aren't the souls of humans who passed on, like the stars. Shooting stars were here well before us. They're more like little angels."

I look past Mrs. Sapienti into the dark hallway behind her. My throat tenses up as if trying to trap the question I want to ask. Finally, it slips through. "Do you think that if I caught one, the shooting star would grant my wish?"

Mrs. Sapienti looks at me for a long time before taking a deep breath. "Shooting stars are complicated beings. They don't always behave how you want them to, and we've no control over how they'll react to a wish."

"Oh." My shoulders slump. The hard plastic digs into my cheek. She stares straight at it, her eyes sympathetic in that way my family looks at me.

"Let me see what I can do to help," Mrs. Sapienti says before leaving.

Chiara sloshes another cookie around in her hot chocolate.

"Maybe we should save some for Alessandro?" I say.

She shrugs. "He'll have plenty to eat."

I push the shooting star from my mind and take a sip of my hot chocolate. Alessandro trudges into Chiara's room, taking off his coat and gloves and tossing them on the floor. "It's freezing out there."

"Are the stars warm?" Chiara asks.

Alessandro plops down on a pillow and takes up the

mug of hot chocolate Mrs. Sapienti left for him. "They're fine." He looks at the plate of cookies and narrows his eyes at his sister. "Hey! How many did you eat?"

"I saved you one."

"One!" Alessandro snatches the cookie before Chiara has second thoughts. "Unbelievable."

Mrs. Sapienti clears her throat. She stands in the doorway. In her hands is a small glass bottle filled with what looks like glittery, shimmery dust. "I'm glad you're warming up, Alessandro."

"Chiara ate all the cookies," he says.

"There are more. I'll bring some up." Mrs. Sapienti turns to me, holding out the tiny bottle.

"Mama! That's a great idea." Chiara jumps to her feet, nearly knocking over the empty plate. "I should've thought of that."

"Dust?" I ask.

"Our family recipe—a secret mix of moon and stardust. The perfect ratio of both. Add this to your favorite hot dish—the heat activates the healing properties— and it'll make you want to dance under the night sky."

I take the bottle from Mrs. Sapienti. "Should I use all of it?"

"You should. And be sure to eat every last bite."

My breath catches in my throat. I clasp the bottle tight. "Thank you, Mrs. Sapienti."

"You're helping these two sweep the sky and collect dust. It's no trouble at all." She clasps her hands together. "Now, enjoy your sleepover and don't stay up too late," Mrs. Sapienti calls out as she disappears down the hall.

"Do you think it'll really help?" I ask, excitement rising in my voice. My head feels light like the zeppelin's big balloon.

"I think so. It's not a one hundred percent fix, but it's a start." Chiara grins. "Who knows? Maybe we'll find a shooting star and he'll grant your wish for you."

Hope swells in my heart once again. I hug the jar to my chest. This could be the little boost my family needs.

Chapter 19

D r. Miles sits across from me in an overstuffed green chair. On the coffee table between us are stacks of thick sheets of paper and freshly sharpened pencils. The clock ticks the seconds away, dragging us through the first few minutes of our appointment.

I stifle a yawn. We didn't get much sleep at our sleepover, and I had to scramble across the light bridge before my mom and dad woke up. Even when we did try to sleep, I couldn't. I kept thinking about finding a shooting star.

Dr. Miles peers at me from behind her gold-rimmed glasses. "How's your weekend been, Luna?"

The air in her office smells like Play-Doh and crayons. The clock loudly ticks out the seconds, echoing through the room.

"Your mom told me about what happened at the mall,"

Dr. Miles continues. "Would you like to talk about it?"

I swing my feet back and forth, hitting the couch with my heels. "I don't like feeling that way," I finally say. "It scares me."

"Can you tell me what you experienced?"

"It was hard to breathe, and my skin felt tight around my bones. Everything felt numb, and I was dizzy." I close my eyes, trying to keep the memories from coming back too clearly.

Dr. Miles scratches something on her notepad. "Panic attacks are scary. How did you manage to calm down?"

I shrug. "I took deep breaths, and that seemed to help with the shaking. It helped me calm down. Then my mom followed me out of the store and she rubbed my back. That made me feel better too."

"That's very good. Focusing on your breathing during a panic attack is a great way to pull yourself out of it. Which you were able to do. We can practice some techniques so you're more mindful of it." Dr. Miles leans forward. "Is this the first time you've experienced something like this?"

"No."

"How many times has this happened?"

I cross my arms over my chest. "Two other times."

Dr. Miles jots down more notes. "When do you usually start feeling like that?"

My feet *thump-thump-thump* against the couch. I stare at the hammock full of stuffed animals. At the stuffed bat with black pebble eyes. The sooner I get this over with, the sooner I can check in with Chiara and Alessandro. They said they'd be awake by this afternoon.

"The first time was a couple weeks after the accident. Once I got home and my arm was still in a cast. I hurt pretty bad and couldn't do any of the things I used to. I couldn't draw or write or play outside." My voice hitches in my throat. Dr. Miles's eyes remain fixed on my face. Her pen pauses on the notepad. She stares but doesn't make me talk. I look at my hot-pink sneakers and focus on their dirty white laces. "I saw myself in the bathroom mirror. I didn't look like myself at all. My arm useless and all bruised. My face covered in an ugly mask. You could still see some of the burns and fresh scars underneath it. I tried picking up one of my pencils and I couldn't do it. That's when it felt like my lungs were tightening. I couldn't be myself. It made me really sad."

My mouth is dry. The Play-Doh and crayon smell sticks inside my nostrils. "The second one happened when my mom and dad first started arguing after the car crash," I say. "I'd just hide in my room and play music so I didn't have to hear them fight."

Dr. Miles nods as her pen moves against the paper on her notepad. "I imagine those were hard for you. Were those panic attacks as big as the one you had at the mall?"

"What do you mean?"

"How would you rate this most recent one against the first two?"

"I don't know."

"On a scale from one to ten. Ten being the worst," Dr. Miles says.

"Worse, I guess. The first was a four. The second maybe a six." I pull at the skin around my fingernails. "This felt like a nine or a ten. It was really bad."

"What made it worse?" Her eyes are soft, kind.

I look at my shoes again, staring at the scuffs and dirt. Worn in and worn down from being out in the world instead of sitting in a shoebox. "Worse because it wasn't private."

"Because it happened at the mall?"

I nod. "And because it could happen again. Everyone was staring. Everyone saw. I couldn't control what was happening. Emily and her friends were whispering and laughing. They said I was . . . ugly. Everyone thinks it. It's why my nonna cried. But I've never heard it said aloud."

"Do you think you're ugly?"

The word pulses through my body as steady as my own heartbeat. *Ugly, ugly, ugly.* That stupid word that, if hurled at you, sticks to your skin like flypaper. No matter how much you try to wash it off, ugly holds fast, collecting more dirt and grime until it's even messier. Until you feel even worse.

"Sometimes," I say. "I didn't really feel that way before the accident. My nose was a little big and my hair a little frizzy, but no one ever stared at me. I don't like the word 'ugly.'"

"Why is that?" Dr. Miles asks.

"I don't want to talk about this anymore. Not now."

Dr. Miles scribbles in her notebook. "Okay, Luna. We don't have to." She looks up at me, her glasses glinting in the lamplight. "Let's try something different."

She scoots her chair closer to the coffee table and pushes a piece of paper and pencil toward me. "I'd like you to draw the qualities you like about yourself."

My eyebrows knit together, but I take up the pencil and stare down at the blank sheet of paper. Pencil poised to draw, but stuck in the air. "It can be anything?" I ask.

"Of course. Anything you like about yourself." Dr. Miles smiles. "You're a terrific artist. That could be a good place to start."

I press my pencil onto the paper and sketch a small paintbrush and easel. "I hope I can start painting soon. Like my uncle Mike," I say. "He painted sunflowers in our deli."

A small drawing of Uncle Mike's face pops up on the

paper. "I'm a good niece. I helped my uncle and dad decorate for Christmas."

The Bianchini Christmas tree takes a space next to the easel. "I like helping around the house. And at the deli when I can."

My pencil hovers over the paper. I think of Alessandro and Chiara. Our trips up in the sky. Slowly, a small flying ship takes shape. Little stars dot the sky behind it.

"What's that mean?" Dr. Miles asks, looking at the zeppelin.

My lips tug upward. "I like adventures. Other people might be scared to try new things, but I'm not."

"There's a lot to like about you, Luna." Dr. Miles sits back in her chair. My pencil moves over the paper, drawing more things I like about myself. A report card for good grades, a head with frizzy curls, a pair of socks with alligators on them. "What do those mean?"

"I'm smart. I like my hair. I'm good at picking out fun clothes."

"Those are all great." Dr. Miles nods. "Difficult moments happen to all of us. Even though we can't control these things, we can remember our strengths to get us through. We all have to learn how to cope with the big, uncomfortable events. It's part of being human."

It might be part of being human, but there's also magic. The shooting star flashes through my head. That fiery ball of light that feels impossible to catch. My heart thumps fast in my chest. I sketch a bright, glimmering shooting star flying high in the corner of the paper.

One simple wish on a shooting star could change everything.

Chapter 20

Rain drizzles against the windows as minestrone bubbles in the little saucepan on the kitchen stove. Nonna's recipe, except I added a secret ingredient. I emptied all of Mrs. Sapienti's mixture into the soup. I swear I can see shimmery bits of moon- and stardust swirling through the tomatoey broth. The wooden spoon moves easily through the billions of beans, bright orange carrots, and chewy macaroni. It smells like any ordinary minestrone—hearty and delicious.

It's not going to fix everything, but I know that even a little bit of magic could do a world of wonders. I pour the minestrone into a bowl and turn off the stove. Steam wafts up and sticks to my mask.

"That smells good, Luna," Dad says from the kitchen table.

I grab a spoon from the drawer and place the bowl in front of Dad.

"Are you sure you don't want any?" he asks.

For a second I consider it. But Mrs. Sapienti said it's best to eat all of it to get the most from the magic. I already get all that dust on me when I'm up in space with Alessandro and Chiara. As much as I can't stand my mask or the pain in my arm, Dad needs the soup more than me.

"I made it for you. Besides, I want a sandwich for lunch anyway."

"Well, sit down with me. Your mom will be home from Bianchini's with cold cuts soon."

I sit down next to him, watching intently as he scoops the first bite into his mouth. I lean forward, eyes narrowed, waiting for the magic to glow around his body like a star.

"How is it?" I ask, my voice barely a whisper.

"Delicious!" he says. "Keep this between you and me, but I'd say it's even better than your nonna's. You did an excellent job, Luna. Thank you."

He slurps down the minestrone, eating faster than I've seen him eat in months. I lean back in my chair, shoulders relaxing. Telling Mom and Dad about the magical next-door neighbors may be impossible, but that doesn't mean I can't make them *feel* the magic. I stare at his wheelchair and the sunken shadows under his eyes. Everyone's been so worried about me. A twinge of sadness stabs my heart. I want to help too.

Dad gives me a lopsided smile and goes back to eating the soup.

This little bit of magic has to help some. At least until I catch that shooting star. It's hard to remember sometimes, but I'm not the only one hurting. My whole family is fractured because of that stupid crash.

My eyes widen. I sit straighter as my new wish solidifies. A wish the shooting star can't refuse to grant. If I wish to go back to before the accident and can stop that awful Wednesday from ever happening, then my dad, mom, nonna, me—everyone—would be back to normal and feeling better.

Dad tips the bowl to his lips, finishing every bite. "That was incredible." A grin spreads across my face, matching my dad's. If even this teensy bit of magic can help him feel better, a wish from a shooting star can do so much more.

Alessandro's heavy broom hits the side of the moon with a soft *thunk*. Scrub, scrub, scrub. Moondust falls onto us like bits of shimmering snow. I have a collection of jars lined up in rows and hold two larger ones, trying to get the dust that falls just out of reach. We get what we can, but there's always more. And when it collects in big clumps in our hair and on our shoulders, Chiara laughs and says a little dust will do us all some good.

The heavens are quiet tonight. Even the baby stars are resting peacefully in their bassinets, exhausted from a long day of jumping from the top of the castle in the forest.

"They're getting stronger," Chiara said with a grin when I got onto the ship earlier this evening. "I think they'll be ready to head home soon."

The ship sways gently, the hole in her side all patched up. The stars are bright and clear. I inhale the cold space air and seal a shimmering jar of moondust.

"We're almost out of jars," I call to Alessandro and Chiara.

"Good thing we're finishing up," Chiara says. She lowers her brush and holds on to the bottom of the ladder while Alessandro carefully climbs down.

Alessandro squints at me, his eyes strained in the lantern light. "You've got moondust on your face."

I wipe at my cheek, and he shakes his head, gesturing to the right side of my face.

"On your mask," he says.

I brush at the mask with the back of my hand. My cheeks heat up, hot enough to make the inside of my mask feel suffocating, despite the chilly night air.

Chiara looks at me. No, looks at the mask. Her eyes narrow. "Why do you wear that anyway?"

"Chiara!" Alessandro shoves his sister's shoulder. "Don't be rude."

"What? I'm just asking a question." She returns her brother's shove.

"It's fine," I say. "Promise. It wasn't rude at all."

"See?" Chiara sticks out her tongue at Alessandro.

"You don't have to tell us anything," he says.

"It's hard to talk about." I cross my arms over my chest and burrow further inside my coat. "We were in a car accident, my dad and me." I stare past Alessandro and Chiara and tell my story to the moon. Her light is soft. A gentle glow in the vast blackness of night. If I squint hard enough, I can make out her face. It reminds me of my mom's or granny's or maybe my own. "He wasn't paying attention. We ran a light and another car hit us." My throat tightens and I take a shaky breath, releasing the nerves collecting in my stomach.

"The airbags exploded, and I don't remember much after that. Fire, heat, darkness. There were screams, but I don't know who they belonged to." I shake my head and close my eyes tight to keep the tears from falling. "I don't know. I woke up in the hospital. Lots of pain in my face and left arm. Pain everywhere, really. Like my whole body was being torn apart and twisted. Totaled, just like our car. We flipped over and over, but I don't really remember that either." I open my eyes. The moon is still there, still listening, patient and calm.

The story rushes from my mouth, as if trying to escape

being played on an endless loop in my mind. "I couldn't draw for a long time. I was in physical therapy to fix everything, but I still feel broken. The mask is supposed to help my face heal. It's like a cast for my face. There are burns and scars underneath, and in January I need to have surgery to fix my nose. It's not healing right." I sigh, exhausted from talking so much. The story lingers in the air, thick and cloying like syrup. I look at Chiara and Alessandro, waiting for a reaction. For them to tease me or look at me with pity or something.

Finally, Chiara smiles and shrugs. "Well, at least you didn't die."

"Chiara!" Alessandro nudges his sister on the shoulder again.

"Well, it's true!" she says.

Laughter rumbles in my stomach and travels up my throat and out from between my lips. A deep belly laugh, one that shakes my whole body. It echoes through the heavens, loud and ringing. Chiara's and Alessandro's laughter joins mine, our giggles harmonizing. I double over, grabbing my stomach and gasping for air. Tears stream down my face. A lightness settles on my skin, cooling it, and seeps all the way down to my bones. I take long breaths, filling my lungs with cold air. The laughter slows and my shoulders stop shaking. Chiara and Alessandro grin, their own laughter coming to a stop. We stare at one another, their eyes on me and not on the mask. They still see me.

I don't remember the last time I laughed like that. Not a polite laugh or a forced laugh, but a real laugh. Carefree and not worried about what's going to happen next. It feels good. For once *I* feel good.

I catch my breath and wipe the tears from my eyes. "I'm just glad to be here."

Alessandro grins. "Good, because we need to get back to work." Alessandro pulls out his trusty moon tracker and fiddles with a few of its doodads to line up a location. "We've got one more stop to make."

"I almost forgot!" Chiara claps her hands together.

"Where are we going?"

"Papa tracked down Ellie's mama!" She organizes the jars of dust in crates. "She's all the way off in Andromeda, but it's not that far away. Ellie's too small to travel that way on her own."

"You're going to bring them together?" I ask, helping Chiara with the jars. "Is that difficult?"

"Ellie's young enough to move to another constellation. Since she's technically not part of the Lynx constellation of stars, just an outer-lying star, she'll be able to adapt," Alessandro explains.

Chiara and I are quiet as we work, carefully placing the glass jars in crates padded with hay.

Ellie's glowing little face greets us as we near the edge

of Lynx. "You're back early," she squeals. "Did you bring me hermit crabs for Christmas?"

"We've got something better." Chiara grins and holds out one of the big silver ladles for her to jump into.

"What is it?"

"A surprise!"

Ellie beams brighter. "I like surprises," she says. "As long as I don't have to wait too long to know what it is."

"This'll take only an hour at most." Alessandro pulls out a piece of paper, reads off a few coordinates, and sets the new location on his moon tracker.

"How did your dad know where to look?" I whisper to Alessandro.

"We asked the other families for help." He smiles. "The Chiavaroli flew up one of the nights we had a storm here to make sure the star we saw through our telescope was actually Ellie's mama."

"That's really nice."

He shrugs. "It's Christmastime. And it's the right thing to do."

We zoom along to Andromeda, flying at top speed. Alessandro's estimation was right. It took us just under an hour to arrive at the constellation. The zeppelin slows down, the ship rocking gently as we come to a halt. Ellie sits up in an attempt to get a better look over the side of the ladle.

"Where are we?" she asks. "This seems pretty far."

"We're at Andromeda." Chiara brings her around to the bow. "Your new home."

"What do you mean?"

"Ellie?" a small voice calls from the right side of the ship. "Ellie, is that you?"

The little star's eyes widen. She squirms around in the ladle. "Mommy?"

Alessandro grabs another ladle and brings Ellie's mom over to us. The star shines a light shade of gold. She looks similar to her Ellie, the same star age since they died at the same time, but her beady dark eyes gleam as she stares at her daughter. "Oh, my sweet girl!"

Chiara and Alessandro carefully let the stars out of the ladles. They float toward each other, colliding, their pointed bodies whirling and twirling around each other.

"Mommy!" Ellie squeals. "I can't believe you're here!"

"I thought I lost you forever. My Ellie."

Ellie looks up at us. She beams so bright I have to shield my eyes with my hands. "Thank you so much!" The little star flips in the air and spins around her mom again.

"You don't know what this means to us," her mom says. "To be reunited after all this time."

"You're not lost anymore. You're finally home." Chiara smiles and pats Ellie's head. "And maybe we'll find a way to bring you hermit crabs!"

"Don't push it, Chiara," Alessandro says.

Ellie giggles. "There's so much I need to tell you, Mommy."

Her mom kisses her on the head and smiles. "We've got all the time in the world."

I stare down at the pair and think of my own parents. My heart twitches, recalling how scary it was to see Dad in the hospital connected to all those whirring machines. A lump forms in my throat. I don't know what I would've done if I'd lost him. How lonely it must have been for Ellie.

The timer rings out, the sharp bell alerting us that it's time to head back to earth.

"We'll return soon," Chiara promises.

The two stars wave their good-byes. Both dazzling brightly against the darkness so that it's miles and miles before we can no longer see them.

Luna Bianchini
236 Marigold Court
Staten Island, NY 10301

Wishing on a Star

Chapter 21

Christmas Eve is the loudest holiday—louder than Thanksgiving. So many kids running around, shaking presents, and sneaking cookies off the dessert table. So many opinions on how to prepare the dishes for the Feast of the Seven Fishes.

At least Dad's been feeling better since the minestrone soup. Mom and I were both surprised at how excited he was to have the feast at our house. That's worth all the commotion.

The kitchen smells of butter and garlic. "The scallops are going to burn if you don't keep your eye on them," Uncle Mike shouts above the noise. He points at the sizzling pan of scallops my aunt Therese is searing. "Quick. Be quick about it!"

Aunt Therese tosses her hands in the air. "If I cook them your way they'll be rubbery."

"I've never made a rubbery scallop in my life."

"Oh, go fuss over your clams casino, will you?"

I sit at the kitchen table, helping my cousins Tina and Gloria run pasta dough through the pasta maker. Our hands are sticky and covered in flour as we hang the ready noodles from coat hangers to dry. The Feast of the Seven Fishes is one of the biggest holidays on our calendar. It's supposed to be a celebration of the upcoming birth of Jesus, but I'm not sure why we also celebrate by yelling. Which is how my family's feast usually goes.

"Take the dry noodles off the pasta rack, Luna, and bring them over to Aunt Giovanna," Tina instructs. "We're running out of hangers."

I run the noodles over to Aunt Giovanna, who adds them to a boiling pot of salt water, then bring the makeshift pasta rack back to the kitchen table, where Tina and Gloria load it up with more fresh noodles.

"Surgery is the best possibility for Luna." Dad's voice travels out from the dining room and into the kitchen, barely audible above the commotion. I slink out of the kitchen and stand just outside the dining room. Both sets of nonni and my mom and dad sit at the table.

"But what if it makes things worse?" Nonna Bianchini says, her voice breaking. She has a tissue in her hand. My nonno puts an arm around her. "What if she doesn't look the same?"

Anger wells up in my chest. But she could be right. I squeeze my eyes shut.

"That doesn't matter, Ma," Dad says. "It's going to help her breathing. It's not just cosmetic."

"But my baby's face," Nonna Bianchini cries. "She was so beautiful."

"*Is* beautiful." Dad pounds his hand against the table. The room falls silent. My eyes widen. Dad's never spoken to his mother like that before. "That kid is more than the burns on her face. She's my brave little girl and has had to grow up real fast. The least we can do is proceed with this surgery and try. Try for her."

A smile tugs at my lips. Mom stares at him, eyebrows raised. I want to throw my arms around my dad and hug him hard for standing up for me.

Granny Ranieri nods. "Medicine and surgeries have come quite far in recent years," she says. "This isn't the worst thing to happen, Favianna."

I run back toward the kitchen. My heart beats fast. If my family's going to try for me, then I'll do the same for them.

We finish off the last of the feast just in time to head to church for Midnight Mass, bellies full of scallops, shrimp Alfredo, clams casino, four different kinds of fish, and pounds of pasta. My stomach rumbles in protest of the piece of cheesecake I ate. Every Bianchini gathering involves stuffing ourselves to the brim.

"Are you all right?" Mom asks as she hands me a stack of Christmas hymnals to pass out to the rest of our family. We stand in the cathedral's lobby, waiting to sit for Mass. The lobby is decorated for Christmas, with a tree in the left corner, garland on the banisters, and a porcelain nativity scene sitting on a pedestal near the cathedral doors.

I pass the stack of hymnals to Gloria, who circulates them among the other cousins.

"My stomach hurts a little bit," I say. "But it always does after the feast."

"Are you feeling okay being here?" She puts an arm around my shoulder and hugs me to her side. "We can leave if you need to."

I look at my family. There's enough of us here that we'll take up at least two pews. My family is loud. They laugh and talk with their hands. Their voices bounce off the walls of the lobby. Even with my bulky compression mask, no one will notice me in a group this loud and animated.

"I'll be fine." I hug Mom back. "I'll let you know if I want to go."

She pats me on the head before turning away to talk to Uncle Mike and Dad.

"Luna," Nonna Bianchini calls over the din of conversations. She's standing at the front of the lobby with Father Clementi, near the cathedral doors. She gestures at me to come over.

Father Clementi is one of the oldest people I know. Even older than my nonni. He smiles at me, his wrinkled face stretching out to reveal his yellowing teeth. Sometimes, when I'm bored during Mass, I count the gray hairs haloing his bald head. If I'm really bored, I count the white ones sticking out of his ears and nose. "How nice to see you, Luna. It's been a while." The lights from the Christmas tree on the left side of the lobby twinkle in his eyes.

"Merry Christmas, Father Clementi." Father Clementi is nice, but it's always weird talking to priests. He teaches religion at my school. He's not bad, but dread still weighs on my shoulders. Whenever any priest wants to talk, it's always going to be some kind of lecture about faith.

"Your nonna says you'll be having surgery in January." He nods toward Nonna Bianchini, who smiles at me.

I shouldn't be surprised that she couldn't keep my surgery to herself. Nonna Bianchini loves to talk. "It's not a big deal." I look down at my black Mary Janes.

"It's important to discuss health matters with a man of faith," Nonna Bianchini says. "We all need guidance in such situations. Wisdom."

"Perhaps it would be best if Luna and I spoke alone," Father Clementi says. "These matters are important, as well as private."

Before my nonna can protest, Father Clementi leads me over to a bench near the Christmas tree and out of earshot of the rest of my family. I stare out the stained-glass window in front of us, barely able to see the stars beyond the colored glass. My heart aches for the stars. If only I could spend my Christmas Eve in the skies instead of discussing my health with Father Clementi.

"So tell me, Luna," Father Clementi begins. "How are you feeling?"

The question digs under my skin. It's the same question everyone asks, as if how I feel about the scars and burns on my face is a mystery. I stare at the creases in my palms. "Like anyone would feel, I guess."

"I had surgery on my shoulder about ten years ago," he says. "I'll never forget how terrified I was. Surgery's a big deal."

"No one's letting me forget that. My nonni won't stop fussing over me. Nonna Bianchini is the worst."

"That's how she shows her love."

"It makes me antsy."

"You're young. You will persevere, Luna. And God will watch over you."

I take a deep breath and clutch the cornicello hanging

from the gold chain around my neck. "Then why didn't he watch over my dad and me during the car crash?" I ask. "Why didn't he keep us safe then?"

Father Clementi nods. "Grief and trauma are part of our lives on this earth. Sometimes they feel unexplainable. People ask, 'Why would God do terrible things to us if he loves us?' That's a hard question." He takes off his glasses and wipes the lenses on the sleeve of his cassock. "These trials are meant to make us stronger. You Bianchinis are tough stuff. I remember when you were a little girl, playing out on the swing set during recess. You were determined to swing over the top of the swing set. Do you remember that one time you almost did it?"

I laugh. "I flew off. Sprained my wrist and scratched up my legs. Mom was so mad."

"You were only seven. Even back then you were brave."

"But what if I'm not brave now?"

"God will light your path. He will give you strength."

The wrinkles on Father Clementi's face look like the crevices in the moon. "I'm tired of people telling me to be strong." I look out the window. If only I could float from the cathedral and up into the sky.

Father Clementi follows my gaze and grins. "The stars are reassuring, you know. A long time ago, sailors used them to get home safely. They're God's light."

Outside, the stars wink a little stronger, as if straining to see through the windows and into the cathedral.

He stands, the bench creaking under the shift in weight. "Time to start getting ready for Mass."

"Thank you for speaking with me, Father," I say.

"I pray for your health and recovery." He passes through the growing crowd of people and disappears through a door on the right.

It's been a long time since I've prayed. Father Clementi always says in religion class God won't grant all your wishes. That's not how prayer works. But he said God listens to us when we're hurting. I clench my hands together until my knuckles whiten and bow my head.

"If you're listening, God," I mutter into my hands, breath hot against my skin, "I know we haven't talked in a long time. But if you can hear me, please fix my face. I'm scared of surgery. If you fix everything now, I'll be normal again and won't have to go through with it."

After a few moments, an usher opens the giant wooden doors to the cathedral and people begin filtering through to find seats. I quickly make the sign of the cross and hop off the bench.

Rocco stops just before the doors, his head swiveling from right to left before his eyes land on me. He smiles. "I've been looking for you everywhere," he says.

"Father Clementi and I were talking."

"We're going to go light candles," he says. "Come on." Rocco grabs my arm and leads me through the throng of people and into the cathedral.

The cathedral is cast in the warm yellow light of hundreds of candles lining the walls and altar. Stained-glass windows are pressed into the stone like finger-prints, each one depicting a station of the cross. We walk down the center aisle between two long lines of wooden pews facing the altar and a large, wall-size organ. Our family stands on the left side of the room, huddled close together in the candles' gentle glow. Uncle Mike hands me one of the already lit votive candles, and I use it to light another. Hot wax drips down its side and lands on a mound of hardened wax from candles that have already burned in it.

Rocco lights a candle, and so do my other cousins. We stand in silence and watch the candles flicker to life. Granny Ranieri utters an "Our Father" in Italian, and soon Papa Ranieri and Aunt Giovanna join her. The prayer envelops us, tugging us closer together under the warmth of candlelight. I close my eyes. I count my slow breaths and the consistent beat of my heart.

Faith, magic, hope.

Faith, magic, hope.

Faith, magic, hope.

Someone squeezes my shoulder. I turn and see Aunt

Therese smiling. "Let's go find seats before it gets too crowded," she says.

My family takes up two and a half pews. I sit on the end, near the aisle next to Rocco, and look over the familiar Christmas songs in the hymnal.

"Hey, where are your parents?" he asks.

I look down our row and at the two pews behind us. Mom and Dad aren't there. They aren't in the cathedral at all.

"Maybe they're in the bathroom," Gloria says, leaning over her brother. "Mass is so long. Granny will probably have to get up a gazillion times."

The organist enters and sits down at the bench. She begins warming up with "O Holy Night." I look over my shoulder. A few people are streaming through the doors; most are already seated.

"I'm going to go look for my parents," I say. I hurry down the aisle, passing families excitedly chatting about Christmas, and enter the lobby.

My eyes widen. Mom is sitting on the bench, cuddled up to Dad in his wheelchair. Both underneath the mistletoe. Kissing!

I run from the lobby and back to my seat at the end of the pew. Mom and Dad kissing! They've hardly hugged since the accident. It must be Mrs. Sapienti's dust mixture. Dad's been feeling good enough to make things better with Mom. And he was able to stand up to Nonna earlier. It *has* to be magic. My body buzzes, my legs shaking against the pew. I clench my fists in my lap. *Don't get your hopes up, Luna.* Still. My heart thrums against my chest. I lean back in the pew, smiling.

Chapter 22

"L una? You still have one gift left." Mom grabs the hot pink and yellow polka-dotted wrapped present I put on the shelf in my closet. Tailee's present. Her mom brought it over yesterday morning. Mom smiles and hands it to me, along with a steaming mug of hot chocolate.

Mom, Dad, and I opened our gifts early in the morning before the rest of the family came over. This year was the first time I didn't receive a doll. Instead, I got new paints, art books, an easel, and some clothes for spring. Dad surprised Mom with a gold heart-shaped locket that has our pictures inside and she hugged him tight.

The family started coming over around midmorning, just in time for pancakes and bacon. The rest of the day was a blur of wrapping paper, Christmas cookies, and lots of food. My cousins and I chased one another outside, hurling snowballs and making snow angels. My grand-fathers settled in the living room with my dad and uncles, while my grandmothers busied about the kitchen with my mom, aunts, and Uncle Mike. We exchanged gifts with the entire family before sitting down to our second feast in two days. By the time everyone started to leave, I was so stuffed that I vowed to never eat another bite of food for the rest of my life.

"Want some cookies to go with that hot chocolate?"

"Maybe just a couple," I say.

Mom laughs and turns to head back to the kitchen. "Open your present," she calls down the hallway.

I cross my legs on the window bench and stare down at the present in my lap. Tailee's pretty handwriting spells out my name with a glittery gel pen. My stomach knots up. This could be the last gift I ever get from her. I tug at the purple ribbon and slip my fingernail underneath the tape on the top and sides, careful not to tear the wrapping. It's nice, heavy paper. I could use it in an art project. The box underneath the paper is simple, white. The top comes off easy and reveals a sea of lime-green tissue paper. It crinkles between my fingers.

Underneath the tissue paper is a framed photo of Tailee and me from Halloween two years ago. We're standing outside her house, our arms over each other's shoulders. She's dressed up as Dracula with a white face, dark bags under her eyes, and blood smeared across her lips and chin. Tailee convinced me to dress up as the Swamp Thing and spray-painted a yellow hula skirt different shades of dark and light green for my swampy monster hair. We ran all around the neighborhood that night and went to every house at least three times.

I press my fingers to the picture. We were so happy. We had no idea what would happen. That I'd hide away from her and everyone else.

I take a breath and sift through the rest of the box. Bobbing up and down on the tissue is a velvet jewelry box. It fits in the palm of my hand. Navy, gold, and square. Inside is half a gold heart with the word "best" etched into it. I look at the jewelry box. At the bottom is a quick note in Tailee's precise letters and gold glitter ink: "You're still my best friend."

"What did Tailee give you?" Mom walks into my room with a plate of Christmas cookies. I pass her the picture and the necklace but hide Tailee's note underneath the tissue paper. "Oh, these are really nice."

"I don't know what to do. I haven't even gotten her anything yet."

"There's still time. Tailee loves you. She'll understand."

"How can I even get her a gift when I can't go to the mall without freaking?"

"You'll figure something out. You always do." Mom

brushes the hair out of my face and kisses me on the head. She leaves the plate of cookies next to me and hands me Tailee's gifts before heading toward the door. "Merry Christmas, honey. Don't stay up too late tonight."

Mom closes the door, her footsteps disappearing down the hallway.

I unclasp the necklace Tailee gave me and put it around my neck. It sits next to Dad's cornicello, and both shine in the lamplight.

Guilt twists around my heart. So much has gone wrong. And it's all my fault. I grab Tailee's note out of the tissue paper and hold it tight.

Chiara taps my window. Behind her the ship floats between our houses.

I open the window, warm air slipping into my room. "What're you doing?"

"The baby stars are ready to be released!" Chiara says. "We weren't gonna go up on Christmas, but Papa really wants us to get them back up there. Come on!"

I grab the leather bomber jacket out of my closet, pull on a pair of boots over my pajama bottoms, and tuck my sketch pad under my arm. I grab the plate of cookies Mom brought up before heading out of the window and hopping into the zeppelin.

It's only a matter of moments before we're soaring high up into the clouds. The city grows farther and farther away until it's nothing more than a glowing speck. The wind blows through my hair and whips against my cheeks.

"Here," Chiara says, holding out a thermos. "It's Mama's hot chocolate."

I open the top and take a sip, letting the sweet chocolate heat me up from the inside. "I brought some cookies. My mom makes the best. Look at the stars on them."

"Ooh, so pretty." Chiara takes a cookie and examines it. "I love the glitter."

We bring the cookies up to Alessandro and sit with him. The clouds break up and the stars shine brighter. They peek through the night, watching the city sleep, watching us as we travel higher into the heavens.

"Are the baby stars excited?" I ask.

"I think so. It's kind of hard to tell," Chiara says. "Alessandro's *definitely* excited."

"It's a lot of work watching after baby stars." Alessandro rolls his eyes. "It's like house training twenty puppies at once."

"But they're so cute! We were lucky that Gemini needed new stars. They can all stay together."

Chiara, Alessandro, and I finish off the cookies. Only some stray sprinkles and chocolate remain on the plate.

"What did you do for Christmas?" Chiara wipes the crumbs from her mouth with the back of her hand.

"We celebrated the Feast of the Seven Fishes on

Christmas Eve and went to Midnight Mass," I say. "My family came over this morning, and we cooked and had snowball fights outside."

Chiara's eyes widen. "That sounds amazing! We've only ever had one Christmas in Italy with our whole family. It was so nice."

"We still have a lot of food," Alessandro says. "And presents."

Alessandro lines the ship up next to a large, dark gap in the Gemini constellation. Chiara was right. They really do need more stars. The closest are about a mile away on both sides.

"Time to get the stars." Chiara springs to her feet. She rushes to the small room that serves as the ship's nursery.

"Will we need goggles when they come out?" I ask Alessandro.

He shakes his head, dropping the *Stella Cadente*'s anchor into a nearby cloud. "Those are only needed when the stars are in a contained area. There's plenty of room for them to shine brightly out here."

Chiara hurries back with a large wicker basket full of beaming baby stars. They bounce up and down, bumping into one another.

"Get the rest, Alessandro."

Alessandro hops down the stairs and disappears into the nursery.

"Luna, will you help me?" Chiara calls from the deck. "They're great at floating now. All you need to do is hold them up and let them flap from your arms. They'll know which spots to fill in the constellation," she says. "But be careful."

I pet one of the stars on her head. She wriggles, her mouth quirking into a smile. "Are you ready, little one?" The star bounces into my arms and I hug her close, her warmth radiating through my body.

"Good! Now hold her high and let her go," Chiara calls.

She holds her own star over her head. The little baby tumbles from her arms before floating higher and higher above the ship. Chiara clasps her hands together. "Look at him go! Great job, little guy!"

The star bounces around in my arms. Carefully, I hold her up as high as I can. She kicks upward out of my grasp, and soon only my fingertips are touching her. The star twirls around just above us, her dust sprinkling down on my head, before she floats up toward Gemini.

"Two down, three to go," Alessandro says. In his arms is another wicker basket with two more baby stars. "Looks like they're doing well."

"They're so happy!" Chiara spins around the deck before hoisting another star from the basket. Alessandro grabs one too, and I pick up the last. "Let's release them on the count of three. One."

"Two," Alessandro says.

The star's warmth spreads from my chest all the way down to the tips of my toes. I hold her over my head. "Three!" I say.

She slips from my hands and zips up to meet the others. The three stars twinkle against the darkness as they whirl around one another, floating farther away until they join the other two. All five baby stars lined up in a row, part of Gemini.

"Glorious!" Chiara jumps up on her tiptoes. She points at the constellation. "Look at them up there. They're going to be great."

"We'll need to check in on them soon." A smile slips over Alessandro's face. "I'm glad they're happy. Thank you for your help, Luna."

The baby stars shine bright as part of Gemini, closing the gap that had darkened the constellation. Alessandro and Chiara prepare the ship for our departure, but I don't move. I hold on to Dad's cornicello, watching the baby stars work together to illuminate the black sky.

Chapter 23

"Hey, look!" Chiara runs toward the other side of the ship. "A shooting star!"

I whip my head in her direction. "Really?"

Alessandro consults his moon device—the one with all the odd-looking attachments—and hurries over to where Chiara is standing. "He's closer than the other one. Only three-point-seven miles away and headed in our direction. He's going to pass us about one-point-five miles to the left."

"I can see his tail." She runs to the closet and pulls out a large net with a long wooden handle. One I imagine could be used to catch giant butterflies. She shoves it into my hands. "You need to catch the shooting star, Luna!"

In the distance is a fiery ball of light hurtling through the heavens. Its tail lashes behind it like lightning cracking the sky wide open.

"He's coming fast." My pulse races, beating so loud in my ears I can hardly hear my own voice.

Alessandro hurries for the wheel. "We're going for it, right?"

He and Chiara look at me as if for instruction. I stare at the net. Its polished handle shines under the lanterns' flames.

"What've we got to lose?" I grip the net tight to focus the excitement pumping through my veins. "Let's do it."

Alessandro makes a sharp left, nearly knocking Chiara and me off our feet.

"Hey!" Chiara yells. "Be careful."

"I'm lining us up so we're in the way." We travel at full speed, dipping under asteroids and dodging space debris. Before we can even regain our balance, the ship comes to a jerking stop and tosses us forward. "You'd better steady yourself," he shouts. "He's going to be here soon."

He moves the *Stella Cadente* so she's in the shooting star's path. Alessandro rushes down from the wheel to the main deck, his moon device in his hand. "Only one-point-two miles now. It's going to come about five feet closer—most likely on the left side."

I squeeze the net's handle until my knuckles go white and my hands ache and lean even farther over the railing. This is the moment I've dreamed of. I can't mess it up now. The shooting star nears, and it's almost too hard to look at him. He burns white-hot like a poker left in the fireplace, and his tail licks at the darkness—searing it with light.

"Ground your feet," Chiara yells. She wraps her arms around my middle, and Alessandro holds on to her to anchor us to the ship.

The shooting star is close enough for me to make out his eyes and mouth. His expression changes as he notices the net only a few yards in front of him, but he is going too fast to stop. I extend the net farther. My mouth goes dry. Sweat beads on my neck and hairline.

He collides with the net and tugs it about half a mile ahead of us. My waist hits hard against the railing, and I groan. Pain shoots through my arms, and the wooden handle rubs my palms raw. I want to let go. The shooting star pulls the ship behind him before he comes to a stop, his tail whipping back and forth like an angry cat's. "Why isn't the net breaking?" I yell, readjusting my grip on the handle.

"It's made of spider silk and moondust. Like the bridge," Chiara says while tightening her arms around me.

The shooting star begins to settle, and the ship lurches forward. Chiara and Alessandro slam into me before the ship swings and tosses us backward. I scramble to my feet and pull the net aboard. The shooting star floats a few inches above the deck, the net still covering him. Alessandro steps forward and pulls the net from the star's body.

"What do you want?" he asks, swiping at the net with his tiny pointed arms. "I was on my way to the other side of the galaxy."

Chiara nudges me toward the star.

I look at Alessandro, who nods.

"Well?" The shooting star looks at me. "You caught me. What's your name?"

"Luna Andrea Marie Bianchini." I straighten my shoulders, hands clenched.

"Where are you from, Luna Andrea Marie Bianchini?"

"Staten Island, New York."

"I can feel your wish radiating off you." His gaze is so intense it's like he's trying to drill into my soul. "I can see it in your heart. You've been waiting some time to catch a shooting star." He spins back and forth. "Please. Ask your wish out loud so that I may hear it too."

"I wish to go back in time to before the accident. When everything was normal," I say. "Before I had to wear this compression mask and needed surgery. Before my dad was in a wheelchair and couldn't go to work. Before my mom had to take care of us every day and was fighting with my dad."

"Luna Andrea Marie Bianchini." The shooting star flies closer to me. So close I can see myself reflected in his dark eyes. "Let me ask: Won't surgery mean you'll no longer need to wear your mask?"

I cross my arms over my chest. "Well, yes. That's what Dr. Tucker says."

"And your dad has been going back to the deli more, correct? He's been feeling better. Happier?"

"I guess so."

"Your mom and dad haven't been arguing as much, either. In fact, it seems like their relationship is growing stronger by the day."

"How do you know all this?"

"I can see it," he says. "Shooting stars know everything."

Panic flares in my chest. "You can grant my wish, right?"

He shakes his head. "I'm afraid I can't give you what you want. Changing time is impossible. But things are already getting better for you and your family."

"What do you mean?" My voice hitches in my throat. "I wish for the accident to have never happened. My dad and I would be healed. Why is that wrong?"

The shooting star comes closer and touches my arm. Alessandro and Chiara back up to give us space. "The things you want changed are in the midst of changing."

"But how do I know they will?" I take a ragged breath.

"What happens when you're unhappy again? Are you

going to make another wish?" he asks. "You need to be patient."

"If you can't make Luna's wish come true, what can you do?" Chiara asks.

"Shooting stars ignite a spark within a human's soul." He spins around in front of us. "When a person wishes for something, we give them the urgency to act to make their wish come true. You, Luna, lit your own spark. You don't need me."

Tears well up in my eyes, and Chiara tucks a tissue into my hand. "I can't fix all these big things," I say, my voice quivering. "I'm just a kid."

"You've already given yourself permission to act," he says. "You're opening up to others through your friendship with Alessandro and Chiara, you're making great strides in your therapy, and you helped your dad with that healing soup." His light grows brighter. "Your soul is ablaze with the changes you've already initiated." The shooting star smiles softly. "Now it's time to continue going forward and confront those problems that are left. Like your relationship with your best friend and your fears around your upcoming surgery."

Tears slip faster down my cheeks. Any dwindling hope for my wish coming true is crushed into a million pieces and scattered through space like stardust.

· · ·

Alessandro maneuvers the ship between our houses and docks it against the tree outside my window. Our trip back down was done in an exhausted silence, aside from the stars' gentle lullaby.

"I'm sorry, Luna," Chiara whispers. "I'm so sorry."

"It's my fault. I wished for something impossible."

Chiara helps me out onto the wooden platform in my tree and opens my window for me.

"Can we come by tomorrow?" Alessandro asks, walking down the stairs to the bow. "Just to see how you're doing?"

I look down. I don't want to see them. The only thing more embarrassing than sharing your deepest wish with others is being denied that wish right in front of them. "I don't want to be up there anymore."

Alessandro squints at me but doesn't question it. "Stop by whenever you'd like," he says. "We'll be home."

Before either he or Chiara can say anything else, I dive through my window, shutting it and the curtains behind me. The *Stella Cadente* lingers just a moment before lifting off into the sky.

It's like losing Tailee all over again. Talking to Alessandro and Chiara was easy, but after they saw me cry over losing my wish, I could hardly talk to them on the way back to earth. I clammed up just like I did with Tailee. How am I ever going to be able to face them again?

And the one shot I had to make everything right with that wish: gone.

"I can't take it anymore," I yell. I snatch up the pillow from my window bench and scream into it as loud as I can, the sound muted by feathers and fabric. All of that hope and faith dashed. Everything gone.

I grab my sketch pad. Those stupid pictures of the heavens, of fantastical trips to the moon, of sweeping stars and floating ships. I rip the pictures out and toss them into the trash. Each one a dumb dream.

I squeeze my eyes shut and hold my breath until my lungs ache and scream for air. I gasp, breathing in deep, aching breaths. The shooting star was wrong. Whatever spark he saw inside me isn't there. Not when everything feels as dark and empty as a starless sky.

My body sags forward, halving itself, curling up as tight as possible in an attempt to disappear into the floor. Tears roll down my cheeks and make my mask feel even clammier than usual. I rip the mask from my face and throw it against my bedroom window. It clatters to the floor, the sound abrasive and reverberating against my heart. My eyes grow too heavy to keep open and I drift into a restless sleep.

Luna Bianchini
236 Marigold Court
Staten Island, NY 10301

An Impossible Wish

Nathan Heyer
18 Gardenia Road
Staten Island, NY 10301

Hi, Luna,

You sent my mom a drawing and she told
me to practice my handwriting in a letter
back to you. My name's Nathan. I'm seven.
I liked your drawing a lot. It was just a
bunch of stars on the page, but they had
little faces. Santa brought me a telescope
for Christmas. He knows how much I like
space. Mom set it up for me and I'd spend
all night looking up at the stars if she
didn't make me go to bed so early. But
sometimes I can't see them. It's either
too bright in the city or the clouds are out.
    I'm trying to see if they have faces like
the ones you drew. None of my space books
say they do and none of those pictures show
them with faces. But your drawing does.
Why'd you draw them like that?
    When I look at your stars with faces,
I think about my dad. He died when I
was three. I don't remember him much,

but Mom says he watches over us. One of the stars in your picture looks like him. It would be nice if he was a star. It would be nice if we were all stars.

—Nathan

Chapter 24

Alessandro and Chiara knocked on my window again the night after my failed wish. They knocked last night too. I kept hiding, buried deep under my rainbow comforter until the knocking stopped and the zeppelin's shadow faded from my wall.

Rain slides down my window in fat drops. It shoots into the snow on the windowsill like darts, making a slushy, wet mess. Too warm for snow this morning. But it doesn't matter. Snow isn't very magical after Christmas. After Christmas, snow starts feeling less like a winter wonderland and more like a burden.

I press my face to the cool glass and stare out at Alessandro's window. The curtains are closed, the room dark. He and Chiara sleep late into the morning after star sweeping all night. And I know they didn't come home until dawn. The zeppelin blocked out the faint blue light of early morning as it docked between our houses.

A sob catches in my throat and I swallow it back, closing my curtains and turning away from the window. I stare down at the sketch pad on my knees. A blank page. Impossibly white and vast. The potential of a new page used to be exciting, but when you don't have anything you want to draw, an empty page feels overwhelming and bleak.

The past two nights have brought nothing but nightmares about the car crash, so vivid I can practically feel the pulsing, endless heat from the collision every time I close my eyes.

If I can't fix my problems with a wish, then how will they get better? It's been months since the accident, and everything is still in pieces. Shattered like thousands of shards of glass.

"We're so worried about her." Mom's voice travels up from the vent in the floor and into my room. "She refuses to leave her bedroom. We don't know if something happened on Christmas, but she seemed fine when I said good night that evening."

"Tell her that Luna's not eating much, either." Dad's voice trails after Mom's. "She needs to eat."

"You want to see her tomorrow? Yes. We can bring her in at nine o'clock. Thank you so much." There's a pause. Mom sighs. "Dr. Miles thinks she might be worried about the surgery."

"I hate seeing her this way." Dad's voice is low and raspy, as if he's been crying. "She was starting to come around."

"I know," Mom says. "I don't know why this is happening."

I walk over to the vent and shut it with my foot, closing off my parents' voices. The last time I saw Dr. Miles was right before Christmas. I stomp over to my bed and curl up in my comforter. I don't want to see her again. I don't want to see anyone again.

The doorbell rings.

"Where is she?" Nonna Bianchini's voice booms up the stairs and against my door. I groan into my pillow and roll over onto my side. Nonna Bianchini isn't like my parents. Where my mom and dad see a shut bedroom door and let me have privacy, Nonna Bianchini will kick it down and pester me until I talk to her. Of course they had her come over. They knew she'd be the only one who could wear me down.

"Luna." Nonna Bianchini bangs on the door. "Luna, I know you're in there and I know you're awake. Let me in, please."

"I'm trying to sleep," I shout. "Just leave me alone."

"Leave you alone? You know I can't do that."

"I need privacy."

"What do you need privacy for?" She scoffs. "You're

twelve. You don't need privacy. When I was twelve I shared a bedroom half the size of yours with my two brothers and two sisters."

I swing my legs off the bed and unlock the door. Nonna Bianchini stands in the hall, her wrinkled face pinched with concern. Her dark gray hair is pulled back in a bun, eyes set with the kind of determination only a grandmother can muster. She doesn't linger too long on my mask like she usually does. Instead her eyes focus on the messy tangle of hair knotted on the top of my head.

"Dad said you only shared it with your twin sister," I say.

"Bah." She tosses her hands in the air, upsetting her purse hanging in the crook of her elbow. "Are you going to let me in, or are we going to talk in the doorway?"

I open the door wider and go back to sitting on my bed. "Mom and Dad called you?"

"They're worried, Luna. You haven't left your room since Christmas?" She looks around my room, at the torn drawings on the floor and the mess of clothes, pillows, and teacups all over. "What happened in here? Why are your drawings ripped to shreds?" She walks over to the ripped-up drawings and frowns. Nonna Bianchini bends down and picks up some of the pieces, trying to put them back together. "Why are you ripping up drawings of your family?"

I shrug. "None of them feel right."

"What is right, though?" She walks over to my bed and sits down, handing me a pizzelle dusted with powdered sugar. "Here, have a cookie. Sugar's good for the soul."

I nibble on the edge. The anise makes my tongue feel fuzzy.

Nonna Bianchini continues. "When I was a girl my mama and papa would get so upset with me over how I acted." She laughs. "They wanted me to fit in. They'd say things like, 'This is America, Favianna, and you must be polite and respectful.'" She gestures, her hand swishing through the air. "I was always too much of something. Too loud, too angry, too excited. But they were too old and too traditional. They wanted me to be their normal, to fit in with what they thought was right."

"Why didn't you?" I ask.

"Because that wasn't me. I was never going to be what they thought was normal," she says. "I don't even think there is a normal. Our family certainly isn't."

I stare at my soft black and green socks. "But you wanted me to be normal. Remember? You were scared of my face."

"I might have overreacted a bit." Nonna Bianchini takes my hand and sighs. "I kept thinking of how hard it would be for you to go through life. Seeing you and your parents suffering makes me suffer. But you, Luna, you're my shining light. I don't want you to hurt, but I also don't want you to get stuck on being normal. It's not healthy." She shakes her head. "Not healthy at all."

"I wanted to make things the way they were before the accident, but I couldn't."

"And that's why you tore up all those drawings?" she asks.

I nod. "I couldn't look at them again, so I ripped them up."

"I'm sorry." Nonna Bianchini rubs my knee. "But you have to at least try to live your life."

I put the pizzelle on my nightstand and curl up on my bed, tucking myself under the covers and hiding from my nonna. "I don't want to try right now."

She sighs, and I feel her get up from the bed. "You're going to have to try eventually, Luna. You might not think you're able to, but you got it in you. You're a Bianchini."

I listen to Nonna walk to the door and shut it quietly behind her. "Finish that cookie!" she yells from the hall.

I press my pillow over my face to block out the inevitable conversation she'll have with my parents. I pull into myself, wishing I were anywhere but here. But where would I go? Not even the heavens are comforting now. *You need to be patient.* The shooting star's voice bounces around in my head, as clear as if he were standing right next to me repeating it over and over. *I'm afraid I can't give you what you want.*

I hurl my pillow across the room and bury myself deeper under my comforter. Hot tears press against my eyelashes and tumble down my cheeks. After everything that's happened, maybe all that Bianchini fight has been beaten out of me.

Alessandro and Chiara Sapienti
238 Marigold Court
Staten Island, NY 10301

Dear Luna,

Chiara and I miss you.

We're really sorry about what happened. We wish we could help you. You're always going to be our friend. And there's always room for you on our ship. You're basically a spazzatrici. Besides, someone needs to keep Chiara and me from fighting all night long.

You wished for things to go back to the way they were before the accident. But we never would have met if that happened. We don't want you to be normal. We want you to be Luna.

Please talk to us again.

—Alessandro and Chiara

Chapter 25

I know you'd rather not be here today, Luna," Dr. Miles says. She doesn't sit on the green chair, but rather sits next to me on the couch, as if she's trying to bond with me. The pencils and paper are lined up neatly on the table, but neither of us is moving for them.

I keep my eyes focused on the clock, back slouched into the worn couch cushions and arms across my chest. Mom and Dad had to beg me to leave my room to come to this appointment. And just because they brought me here together, just because they think this is a good idea, doesn't mean I have to talk. Even if Dr. Miles helped in the past, I don't want to be in therapy anymore. I'm tired of talking. Anger churns in my stomach, making my whole body feel hot.

"Your parents said something happened on Christmas?" Dr. Miles continues.

"Yep."

"Did someone say something to you during the day?"

"Nope."

"Luna, it's important to discuss what's bothering us. It helps us understand our feelings and how we process things."

I throw my hands into the air. The anger forces its way out of my mouth. "I'm so sick of all of this. I'm tired of still feeling awful after the accident. I'm scared of my surgery. I'm worried about my dad getting better and my mom being stressed all the time. I still feel anxious. I still feel overwhelmed. I'm tired of not feeling like myself." My head begins to ache from the compression mask. I bury my face in my hands and sigh.

"I'm not strong enough to make things better on my own."

"That's not true," Dr. Miles says.

I peek at her from behind my hands. She stares at me, her green eyes intent behind her glasses.

"You don't have to make things better all on your own. It's not your responsibility. You have a family who loves you and wants you to feel good," Dr. Miles says. "Being strong doesn't always mean being tough or ready to fight all the time."

"I always thought that's what I had to do."

"You don't, Luna. Strength also means being open to

your emotions. Sometimes people think this is weak, but it's not. It means you're able to address your feelings. When you acknowledge your emotions, you can find ways to grow and work through the things that make you feel bad."

"How do I do that?"

Dr. Miles pulls the coffee table closer to us and picks up a pencil. "One thing you can do is start doing things you like again. We can start slowly with an easy list, and your mom can put them on a schedule for you. Like taking art classes."

"I'd love to do that again."

Dr. Miles jots down *art class* on the paper. "That's great. What else?"

"Baking with my mom," I say.

"Maybe your cousins can come over to help too."

"I think I'd like that. I also like going to the park down the street to swing on the swings or just draw outside. I used to do that with my cousins a lot."

"That'll help get the blood flowing. Excellent idea," she says. "What about going to your family's deli to do your homework and to draw?"

I slouch back into the couch and watch Dr. Miles make my list. "But every time I go somewhere people stare at me."

"People may always stare," Dr. Miles says. "You can't change that. But you can change the way their staring makes you feel. You are in control of your reaction to things. Reinforce your positive self-talk and think about the qualities you like about yourself—like the ones you drew. Remember that report card and the flying ship you sketched to show you're intelligent and adventurous? By focusing on positive thoughts, even when people stare, you'll build your self-confidence."

"I haven't seen Tailee in forever," I say. "I think I'm more scared to talk to her than I am of my surgery." I lean forward and grab a pencil and a piece of paper, drawing aimless squiggles across the page.

"What about talking to her scares you?"

I shut my eyes tight. "She'd come over and it was like the words got stuck. The old Luna was shouting up from my belly and couldn't get past all the doubt and worry clogging my throat," I say. "I couldn't stop thinking about what *she* thought of me, even though Tailee isn't like that at all."

"You never knew how she felt about your appearance and rather imagined what she might think based on how *you* feel about your appearance," Dr. Miles says without looking up from her drawing. "You should talk to her again and see for yourself how she feels."

"But what if I'm too scared?" I ask, my voice small and trapped under a sea of tears. I blink several times, trying to keep them from falling. "I already feel like I've pushed her away."

"Let's work on a script." Dr. Miles sits back on the couch. "Thinking through what you want to say will help you feel less anxious. I'll pretend to be Tailee."

"Should I just start talking like if I was talking to Tailee?"

Dr. Miles nods.

"Hey, Tailee." A lump forms in my throat. "I didn't act like a good friend and I shouldn't have ignored you. It wasn't a nice thing to do."

"Good," Dr. Miles says.

I open my mouth again, but nothing comes out. The words feel stuck. Dr. Miles coaches me through some breathing techniques, and slowly the words start to break through. We go over the script a few times, and each time it's easier to repeat. The words flow faster and don't sound as rehearsed. The anxiety is still there, but it doesn't make me feel as trapped.

"What happens if this doesn't work?" I ask. "If Tailee says something I don't expect?"

"It's okay not to follow the script to the letter. Think of it as a guide."

"I'm still nervous about talking to her. What if I can't do it?"

"It takes a little courage, and the good thing is that everyone can be courageous." Dr. Miles turns over her paper and draws a small candle sitting on a table in the middle of the paper. She shades the rest of the white space with the side of her pencil, coloring everything in a thick darkness except for a halo of light surrounding the candle's tiny flame. "Like a small spark, courage catches. The more you use it, the greater it grows." Dr. Miles erases more of the pencil shading around the candle until only a faint reminder of it remains. "The thing is that you have to believe it's real, and the only way to do that is to use it."

"What if I'm not ready?"

"There may never be a time when you're ready. But it's good to try. Talk to your parents first. They want to understand the way you see things and help you."

I nod. "I think I can do that."

"You can. And you can tell me all about your progress in our next appointment. Make it your goal to spend less time in your room and more time with your parents before we meet next. Talk to them about your list of activities. And tell them how you feel." Dr. Miles smiles and hands me a pencil and a fresh sheet of paper. "But now let's just draw. Whatever you'd like."

I scooch closer to the coffee table and begin drawing the stars. The scene comes quickly, as if my hand knows what to draw before my head does. Hundreds of tiny stars illuminating the sky, bright enough to dull the darkness. In the bottom left-hand corner is the *Stella Cadente* with its huge black balloon and polished wood body.

Will Linksy
358 Rose Lane
Staten Island, NY 10301

Hello Luna,

I wanted to thank you for your drawing.
I'm not much of an artist and don't
really have an interest in art. I'm not the
kind of guy who likes spending time in art
museums or at galleries. So I'm not sure if
I'll say the right thing.

The drawing you sent me was of a little
girl sitting in a zoo in one of the animal
pens. Her face is burned and people are
staring at her, pointing and laughing. It
really made me upset. Your drawing struck a
nerve with me, and I finally realized why.
I felt like that girl when I was a kid.

I was teased constantly as a kid for
being overweight. It was terrible until I
got out of middle school. I made friends
with people who felt different like me.
Some kids still made fun of me, but my
friends didn't care what I looked like. So
I was doing something right. I didn't have

to listen to those who called me names.

I don't know if this picture is self-reflective, but if it is I'm sorry you're getting teased. It's not fun and can feel like it'll be that way forever. But it won't be. Let people stare. Honestly, they're probably trying to sort out their own issues too. If they have a problem with how you look, that says more about them than it does you.

Thanks for your drawing, Luna.

—Will

Chapter 26

New Year's Eve is my third favorite holiday. Mainly because it's quiet, usually just Mom, Dad, and me. Tailee used to come over to celebrate with us too. We'd get to stay up late and watch the countdown on TV. Mom also buys a feast of frozen appetizers and supplies to make double-fudge caramel ice cream sundaes with extra nuts, extra whip, and extra, extra cherries. Sometimes we shred old newspapers for streamers and bang on pots and pans at midnight, but we haven't really done that since I was little.

Tailee won't be coming over tonight. Even though I've tried what Dr. Miles said—leaving my room more and talking to my parents—I still haven't had the guts to call Tailee. It feels like it's too soon. Maybe talking to Tailee can be one of my New Year's resolutions.

A sharp knocking at my window makes me tumble

backward onto the floor and land on a stack of books. I scramble to my feet and rub the sore spot on my lower back. Chiara's dark curls are covered with snow, a scowl across her lips.

"What's going on?" I ask, opening the window and letting her inside.

She crawls onto the window bench and hops down onto the floor. "What's going on? *With me?* What's going on *with you*, Luna?" Chiara tosses her hands in the air. "Why are you ignoring us? Alessandro wrote you a letter and I told him what to say." Her expression softens. "We said we were sorry."

Chiara's outburst hits me like the first humid day of the summer. I take a step back to make room for her questions. All of her frustration reminds me of the long, awkward pauses that dominated my talks with Tailee.

"You don't have to be sorry," I say. "You didn't do anything." I look past Chiara's shoulder and out into the snowy night, unable to look her right in the eyes. "It wasn't fair of me to not explain. I felt stupid and embarrassed. I thought I could fix everything with a wish."

"You shouldn't feel embarrassed, you know. I would've wished for the same things."

"He said I have the ability to make things better." I close my eyes, imagining the shooting star explain to me why my wish won't come true. "But I don't know if I do."

"That's silly," Chiara says. "Of course you do."

"You're serious?"

"You've got faith in magic and in the spazzatrici. Enough faith to make you get into a flying ship. Most people pretend they don't see us and explain it all away. You believed. It's easy to ignore stuff, but you faced it head-on. That's huge."

It was hard believing in magic when I first saw Chiara make that tiny furniture grow with a snap of her fingers, but I *knew* what I saw was something special—even if it didn't make sense. Faith's a deep-down feeling. Believing even if it seems impossible. If I can believe in flying ships and the spazzatrici, I can believe in myself and that things will work out like they should.

"Thanks, Chiara." I squeeze my cornicello between my fingers.

"Just don't ever leave like that again. You can't disappear no matter what," she says. "Promise?" Chiara's dark eyes are wide, her mouth a straight line. The same serious face she uses on her brother.

I laugh. "Promise, Chiara. And if I ever disappear, just come over and talk some sense into me."

She nods. "Mama says I'm a good talker," she says. "Why are you holding on to your cornicello?"

"Oh. I forgot I was holding it." I shrug. "I do it a lot."

"I do that too!" She smiles and pulls the thin gold

chain from under her pajama shirt. At the end of the chain is her cornicello and a large, old-looking pendant. It's diamond-shaped and a tarnished bronze. It looks heavy.

"What's that?" I ask, pointing at the pendant.

Chiara pulls it closer for me to inspect. "It's the spazzatrici crest." Imprinted into the metal is the outline of a human body, and inside it is a cluster of tiny, sparkling diamonds. Written above the body's head is the phrase "*le stelle vivono dentro di noi.*"

"*Le stelle vivono dentro di noi?*" I stumble over the phrase, trying to get the pronunciation correct. "What's that mean?"

"It's the spazzatrici motto. It means *the stars live within us.*"

Glass shatters. Dad's swearing carries up the stairs.

Chiara and I jump.

"I've got to go," I say. "I'll see you soon."

She opens the window, and a blast of air blows through my room. Chiara waves good-bye before hurrying across the light bridge she built between our houses. I shut the window and close the curtains before running downstairs and rounding the corner into the living room.

Dad's face is red. His hands are fists in his lap. Next to him on the ground is a shattered glass. Water dribbles down from the end table and onto the floor. "I couldn't reach the glass and the thing fell over."

"Frank? What happened?" Mom's right behind me. Her eyes dart around in search of an emergency.

"It's nothing." He tosses his hands in the air. "I'm just so sick of not being able to get around."

Mom disappears and comes back with paper towels and a dustpan from the kitchen. "It's okay, Frank."

I wipe water from the end table and floor while Mom sweeps up the glass.

"I just want to be able to do things on my own," Dad says. "And to help both of you for a change."

"I'm sorry," I say, cleaning up the last of the water with a sopping paper towel.

"It's my own damn fault. I shouldn't have been so careless." Dad pounds his fist against the armrest, new tears welling in his eyes. "Why won't my body work the way it used to?"

I sit next to him on the couch and reach over to hold his hand. Mom puts the dustpan on the ground and balances on the edge of his armchair, her arm back around his shoulders. He squeezes my fingers. I take a deep breath. Dad cries even less than Mom. It's hard watching your parents cry. Sometimes they need you more than you need them.

"You've been getting better," I say. "Mom said you'll be out of the wheelchair and walking with a walker soon."

"Walkers are for grandpas." He covers his face with

his hands and sighs. "I shouldn't have taken you to your art class that day."

Mom rips a paper towel from the roll and wipes the tears from her cheeks. Tears she's been holding on to for months. Her cheeks are blotchy, eyes watery and red.

"Not being in that car with both of you has driven me nuts. It keeps me up every night, you know." Mom sniffles. "Every time we get in a car or you go work at the deli or I have to leave Luna home alone, I'm terrified something bad is going to happen. My mind goes to the worst places and I feel like I have to be with you both at all times because what could happen if I'm not? I don't want to lose either of you like I lost Marie." Even though she wasn't in the crash, she's still hurting.

"You've sacrificed so much to take care of us, and I don't want you to have to worry anymore," Dad says. "I'm glad you weren't in the car. I was just so angry that day. We were arguing again, and I wasn't paying attention. Stupid."

"Again?" The word catches in my throat. "All of that started *after* the accident."

Mom and Dad exchange a look. Mom shakes her head.

This information slices through my mind, reopening old wounds. All the late-night arguments that passed underneath my bedroom door and banged in my eardrums. I pushed their fighting deeper and deeper down under the surface of my mind until they became misplaced, confused with the arguments that picked up after the accident. I didn't want to know what was happening, so I chose not to see the truth.

"When did it start?" I ask, unsure if I want to hear the answer.

"Over a year ago," Dad says. He stares straight ahead, unable to look at me. "It got really bad last November."

Memories of their arguments rise to the surface of my mind like dead bodies. Hazy and unclear, but still real. Last November *was* bad. I listened to music nonstop that month, my headphones practically glued to my ears.

"I didn't want to see any of that." I ball my shaking hands into fists. "I just blamed it on the accident."

"That made things worse at first." Dad rubs Mom's knee.

"But it started getting better. We've been talking more. We found a good counselor and started going once a week after your dad's checkups. Talking to someone has helped. We've made progress."

As much as I didn't want to see Dr. Miles in the beginning, the exercises and the talking we've done have started making me feel better too. "Therapy really isn't all that bad," I say. "We're *all* making progress."

Mom puts her hand on top of Dad's. The gold wedding band gleams on her left ring finger. "It's coming along one day at a time."

Dad wipes the tears off his face. "I'm sorry for not always putting you and your mom first. I lost sight of our family."

Tears sting my eyes. "No, you didn't."

"I wasn't the only one hurting, you know?" Dad says. "Sulking doesn't help. I realize that now."

"I've been bad about that too," I say.

"Your poor mom. Having to deal with two very sensitive and hot-headed Bianchinis." Dad frowns. "I wish I could take your pain away, Luna. I wish I could make things right. I'm so sorry you're hurting."

"I tried, you know." I squeeze my eyes shut and think about my wish, tears hot on my face. "You all want me to be this brave girl. But I'm scared. All the time. I can't pretend that I'm not anymore."

Mom's hand is on my shoulder. I open my eyes and she's kneeling in front of me, Dad leaning forward, his hand on my other shoulder like we're in some group huddle.

"Luna, you don't have to pretend," she says. "We can't keep our feelings from each other anymore. We need to talk to each other and listen when one of us is hurting. That's how we can be brave. By helping each other out."

"I just want to be okay for you and Dad."

"You don't have to be okay all the time. Being tough isn't about bottling things up. It's about expressing your emotions and finding a way to work through them."

"That's what Dr. Miles said too." I wipe the tears from my eyes. "She said strength doesn't mean being big and brave all the time. She said it's important to feel emotions—even if they're sad ones—so you can grow." I hold on to my cornicello. Alessandro said something like that about magic too.

"She's right, you know." Dad pulls me toward him. "You're allowed to be scared and feel bad. I never meant to make you feel like you couldn't. You're not alone, Luna."

"We love you so much," Mom whispers. "We'll get through this together."

The torn-up drawing of my family begins rearranging itself in my mind, taping itself together again. This time the Luna in the drawing doesn't have her same old face. But she isn't wearing her mask, either. Her face is burned, but not nearly as bad as my face is now. A new Luna.

Our foreheads are pressed close together, Mom's and Dad's skin wet with tears just like mine. We stay like this for a while, warm and quiet and holding on to each other.

Slowly we let go of one another to wipe away the tears.

"You and Nonna always say the Bianchinis are made of tough stuff," I say.

"Because we come together as a family." Dad nods. "*Le stelle vivono dentro di noi.* There's nothing tougher than a star. Every inch of us made up of that same stardust that fills the cosmos. It's in our blood. Our bones. Our hair. Every living thing, even the plants and animals." Dad looks down at his legs and pats his thighs, smiling. "That's special, isn't it? It must mean something. Maybe the heavens are closer than we realize."

Le stelle vivono dentro di noi. Just like Chiara's spazzatrici crest. I grin, the lilting Italian phrase squeezing my heart.

Mom and Dad settle in together on the armchair, and Dad turns on the TV to the New Year's Eve countdown. Still a few hours to go until the New Year. I get up and make my way into the kitchen for a glass of water. Outside, the sun has set. The moon smiles down on Staten Island and casts her bright yellow glow across the tops of the houses. The stars wink in the night's sky, watching over us and part of us all at once.

Anne Castillo
22 Gardenia Road
Staten Island, NY 10301

Dear Luna,

You sent me a picture of the entire downtown
Manhattan skyline lit up, the way you'd see
it from the ferry. It's the stars that make
this picture magnificent. They feel alive.

Your drawing took me back to the day
I married my husband. Our ceremony was
quick, but we celebrated long into the night.
We danced through Central Park until our
feet were sore and the only music left was
our delirious happiness.

On our way back to Staten Island, we
held on to the ferry's railings and just
stared at the skyline. All of those glittering
lights. I wanted to soak it all in until it
became one with my bones.

Tony passed away a year ago, and losing
him has been the hardest thing I've ever
faced. Some days are angry. Some are sad.
And even a few are happy. He's never far
from my mind.

I like to think he's standing on the Staten Island Ferry with me by his side as we watch New York City, the entire universe, shine for us.

Thank you, Luna.

With love,
Anne

Chapter 27

I didn't get much sleep last night. But I didn't think I would the night before my surgery. Even when I do the breathing techniques Dr. Miles and I practiced, I'm still nervous for what's to come.

Threads of blue, early-morning light peek in through the window. I swing my legs over the side of my bed, tuck Jean Valjean under the covers, and open the curtains.

The neighborhood's just starting to wake up. People juggle coffee cups and purses as they get into their cars and head to work. I tug on a pair of jeans and zip on my jacket.

Tailee's front door is sunflower yellow. I take a deep breath. No more wishing. Bravery is working through your fears. The doorbell buzzes under my finger and rings throughout the house. Tailee's dog, Pepe, starts barking. Mrs. Ruiz yells at him to be quiet. She opens the door, half ready for the day with her bathrobe still on but makeup finished. Her eyes widen. "Luna? What are you doing here? It's barely seven. Come inside."

"I'm sorry it's so early," I say, not moving from the front porch. "But I can't come by later and wanted to catch you all now. Is Tailee up?"

"She's getting ready for school." Mrs. Ruiz hesitates a moment before calling up the stairs. "Tailee! Come down!"

Footsteps thump down the stairs. "What is it?" Tailee's voice is still groggy with sleep.

Mrs. Ruiz nods in my direction. Tailee looks right at me, her large brown eyes locked on my face as if debating whether or not I'm really standing in front of her.

"Hey, Tailee."

Mrs. Ruiz leaves us without a word, Pepe barking after her. Tailee closes the front door and wraps her arms around herself to stop from shivering. "What are you doing here?"

I close my eyes, willing myself to stay put and not run all the way home. The script Dr. Miles and I rehearsed over and over bubbles to the surface of my brain. "I didn't act like a good friend and I shouldn't have ignored you. It wasn't a nice thing to do. It was hard for me to talk after the accident, and I started to clam up and not act like myself." I swallow and keep my eyes squeezed tight. The rest of what Dr. Miles and I practiced flies from my mind.

Silence.

Keep going, Luna, I think. "I got your Christmas present and I'm going into surgery today and wanted to say thank you." I shuffle from side to side, old snow crunching under my boots. "It's okay if you don't want to be my friend now after everything." I open my eyes. Tailee's still standing there, her lips pressed together.

The crisp air seeps under my jacket and chills my skin. Tailee shivers, her giant Rutgers hoodie doing little to keep her warm. She shakes her head. "Luna, I *want* to be your friend, but it feels like you don't want to be mine. You cut me out." Tailee tugs a gold chain out from underneath her hoodie. The other half of the best friend pendant she sent me dangles in the air. "You looked so angry outside the deli that day I saw you. It made me mad because I tried to be there for you."

"I know you were there for me. Even when I wasn't a good friend to you."

"You weren't. At all." Her voice hitches a bit. I look up, and her eyes are narrowed. That same look she gave to the boy who pushed me down on the playground years ago. I flinch. It doesn't feel good having Tailee look at me like that.

"I'm sorry. I'm going to get better at trying," I say. "But I'm not going to be the old Luna. I can't pretend to be that happy or relaxed when I'm not there yet. But I'm learning how to feel better and how to express myself.

The new Luna won't be so bad. I promise."

Tailee tilts her head to the side as if trying to see through me to the truth. "I missed you. I know you've been through a lot, but you could've trusted me."

"I should have," I say.

I stare past Tailee at the Ruizes' cheery yellow door. It looks out of place surrounded by dirty and melting snow, but it still somehow fits.

"Can we try being best friends again?" I ask, my voice soft. "I promise I won't disappear."

A chill kicks up and Tailee blows into her hands, rubbing them on her arms.

"I think so," she says. "I love you, Luna. As long as you pinkie promise to let me know what's going on. Let me be there for you."

I stick out my pinkie, and Tailee wraps hers around mine, squeezing tight.

"You said you've got surgery today?"

"Yeah, and I'm terrified. What if I never look the same?"

Tailee shrugs. "You'll still be you."

I wrap Tailee in a big hug, squeezing her tight. She wraps her arms around me too. Relief floods my body. "I'm sorry for not giving you a chance." We pull apart, and it feels like I could float away. "I should've known."

"You definitely should have," she says. "You're my best friend. I don't care if you have three heads and forty toes.

It would be kind of cool if you did actually."

I roll my eyes. The smile on my face is so big that it's starting to hurt. "Maybe I'll ask Dr. Tucker if he can give me a pair of wings."

She scrunches her nose. "Then you'd have to cut holes in all your shirts."

I look down at my watch. Mom will be mad if she knows I snuck out. "I need to go, but can I call you once I'm feeling better? Can we have a sleepover soon?" I think about Alessandro and Chiara. About the spazzatrici. "There's so much I need to tell you."

Tailee nods, her own lips turned up in a smile. "Just don't take months this time. Please?"

"Deal."

We hug again once more before I run back home. My heart races as I speed around the corner and down my street. Chilly air whips against my face and wraps around my body, but I don't feel cold. Not at all.

I take the stairs up to my house two at a time and swing the door open. "Luna Andrea Marie Bianchini, what on earth were you doing outside?" Mom yells from the kitchen as I race down the hall to my bedroom.

I pause and run back to the stairs. "I went to Tailee's! We're going to be friends again."

"Really?" Mom laughs. "Good. But you still shouldn't have been outside."

"Sorry." I run back down the hall to my room.

"We need to leave soon. I just need to finish getting your dad ready." Mom's voice trails after me.

I hurry into my room and grab my hoodie off the window bench when a piece of paper fluttering in the breeze catches my eye. Attached to a rock sitting on my windowsill is an envelope and a small brown package. I open the window and grab the letter and package, staring at Alessandro's darkened window. Scrawled in his now familiar handwriting is my name and a little drawing of the moon. Underneath, he wrote: *Open the package first.*

I slide my thumbnail under the tape holding the crisp paper together and tug the small rectangular case out. It's a beautiful blue velvet, similar to the jewelry box Tailee's best friend necklace came in. It opens with a small creak. Sitting on a silk pillow is a spazzatrici crest, just like Chiara's, except it's on a silver bracelet.

Dear Luna,

Good luck today. Even though you don't need it.

Love,
Alessandro and Chiara

P.S. We hope you like your gift. It's made from moon rock. Just like ours. You're an honorary spazzatrici and should have the crest too.

I put on the bracelet and shake out my wrist, watching as the small diamonds in the crest glitter in the sunlight.

A knock bounces off my bedroom door. I quickly take off the bracelet and put it back in its box, along with my cornicello and Tailee's best friend necklace. Dr. Tucker said no jewelry would be allowed during surgery. Mom pokes her head in. "Ready?"

I nod.

She smiles again, this time a little more forced. As if she's putting on her brave face just for me. Mom probably got as much sleep as I did.

We make our way down the hall. She takes hold of my hand and squeezes. I squeeze back.

Luna Bianchini
236 Marigold Court
Staten Island, NY 10301

Chapter 28

It's been three weeks since my surgery and tomorrow's my first day back at school. Even though sleeping has gotten easier and the nightmares are happening less and less, there's no way I'll get any sleep tonight.

I drag my desk lamp closer to the last page in a big book of spazzatrici drawings. The silver and gold sparkle in the lamplight, threading together to create a tapestry of brilliantly shining stars on the rich black background of space. I smile and put down my pencil, carefully closing the book. *Le Spazzatrici* is scrawled across the cover in gold cursive. Tailee's very late Christmas present.

I grab my mug and stare at the window. My reflection looks back at me. It's not the face I had before the accident, but it's not the one I had right after, either. Dr. Tucker said I didn't need to wear the mask anymore.

There's some swelling and bruising from surgery. There're scars and burns left behind, and Dr. Tucker said my nose will have a little bend to it. Not the Bianchini beak, but that's okay. This new face and I are still getting used to each other, but we're settling in. Patience, like the shooting star said.

There's another surgery I need in the summer to help correct some more breathing issues. But I'm not as scared anymore. Plus, Dad said we could plan a trip to Italy once he finishes up physical therapy and my surgery is over. I hold on to my cornicello and take a sip of my tea.

Drawing comes easy tonight. The four spazzatrici towers revealing themselves as the sketch progresses. Sharp, tall towers like I saw in Alessandro and Chiara's book. In one of the windows is a pair of spazzatrici, peering up into the glittering night sky through a giant telescope.

A soft knock on my window rouses me from my drawing. I look past my reflection to see Alessandro waving wildly from the platform in my tree. The ship floats behind him, lit up by hundreds of fireflies.

I open my window and let the familiar warm breeze into my room.

"Hey," I yell.

"It's been a long time," Alessandro says.

"It has," I say. "What're you doing out here?"

I lean farther out the window. The air tickles the right side of my face. I smile. The sweaty mask really is gone for good.

"It's nice seeing you happy." Alessandro notices the spazzatrici crest hanging from my wrist. He grins. "Heading up to the heavens one last time."

"What do you mean?"

"We're leaving for home tomorrow." He nods back toward the *Stella Cadente* bobbing up and down behind him.

Leaving. The word echoes across the short distance between us. My heart flutters in my chest like a moth bumping around a streetlamp. "But you can't leave." I shake my head. "Not yet."

"We can write each other," he says. "It's not like we'll disappear."

"Will you come back to Staten Island?"

Alessandro shrugs. "I don't know."

"Yeah, well, writing's not the same as hanging out every night." I stare at my hands. "I'm really going to miss you."

He burrows his flushed face beneath his jacket collar.

"Do you have a second?" Before he can say anything, I rush over to my desk and tear out one of the pages from Tailee's *Le Spazzatrici* book. "I drew this for my friend, but it's of you. So you should have it. I can draw her another picture."

The blush creeps farther up Alessandro's face upon looking at the drawing. "That's me?"

"It is," I say. "Flying around in your ship."

"The hero of the heavens." He reads the caption aloud.

"Well, you pretty much are."

"I'm sorry about the shooting star." Alessandro scratches the back of his neck. "Maybe next time we can help you catch another one. One that'll grant your wish."

I peer up at the sky. The moon and stars watch us from the heavens. "It's okay. I didn't need the wish anyway. He was right. I can do it on my own."

"I'm glad you're figuring it out."

The breeze picks up, rocking the ship back and forth under its giant black balloon.

"Where's Chiara?" I ask.

"She's getting the ship ready. She said you'd better come up with us or she's going to need to have a talk with you again."

I grin. "Let me grab my coat."

"And your sketch pad?"

"Of course."

Alessandro takes hold of my hands and helps me aboard. As I step onto the *Stella Cadente*, the warm air vibrates around me. Back in my bedroom, the pages of Tailee's *Le Spazzatrici* book flutter on my desk. One last adventure to the sky and then they'll be gone. My chest tightens.

Not gone forever. As long as I remember to look up, I'll see them, flying among the stars.

Acknowledgments

There are so many people I want to thank for helping this book become a reality. A real live book! First and foremost, I'm endlessly thankful for Dhonielle Clayton, Sona Charaipotra, Victoria Marini, and the rest of the Cake Literary team. They made my dream of becoming a published author come true and I get a little teary-eyed whenever I think about them. They guided the entire process, providing a listening ear (for ideas and for venting). Words cannot describe what they mean to me.

To my lovely editor, Liz Kossnar, who did so much to make this story what it is. I'm forever grateful for her encouraging notes and for kindly telling me when something wasn't working. To Kate Zelic for reading over all the therapy scenes. To the fabulous Simon & Schuster team: Andre Wheeler, Justin Chanda, Jenica Nasworthy, and Lucy Ruth Cummins, Milena Giunco, and Dana Wulfekotte. Thank you all for bringing this book to life and loving Luna as much as I do.

To my sweet and (mostly) patient fiancé, Dan Gardon. He's one of my biggest supporters and helped me buckle down and finish writing this book. No matter how much I'd whine or procrastinate, Dan did his best to keep me focused. And most of the time, I'd listen to him and get back to work (maybe not *most*, but a good number of times). He cheers me on, supports my dreams, and always makes sure our cats, Gloom and Doom, don't pester me too much when I'm writing. He always listened to me read things out loud without getting too annoyed when I went off on tangents about things like what a shooting star sounds like and if magic is powerful enough to keep a human from exploding in outer space.

I'm not sure where I'd be without my sisters, Andrea Cannistra and Allyson Lynch. I realize I was the pesky little sister growing up (very much a Chiara) and we didn't always see eye to eye, but I'm so happy I had them to protect me and prepare me for the world. You still look out for me and keep me going strong. They're the best sisters a girl could have.

My dad, John Cannistra, has done so much to build me up. He never once doubted my dream to become a writer and he's always quick to remind me of how proud he is. Being his daughter has made me a brave, ambitious, and resilient person. I'm so thankful for him caring so much about me.

Anne Ursu, Swati Avasthi, Kelly Easton, Laura Ruby, the Hamline Hamsters, and all the other faculty, staff, and students at Hamline University pushed me to be the best writer I could be and made me go beyond the surface level and straight into the heart of what matters. There were so many times I didn't feel like I could write, but they taught me to push that voice aside and keep going. I'll never forget my first day at Hamline and how nervous I was. But they all taught me to be kind to myself and helped me find my voice. I wouldn't be the writer I am without them.

None of this would have been possible without my big, beautiful family—the Cannistras and DeSarios. Growing up with so many people all up in your business seems like a pain, but really I couldn't be more grateful. They're all so important to me and I'm lucky to have them in my life. This book is for them.

Even though she wasn't here to see my first book printed, I want to thank my mom. She always encouraged me to write and was so proud of all my stories and poems—even hanging them up in the kitchen (much to my embarrassment). She taught me to be creative and to take risks. She was a bright light in my life, and I'm sad I can't share this moment with her, but fortunate enough to have her as my mom.

And to my readers: Thank you for reading my debut novel. It's scary taking a chance on an idea and putting your soul out there for all to see. I'm so grateful you picked up my book. I hope it brought as much magic to your life as it did mine. I love you all.